Come As You Are

Novels

Going Bicoastal

Home Field Advantage

Cool for the Summer

Just Visiting

Under the Lights

Behind the Scenes

Anthologies

(AS EDITOR)

At Midnight:
15 Beloved Fairy Tales Reimagined

That Way Madness Lies:
15 of Shakespeare's Most Notable Works Reimagined

His Hideous Heart:
13 of Edgar Allan Poe's Most Unsettling Tales Reimagined

(AS CO-EDITOR WITH JENNIFER IACOPELLI)

Out of Our League:
16 Stories of Girls in Sports

Come As You Are

A NOVEL

Dahlia Adler

WEDNESDAY BOOKS
NEW YORK

This is a work of fiction. All of the characters, organizations, and events portrayed in this novel are either products of the author's imagination or are used fictitiously.

First published in the United States by Wednesday Books, an imprint of St. Martin's Publishing Group

Printed in the United States of America. For information, address St. Martin's Publishing Group, 120 Broadway, New York, NY 10271.

www.wednesdaybooks.com

Designed by Devan Norman
Ivy art © Tanrach/Shutterstock
Case stamp art © Kalinin Ilya/Shutterstock

The Library of Congress Cataloging-in-Publication Data is available upon request.

ISBN 978-1-250-87169-5 (hardcover)
ISBN 978-1-250-87167-1 (ebook)

Our books may be purchased in bulk for promotional, educational, or business use. Please contact your local bookseller or the Macmillan Corporate and Premium Sales Department at 1-800-221-7945, extension 5442, or by email at MacmillanSpecialMarkets@macmillan.com.

First Edition: 2025

10 9 8 7 6 5 4 3 2 1

To all the characters who refuse to be forgotten,
and all the writers who refuse to forget them

Come As You Are

Chapter One

THERE SHOULD BE A RULE that if your parents name you something like Everett Owen Riley, they should have to double—nay, *triple*—check things like, say, whether your new boarding school has put you in the correct dorm.

Right about now is where mine would be hearing from my lawyer.

"But you're a *girl*," Archibald Buchanan says for the millionth time since I showed up with a duffel of extremely scary bras.

"Well, I'm glad to see Camden's education is as stellar as promised."

He blinks at me. And I blink back. And it's a good old-fashioned standoff, except that I'm on the wrong side of the door, and he's on the side where I'm supposed to be, and somehow not one person has come to address this situation.

I try again. "Look, Archie."

He winces.

"Do you not go by Archie?"

"I do, it just sounds so . . . ugh coming from you."

"Now I see why they paired us up. They must've known that we were soulmates."

Looks *can't* kill, right? I know "If looks could kill" has been a saying for a long time, and the implication is that they can't, but Archie looks like he has a whole lot of money, and I don't know if quirky little sayings apply to people like him.

The ability to pinpoint the exact moment when the light goes out of his cold green eyes and he gives up entirely is what makes me an excellent poker player, and it's because I see this happen that I manage to wedge my foot in the door before he can close it in my face completely. "Look. I obviously don't want to be sharing a room with you either, and given they don't have coed dorms in this place, I'm not really worried about that happening. But I *would* like to put my stuff down while we wait for someone to come fix this mess. So can you please let me in, and then you can call the cops or whatever rich people do when they catch a glimpse of the poors?"

I'm definitely getting "Let's be friends" vibes from his scowl. Or, at least, it's enough to get him to let me all the way inside.

Once I'm in, though, he's out. "I'm going to find the dorm head," he barks, as if I have intentionally put us in this position because I was just *dying* to be surrounded by boys, when in fact most of the drive for coming to Camden was to get a fresh start away from the *last* boy and everything wrapped up in him. "If he can't straighten this out right now, my parents are going to have a *word* with the administration when they get back from the parents' breakfast."

Of course his parents are here. Of course they'll fight for him. Of course he didn't have to drag his duffel bag on a bus and then a cab to get here because his dad couldn't take off work and his mom had fifty excuses, all of which sucked.

The thing is, I *know* I didn't screw this up; I reread every single page of my transfer application to Camden Academy so many times I started seeing it on the insides of my eyelids while I slept. I meticulously researched the dorms, making sure I wasn't accidentally checking off anything for freshmen, seniors, boys, or millionaires (seriously, *why* does Hillman House have suites with fireplaces and claw-foot tubs?) when I put down Lockwood Hall as my first choice and Ewing Hall as my backup. As pissed as my parents were about my begging to go to boarding school when I was already at a perfectly fine public school, I wasn't taking a single chance on mistakes.

So how the hell did I end up in Rumson?

It doesn't matter; Lockwood is so close by, the two dorms literally share a patio, and I already see Archie returning with a ginger-goateed gym teacher type with a smooth white head and a navy-blue Camden polo straining around his biceps. I'm sure this will be resolved in minutes.

"You there," Ginger says to me in a thick Boston accent, motioning for me to come back into the hallway. "You're in the wrong place."

"I'm aware," I say as nicely as I can, "but no one's been able to tell me yet where the *right* place is."

"What're you talking about?"

"This is my room." I hold up my assignment. "This is also clearly *not* meant to be my room, and so I need a new room. And a new dorm. And a new dorm head."

He squints. "That assignment says Everett Owen Riley."

"Yes."

He looks at me, and I can see it's not computing.

"My name is Everett Owen Riley. This is my assignment. It is wrong. See right here where it says Rumson Hall? Clearly, I should not be in Rumson Hall."

"It also says your roommate is Archibald Buchanan," Archie adds with a scowl. "You didn't notice that?"

"Obviously not." And it's true, I didn't, because I barely glanced at my assignment before now; I didn't even know it listed a roommate. Given I didn't know anyone here, I didn't really care *where* I ended up. I'd picked Lockwood over Ewing with a rousing game of eenie meeny miney mo, not because it mattered where I slept, or whether my roommate's name was Chloe or Padma or Talia.

Even Camden Academy itself was a relatively meaningless choice within all the in-state options. I mean, yes, I researched to make sure it had decent academics and extracurriculars, but there was only one criterion I really cared about: it wasn't Greentree High, which meant I was nowhere near any of the people who'd broken my heart and sent me running for a fresh start where no one knew me and vice versa.

My parents also cared about exactly one criterion—

financial aid, which the school kindly provided me—and so Camden it was.

"You're in the wrong place," Ginger repeats unhelpfully.

"Yes, we have established that. I was assigned to this room by someone who clearly thought from my name that I was a boy, and they were wrong, and now I need a new room in a girls' dorm. Are we all caught up?"

Ginger eyes me like I've said something extremely shady, but he does it while picking up his super cool walkie-talkie and repeating the scenario to whatever unlucky bastard is on the other side, having to deal with logistical screwups like this in the middle of an already hectic orientation day. Ten minutes of silent standoff later, during which Ginger has to keep darting out to shake parents' hands and help kids find where they're going, someone with an even bigger beard—and so I assume more authority—shows up.

"This is a problem," says Beardy. "Your name is Everett?"

"Evie."

"What?"

"Evie. I know, the long *E* isn't intuitive with Everett's short *E*, but it's what I prefer to be called. Possibly because Everett has a way of landing me in situations like this."

There's a gruff acknowledgment, a squint like maybe all the blond from my frizzy cloud of hair has seeped into my brain, and then, "Okay, Evie. Are your parents at the breakfast?"

"They couldn't make it today. It's just me."

He frowns. "And you're a sophomore transfer?"

"Yes, sir." I have no idea where the "sir" comes from. It

feels like something Archie would say. It might be because in contrast to Ginger's Bostonian accent, Beardy's is crisp and bordering on posh, and it demands some propriety. Which is not my strong suit.

It also occurs to me that no one wears name tags in this place. They should really wear name tags at orientation.

"Lockwood, Ewing, Hillman, and Baker are the options for sophomore girls," he says, as if he's talking to someone who didn't do her research before uprooting her entire life and throwing herself into a school she hadn't even heard of three months earlier.

"I know. I put down Lockwood and Ewing."

"Well, Lockwood and Ewing are both full to capacity."

"Okaaay," I say slowly, "so put me in Baker or Hillman."

"Those are also full to capacity. It's a great year for Camden Academy," he says proudly, as if I'm gonna cheer on the very fact that's screwing me over.

"Maybe Mercer?" Ginger suggests, and I can't remember off the top of my head whether that's a freshman dorm or a senior one, but I really and truly do not want either one.

"Lemme save you the trouble here," Beardy says to him, a note of irritation entering his voice. "Every single room—girls' and boys'—is full this year."

"That can't be," Archie says coldly.

Now the men are exchanging glances and then looking at me like I'm some kind of problem child, like I caused this, like I wanted to have to practically run away from home and deal with *this* on top of a thrice-broken heart. Because of course, Evie is always the problem. My sister, Sierra, could set my house on fire and convince the rest of the town I did it to keep myself warm.

I came here to escape that, to escape *her.* And if being myself isn't helping me achieve that sufficiently, then maybe I need to take a page from her book.

Putting on my stone-coldest expression—the very one I wore when I told Sierra to get out of my life for good—I cross my arms in front of my chest and look Ginger squarely in the eye. "Not to agree with him on something, but it really can't. You accepted me here. You took my parents' money. You took me in as a student—as a *boarding* student—and that means you have an obligation to fulfill. So I'm sure you'll figure it out. Quickly."

My sudden frostiness seems to stun them all into silence, and finally, there's some action. Beardy starts arguing with someone on a walkie-talkie, while Ginger starts pleading with someone else on his. Then a bell rings, and Ginger swears under his breath.

"We've got dorm orientation right now, and I don't have any more time to deal with this. Just come to Rumson orientation and we'll figure it out afterward."

"You want me to come to orientation for a boys' dorm?"

"'Want' is a strong word, but yes, that's what we're doing. Come on."

"Don't you dare tell anyone you're my roommate," Archie warns me as Ginger hurries ahead, leaving us to follow in his wake. "This is not lasting past the hour."

"I promise not to cramp your style around the other guys," I vow with a hand over my heart.

"Oh, shut the fuck up."

We walk the rest of the way in silence, and you know? It's just really nice to make a friend on your first day.

There are already a bunch of legitimate Rumson residents chilling in the lounge by the time Archie and I arrive on Ginger's heels, and I'm left alone in the doorway so fast I can actually hear the breeze Archie leaves in his wake. A quick scan of the room shows a few guys who look about as fun as Archie does, a few clusters of dudes reconnecting after a summer apart, and exactly one guy sitting solo who looks like I feel, sporting a Nirvana T-shirt and appropriately looking like he'd much rather be hanging out with Kurt Cobain right now.

Ding ding, we have a winner.

I let myself into the room as quietly and unassumingly as I can, heading right for the empty chair next to my grungy new dormmate. But it's hard to make a subtle entrance when your hair's the color of corn and requires its own zip code, especially if you're the only girl in a room full of guys. The whispers and stares follow me all the way over, and I know it's only a matter of someone deciding he's funny enough to be the one to fire the opening line.

Thankfully, the hypothetical comedian doesn't get a

chance before Ginger declares "Everyone pipe down!" with all the authority of, well, a gym teacher in charge of a bunch of teenage boys. "As you all know by now, I'm your dorm head, Mr. Hoffman. Welcome to Rumson Hall."

"Yes, welcome to Rumson Hall!" some loser says directly to me with a huge-ass grin on his doofy face. "I see they've finally listened to my request to have someone in-house to do our laundry."

Ugh, there we go—let the assholes begin. "As if I would go within fifty feet of your skid marks."

"I don't think she's here for laundry," another d-bag says with a suggestive waggle of his eyebrows.

The room erupts before I can get a word in, and while Ginger—Mr. Hoffman, which apparently I should've known? How?—quickly tries to regain control, I close my eyes and tune everything out.

This part doesn't count. This isn't my dorm, this isn't my dorm head, these aren't my dormmates, and this isn't my new beginning. Whatever happens in the next hour before they figure out where I'll be staying . . . it simply doesn't count. It's part of the crappy phase one of my high school life, and phase two begins when my rightful housing does, and not a moment sooner.

The thought is . . . liberating.

"You make friends fast," Nirvana Boy says, doing some annoying flicking thing with his nails.

"I'll teach you my secrets if you ask really nicely."

He emits a choked snort, as if he did not expect me to

amuse him. Not on purpose, anyway. Still, of all the guys I've spoken to so far today, I guess he qualifies as the nicest. "I'm Evie."

I'm spared the barest of glances through the longest set of eyelashes I have ever seen. "Salem."

"Like the Witch Trials?"

"Exactly like the Witch Trials." He stretches mile-long legs out in front of him, crossing one scribbled-on Van over the other. "The witch being my twin sister, Sabrina, who spent most of our childhood using me as a test project."

"I take it you've been the subject of more than one of her dabbles in the craft."

"My sister's never met a 'shut my brother up' spell she didn't like."

"And I assume your real name is a CIA-level secret."

"Nah, just an expensive one." He rubs his fingertips together, and despite myself, I feel a smile ghost over my lips.

"If it helps, my name's really Everett, which probably answers your next question."

He raises an eyebrow, and I watch with fascination as it disappears beneath his dark, shaggy bangs. "I didn't ask you a first question."

"Well, there are about sixty people in this room and I'm guessing I'm the only one who shaves with a Venus Embrace. Were you really not wondering what I'm doing in an all-boys dorm?"

"I try to mind my own business."

"Well, you're the only one. Anyway, my roommate wasn't terribly happy about my placement." I nod subtly toward

Archie, who's glaring daggers at me from across the room, clearly having figured out that I'm not keeping our little secret. "Who's yours?"

No subtlety for Salem; he just waves a hand in the direction of a cute blond guy with biceps to spare peeking out of the sleeves of his Yankees T-shirt. "They put me with Matt fuckin' Haley, of all people."

The name means absolutely nothing to me. "What's the matter with Matt Haley? Are you a Red Sox fan?"

"No, I'm a fan of not having a roommate who screws a new girl every night, six feet away from me." He pulls one of his Vans up to cross his other knee and picks at the black laces as if they'll leach some of the annoyance out of his body. "At least three different guys have already made sure to tell me that they hope I like 'the Matt Haley soundtrack.'" He sighs. "I don't even understand why a junior who obviously has friends of his own is rooming with a sophomore transfer. I was hoping *he'd* ask for a switch, but—"

"Hey, I'm a sophomore transfer too. Look at that—something in common. We're destined to be best friends."

He glances up at my blond frizzball. "I'm gonna be honest. I have no fuckin' idea how to braid that, so you're gonna have to do mine first."

My laugh-snort gets me a dark glare from Hoffman, who was clearly hoping to forget the problem of Me existed.

"This whole dorm thing is bullshit," Salem mutters.

"I mean. I am very much suffering from exactly the same bullshit."

He laughs, a quick, quiet puff of breath. "Yeah, I guess you are. Thanks for putting things in perspective. Your situation is way shittier."

Well. That is not really what I was going for, but I guess I'll take solidarity where I can get it.

Chapter Two

TURNS OUT, THERE *WAS* ONE free room on campus. After sitting through the rest of orientation and then waiting on the bare mattress in my soon-to-be-former room while Hoffman and Beardy (a.k.a. Mr. Dempsey, a.k.a. the housing director) conferred with everyone possible and Archie glared at me like I was leaving Girl Germs on all of his overpriced stuff, I learned that Lockwood and Rumson are each outfitted with one wheelchair-accessible room. Lockwood's is already taken by an actual wheelchair user, but Rumson's was taken by . . . Mr. Hoffman's bike.

So, Rumson's my official residence after all.

At least I have my own bathroom.

Does this mean phase two of my high school life has started now?

Or does it mean that it never will?

Even with my door closed (but not locked, per Camden

rules for "safety reasons") and Blackpink blaring through my laptop speakers while I make my bed and put my clothing in the provided dresser and small closet, I swear I can hear the entire school talking about me. I'd envisioned doing the moving-in part with a roommate, then wandering the halls and meeting other girls, checking out the lounge, maybe finding other people who like card games and rom-coms and planning fake trips to places they'll probably never go. And it isn't that I'm afraid I've made a mistake by coming here, exactly, since there was no way I could've stayed at GHS . . . but I'm not exactly sure I've traded up, either.

A knock sounds at the door, and I groan under my breath, positive it's Hoffman and praying that if I don't answer, he'll just go away. Of course, he knocks again, so I drag myself over to my computer to turn down the music and swing the door open, only to reveal . . . Matt Haley?

"Hey there." He flashes me the smile that has apparently dropped a thousand pairs of panties. "You must be Evie." He holds out a hand, and for a moment, I hear Salem in my head, warning me not to shake it, because I absolutely do know where it's been.

But Matt's being friendly, and Salem doesn't strike me as someone who knows the meaning of the word, so I take it. "I am. Matt, right?"

"I see my reputation has preceded me." If possible, his smile widens even further. "You need help with anything?" He peeks his head in, and I let him; there's really nothing to see. "Looks like you've still got a ways to go."

"Actually, I'm just about done." I'm sure other people have

photographs and posters and all sorts of fun things on their shelves and walls, but I wanted as few reminders of home as possible. All I've got with me are some comfort reads, the deck of cards I never go anywhere without (my Emotional Support Deck, my former best friend Claire used to call it), a backup deck, and the stuffed panda I couldn't make myself leave behind.

His smile falters into an O. "Is this seriously all you brought?"

"Of course not. My driver will be coming around with my queen-size canopy bed within the hour."

He gives me a funny look, I guess unimpressed by my British accent, and then shrugs and asks if he can come inside.

Technically, guys and girls are only allowed in each other's rooms during intervisitation hours in the evenings, but even more technically, that's a dorm-based rather than gender-based rule, so I guess it's okay? Neither Hoffman nor Dempsey had time to get into the finer logistics, especially since Hoffman was busy pouting that his precious bike would have to live in the bike racks with the—ew—students'.

I step aside and let him in.

"You didn't bring any pictures?"

"Who prints pictures these days?" I ask airily, holding up my own phone. "I brought plenty."

It's a lie. I deleted almost all of them and hid the ones I couldn't bear to part with but also couldn't look at ever again.

His mouth twitches like he doesn't quite believe me but he's wisely decided to drop it. Clearly, he's got bigger fish to fry. "Listen, I wanted to run something by you. Not that I need you to do anything," he adds quickly. "It's just . . . you're not a narc, are you?"

"Me?" I blink. I don't even know what to say to that very unexpected question.

"I didn't think so. You seem like a cool girl." It's a canned line, but combined with his most charming smile and the biceps peeking out of his sleeves, I'm starting to Get It, even if he and his whole thing are not my type. "So, listen. I've kinda got an in at the housing office, and I specifically chose my room for its . . . discreet location. Every now and again, I get after-hours visitors who'd really like to be able to come and go as they please."

"And you want them to come and go through my room? That's—"

"No, of course not." He points at my window. "I have a rope ladder. But it *will* go past your window. I just wanna make sure you'll be . . . looking the other way."

A rope ladder. Jesus. Salem was not kidding. "We're talking fully consensual visitors?"

"Always," he says firmly.

I shrug. "Then it's fine with me. It's your roommate you're gonna have to work stuff out with."

"Psh, Salem I can handle. You're the one who makes me nervous," he says with a wink. "Glad you're chill." He gives me a little punch on the shoulder, and I'm mad that I don't hate it. "I gotta run, but I'll catch you later. I owe you one."

He slips out, and I just shake my head and turn my music back up. I know Matt was just buttering me up to buy my silence, but I can't pretend I didn't like being called "chill" and "a cool girl." Back in Greentree, next to Sierra, no one would ever think of me as the cool one—not when she was dancing on tables at parties or kicking ass at beer pong or snagging every single guy (and occasional girl) in sight. Certainly not when I was working so hard to be the best girlfriend I could be by making Craig and his stupid friends snack platters while they played video games. Or when I was so committed to helping Claire with her art that I'd spend entire yawning afternoons modeling for portraits. Or all the times I put my own studying and hobbies on hold so I could help them with math (Craig), English papers (Claire), or bio (both).

God forbid I be anything but the perfect girlfriend, perfect best friend. But then, a boyfriend and a best friend were the two things I had in life that my sister didn't, and it was impossible not to want to hold them close.

Of course, she took them anyway.

But here . . . there's no Sierra. I don't have to prove I'm "good enough" to earn my space in her shadow. And now I have something *no* other girl on campus has or will have: a room in an all-boys dorm. So maybe this isn't ruining what's supposed to be the perfect reset of my life.

Maybe it's actually the perfect opportunity to do things differently.

How? I don't know yet. But that's okay. I'm a blank slate with nothing but time to figure it out.

Or not. Because everywhere I go for orientation events today, people seem to know who I am.

On the group tour, a couple of my new dormmates I recognize from orientation suggest with dancing eyebrows that we work out a shower schedule.

At the campus store, a guy I've never seen before suggests I see if they carry boxers so I can better fit in at Rumson.

Another pointedly lets me know that he's heard I have my own private room, emphasis on *private*.

I don't know how news got around so fast, or why all these people have to be so fucking creepy, but the entire morning is filled with pointing and whispering and strangers greeting me with variations on "Hey, aren't you the Rumson Girl?"

That's me: the Rumson Girl. Exactly what I've always dreamed.

"It's Evie, actually," I tell the guy who stops me in Beasley Dining Hall, a.k.a. the Beast, where I'm just trying to get some lunch fuel to get me through the rest of this day.

"Yeah, I heard about you. Heard you're Archie Buchanan's roommate," he says with a shit-eating grin, punctuated by a huge dimple. He's got the same kind of overly styled look Archie does, and the same vibe exuding way too much money.

"You heard wrong," I say, sidestepping him neatly in my quest for the baked-potato bar; there is no way I'm letting this dude get between me and my bacon bits.

"Does that mean you're still in need of a bedmate?" he calls after me, but thankfully, he doesn't follow. I shudder the interaction off me and get in line behind a broad set of shoulders in a striped polo. I'm balancing the tray in one hand

and sneaking a piece of smoky bacon into my mouth with the other when I hear the cutest accent in the entire world, sweeter than maple syrup, saying, "Why thank you, ma'am."

I look up, having to see the face that belongs to those four words, and I am *not* disappointed. Striped Polo looks like walking, talking sunshine—healthy golden tan, healthy golden hair, and a smile warm enough to ward off the New Hampshire chill I know from experience will be here before we know it.

He looks like he grew up on a farm, or at the very least is definitely not from around here; not one single thing about him reminds me of a certain ex, including the way he catches my eye and gives me a nod and confident smile as he walks past.

What is it they say? The best way to get over someone is to get under someone else? Well, Craig Larson is definitely in my rearview, and Farmboy shows some interesting potential.

Here's hoping *he* doesn't know me as the Rumson Girl.

"Your drool is gonna stain the linoleum," a voice behind me says as I watch Farmboy take a seat at an otherwise full table, squeezing in next to a girl with a neat French braid.

I whirl around to see Salem standing behind me with a green apple in hand, no tray. "So's your jealousy."

"That doesn't even make sense."

"Neither do you." But I appreciate the wake-up call, noxious as it was, and I finally move again, taking a seat at an empty table. Salem joins me a minute later, having added a tall cup of Coke to his nutritious lunch. "Is that really all you're eating?"

"My mom says it's not polite to comment on others' food," he informs me, taking a big bite of apple that sprays juice squarely on my cheek.

"Yeah, clearly your mom raises charmers." I wipe off my face and return my gaze to Farmboy's table. French Braid is practically in his lap, which I'm *sure* doesn't mean anything. They're probably cousins, or even siblings. They kind of look alike, if you squint hard enough until all you can see is that they're both white.

"You're pretty superior for someone who gave my roommate the green light to hang a sex ladder from our window."

"As if you won't find any way to benefit from that." I roll my eyes away from Farmboy and dig in to my baked potato. *Mmm*, the ultimate comfort food. "You're living on a campus full of horny teenagers with minimal supervision. Go wild."

"Oh yeah? Is that what you plan to do here? Go wild?"

"Oh no, Evie Riley does not go wild," I tell him, gesturing with my fork. "My sister does that enough for the both of us. I am the one who behaves and then gets treated like shit as a result." Whoops, maybe a little too much information there. Thankfully, I'm talking to someone who definitely does not care and will not be internalizing any of it. "But I'm not gonna begrudge Matt enjoying himself. Unless I have to listen to squeaky springs through the ceiling. Then I may have to get him expelled."

Salem eyes me like he's not sure I'm kidding, and I just shrug and take another bite. Farmboy is a nice fantasy, but when it comes down to it, what am I really gonna do—make an excuse to talk to him, maybe exchange names, and then what? I was with Craig for six months, and most of that time was spent holding hands at school and hanging out with his friends in his basement while they played video games. I wouldn't know how to "go wild" even if I wanted to.

People would probably be so disappointed in the Rumson Girl if they knew.

I spend the rest of the afternoon buying my books and meeting with my academic advisor, and after, I have just enough time before our individual grade activities start to let myself into Lockwood to catch a glimpse of where I was supposed to be, and hopefully meet some of the girls I was supposed to be living with.

It's a twin building to Rumson, so the blueprint is the same in mirror image, but it's easy to see little differences right off the bat—a vase of fresh flowers in the entryway where Rumson has nothing, cute signs on the doors as opposed to hastily scrawled names on whiteboards, the smells of scented candles and hair products rather than sweat and cheap cologne . . . This is definitely where I was supposed to be.

I try to ignore the slowly building ache in my heart that feels like envy and nostalgia had a really ugly baby.

Scanning the door signs, I murmur the names of the girls who'll be my classmates (and hopefully eventually dormmates, if I have my way) for the next three years—Cassie and Emmy and Mika and—

A yelp, followed by "What *is* that?"

Well, sounds like someone might be having a worse first day than I am. I don't wanna be nosy, but, well, I could stand to feel a little better about myself right now, so I shuffle back through the hall until I find the room I'm looking for ("Heather" and "Sabrina"), which is pretty easy to do since one girl looks like she's gonna pass out and the other one is holding something furry and black and almost definitely not dorm-sanctioned.

But is it alive? That much I can't tell, although the goth girl is holding it like a precious baby.

"It's my familiar," she says in a hurt voice, petting the Thing, and it hits me in a rush of coal-black hair and milk-white skin that this absolutely has to be Salem's twin. "His name is Checkers. And he's only the stuffed-animal version of the real Checkers, who's home with my parents, so chill out."

Heather breathes a sigh of relief, and I guess I do too, because she turns to me suddenly, her neat French braid swinging against her shoulder. Which is when I realize that it's the same girl from the Beast—the one who was sitting with Farmboy. She immediately breaks into a warm, welcoming smile, a glaring contrast to Sabrina's resting witch face.

"Hi! I'm Heather. This is Sabrina. Are you on the first floor too?"

"Yes, but different dorm." Might as well test the waters for how this is gonna go over. "There was a whole screwup with my name—I go by Evie, but my name is Everett—and now I'm in Rumson. I have my own room and bathroom, so at least I don't have to deal with pee all over the seat and whatever other grossness I'm about to learn boys do."

"Oh, the limit does not exist," Sabrina says dryly, and as she rolls her eyes, I see they're exactly the same stormy gray as Salem's.

"You're Salem's twin, right?"

If I hadn't been sure before, the identical way her eyebrow rises a thousand feet in the air answers my question before the words "How the hell do you know my brother?" can even leave her mouth.

Oh, how to even begin answering that . . . "We met at dorm orientation. He seems like a nice guy. Sort of." Nice enough, anyway. "We just had lunch together, too. Also sort of."

She snorts. "If he was nice to you, he must think you've got decent weed."

Ah, someday I think Sabrina and I are gonna have a lot of lovely talks about siblings who suck.

"So they put you in a boys' dorm?" Heather furrows her neat brows. "That's a pretty nerve-racking first day, isn't it?" Then I guess she realizes I'm still standing in the doorway, looking like a creeper. "Come in, come in."

I do, and immediately take in the way their room looks as if each half is in a different universe. There's no confusion over whose half is whose, either, unless Heather is way more into pentagrams than she lets on. "It was not a great start!" I concede, grabbing Heather's desk chair for myself.

"What's the deal with your hair?" Sabrina asks, eyeing me like an exhibit at the clown museum. "It's fascinating."

"Sabrina!"

"No, no, it's fine," I assure Heather, tugging on a springy

blond curl. "No one's ever that direct about it. I mostly get a lot of staring and an occasional 'Is that real?' It is, for the record—not just me going wild with a curling iron."

"Well, it's pretty epic," says Sabrina, and I can't tell if it's a compliment.

I offer a "Thanks?" anyway, and she nods, so I guess it was.

"So what's it like living there?" Heather asks as she pulls a bunch of random stuff from her bag, including a stuffed unicorn, a stack of picture frames, and an extremely well-loved fantasy novel I recognize as being one of Claire's favorites. For a brief moment, I miss my former best friend, and the way she'd drag me to the bookstore every single time a new sci-fi novel with a Black main character released, how she'd call them her "supreme autobuys" and hug them to her chest.

Then I push her out of my head so I can answer Heather. "It's still new, but I have a feeling it's going to be very . . . loud. And that I should really stock up on scented candles, or at least air freshener. I've never been so grateful not to have to share a bathroom in my entire life."

"I've never actually had my own bathroom," says Heather, arranging the frames on her shelves so I can see an array of photographs of her with a pair of girls who must be her little sisters and a woman who looks like Heather with a "You in Twenty Years" filter on. It's an entire family of French-braided doppelgängers. "Our apartment only has one bathroom for the four of us, which was another point in favor of boarding school. At least here, when we share, there's more than one shower."

"Yeah, I definitely don't miss sharing with my sister," I mutter, watching Heather arrange the stuffed unicorn on her pillow.

"And I will not miss Salem being obnoxious about my hair being everywhere." Sabrina grips her wild mass of black waves in one hand and swings it over her shoulder. "I guess boarding school does have its perks."

"Salem mentioned being a transfer," I say to Sabrina, "so I guess you are too?" She nods, and I look to Heather.

"Not me," she says, pulling the last few items from her suitcase and closing it up. "I was here last year too, and I loved it. Don't worry, I wasn't sure about it either, at first. My mom was having such a tough time being there for all three of us, and my grandma suggested it might be easier on everyone if there were one fewer kid to shuttle around everywhere. My sisters both cried at the thought, but I like trying new things, so, I said I'd give it a shot, and here I am again the next year. You'll both love it as much as I do, I'm sure of it."

"I like your confidence," I tell Heather, both of us ignoring the way Sabrina rolls her eyes. "I did choose to come here, so I definitely hope to like it, but I, uh, did not choose the whole boys' dorm thing, or to have random assholes on campus cracking jokes at me like I begged to live there so I could catch glimpses of bare boy ass in the showers."

She seems to think on that for a second before offering a hopeful shrug and a "This too shall pass?"

"Here's hoping. But now you're both required by law to be my friends, so that I don't become completely warped and maladjusted. I've already spent way too many hours of my life watching boys play video games in dank basements, thank you very much."

"Deal," says Heather sweetly, and I take Sabrina's grunt to mean the same.

I help them finish unpacking and get their luggage into storage, and by the time we're done, the big orientation icebreaker dinner is nearly upon us. I'm feeling grungy and dusty from the combo of the bus ride this morning and the whole rest of the day, so I say goodbye to Heather, Sabrina, and The Dorm That Should Be Mine and head back across the patio to Rumson so I can rinse myself off and change into something that'll hopefully make a better first impression.

The whole time, I try not to feel bitter that if I just lived where I was supposed to, the three of us could get ready together, help one another pick outfits, do one another's makeup . . . it's exactly the kind of thing I pictured when I applied to boarding school.

Instead, I'm gonna have to walk through clouds of Axe body spray and guys loudly calling one another "Asswipe" on the way to my room, where I'll change while double-checking about twelve times to make sure the door is locked.

New start, yaaaaay.

Chapter Three

I NEVER GOT OUT THAT MUCH in Greentree, but on the rare occasion I *did* go somewhere more interesting than Craig's basement, FaceTiming with Claire for outfit consultation was a must. If Sierra was feeling charitable, she'd toss something at me that would look a thousand times better than what I was already planning to wear; if she wasn't, she'd just make a comment that made it clear I needed to change.

This is all to say that despite my desperately wanting to look cute and approachable and like someone you'd want to know beyond "Oh, that's the Rumson Girl," I have never been very skilled at getting myself ready for social things.

Too bad the icebreaker dinner is not optional.

I'd planned to wear a lilac dress that I'd bought for Claire's family's Easter dinner last year, but looking at it now, it's too fancy. And my blue top isn't nice enough. And I'll be too hot in my red sweater. And the last time I wore this star-patterned shirt, Sierra approached me very seriously to ask when I was making her an aunt, because it made me look about six months along.

For a minute, I wish I could just dress like everyone else in my dorm—throw on a pair of jeans and a polo and be done with it. And technically, I could, but that would not yield the look I was going for. Finally, I dig up a black-and-white polka-dot top I feel decent about, and just pray that Sierra was being genuine when she told me it looked cute with my red belt and black jeans, even if it was "in a Minnie Mouse kind of way."

I slip into my black Converse and spend a solid fifteen minutes trying to make my hair cooperate before I finally give up and head out into the late-summer night, only the slightest of chills in the air.

Since the Beast isn't big enough to house all the students at once, the icebreaker is at the Student Center, which is thankfully an impossible building to miss. I figure if I show my face for five minutes, claim my name tag, and choke down a sandwich, I'll have fulfilled whatever obligation I have to attend.

Positive attitude, my mom's voice warns in my head, and it has the effect of making me stand up straighter and paste a smile on my face. She didn't like the idea of me coming here at all, but when she finally relented, she told me that if I did go, I'd better do it with a positive attitude. And I know she isn't here to watch me, but she isn't wrong, either.

You look cute, I tell myself as I walk up the steps, my thumb gliding over the top of the Emotional Support Deck in my pocket. *You look cute, and your outfit is cute, and you already made a couple of friends, maybe, and your dorm-room situation will get straightened out—it has to. Everything is fine. You are fine.*

I pull open the door and head straight for the sign-in desk, where a girl with a round face and a big smile asks my name and then hunts for my badge. "It's not in here," she says, her lips drooping into a frown as she riffles through the envelope. "You said your last name is 'Riley'?"

Deep sigh. "Check the boys' folder."

She does, and lo and behold. "That's so weird," she says with a furrow of her eyebrows as she hands me my name tag and watches me plaster it to my shirt. "How— *Oh*, you must be Rumson Girl."

I grimace. "Please, my friends call me Rummy."

The only familiar face in the room when I arrive belongs to Matt Haley, and he's thoroughly occupied by a pair of gorgeous girls who look at him like they plan to give that rope ladder a workout tonight. Clearly, I won't be interrupting, so I take myself over to the drinks table instead and pour myself a Sprite.

"You're Evie, right?"

I nearly spit out my drink at the sound of that familiar accent, but I manage to choke down the bubbles and only halfway resemble a gaping fish as I turn around to face Farmboy, a.k.a. (per his name sticker) Lucas Burke. "Right. Wow, it's nice to hear my name and not 'Rumson Girl,' so thank you for that."

The regrets at mentioning my stupid nickname and predicament settle in immediately, but Lucas just laughs. "It's a pretty name," he says, clearly determined to make me melt into the floor. "But 'Rumson Girl' is cute too. You're a celebrity on your very first day."

"Not exactly what I want to be famous for." Although there *is* something nice about the fact that Lucas has heard of me.

"There are worse things." He pours himself a cup of Coke, and we clink "glasses." "You've got your own room, right?"

I brace myself for a gross line to follow, but he's just looking at me with friendly interest, as if we are normal people having a normal conversation. How novel. "I do. That part is definitely mostly a perk."

"Mostly?"

"I was kind of looking forward to sharing," I admit, watching his throat as he takes a swallow of his soda. "Making an instant friend. I don't know anyone here. I just transferred."

"Ah." Lucas's lips curve into the most charming of smiles. "Well, I will very happily be your friend, if you're looking."

The way he says "friend" feels a little . . . loaded, but maybe I'm imagining things, maybe even hearing what I want to hear, if only a little bit. He is *very* cute, and being *very* friendly, and singling me out in a packed room.

I am *never* the one singled out in a packed room.

"That sounds nice," I say, and I let it sound a little loaded, too, because flirting is fun and I am *extremely* single. "And what is it friends do around here?"

As soon as it comes out of my mouth, I realize it sounds a whole lot flirtier than I was going for, but Lucas doesn't seem to mind. "There are so many options," he says, putting his cup down. "Especially with a girl who's got her own room."

Oh. Well. He's just moving right past flirting and into . . . I don't know what, but it's got my heart beating double time in my chest, and my nerves tingling with something that could be nervousness or excitement or possibly even some horny combination of the two.

Craig and I didn't fool around a whole lot. We'd make out, sometimes he'd touch my boobs, but mostly the effect was of a puppy pawing at me for a treat. Honestly, I thought maybe he just wasn't that interested in sex stuff.

Until I caught him with my sister and realized that what he wasn't interested in was me.

So now, having someone look at me the way Lucas is looking at me, gaze flicking between my chest and my mouth, lip caught between his teeth in a way that makes me wonder if he even knows he's doing it . . . yeah, I'm feeling pretty good. Turns out it's kinda nice to have someone confirm you're not a troll when that's exactly how your ex left you feeling.

I think about earlier, at Rumson, how channeling Sierra and her attitude was the thing that finally made people listen to me.

And I think about how Sierra would already be halfway back to her room with Lucas in tow.

And I think about how Sierra has always, *always* come out on top, no matter how terrible her choices seem to be.

And I think that maybe, if I want to get out of her shadow, as I came here to do, it's time to make some big moves for myself.

I take a deep breath, put my own cup down next to his, and flash what I hope is an alluring smile. "Well, I happen to be just such a girl. Would you like a tour?"

My heart pounds as we slip out of the Student Center and head toward Rumson, even though no one's paying attention to two students milling about campus when there are so many still making their way to the Student Center. No one even looks twice as we enter Rumson, and no one's there to see me lead him to my room and close the door behind me.

Now that we're inside, I have no idea what I'm supposed to do or say; I hadn't gotten quite that far in my determination to be fiercely adventurous. But Lucas seems perfectly comfortable glancing around my room, and though I wait for the inevitable "Where's all your stuff?," it doesn't come. Instead he just says, "You're cute."

Heat rises into my cheeks with a vengeance. "Am I?"

"You know you are, Rumson Girl," he says with a grin, and it's the least I've ever hated that nickname. "I would get in a lot of trouble if there was a girl like you sleeping right across the hall from me."

"What kind of trouble?" I try not to wince at how shakily my voice comes out, but he just sounds so . . . confident. Adult. Like someone who gets into trouble often, and likes it.

And the way he's looking at me, it's like he thinks maybe I'm that kind of someone too.

Which, I guess I can't blame him for thinking. I did invite him here, and I did close my door—or at least I think I'm the one who closed it. But now that we're here, alone, it strikes me that I know nothing about Lucas, and he knows nothing about me, and the idea that we've escaped together to my room is just so absurd that I can't help it—I start to laugh.

I'm immediately shut up by his mouth on mine.

It's so sudden, so surprising, that I don't even know what to do, but if he notices that I'm not kissing back, that my arms are still at my sides, it doesn't show. Finally, muscle memory takes over; after all, it isn't all that different from kissing Craig. Lucas has similarly soft lips, uses too much tongue . . . it doesn't take all that much effort to let my mind transport back to Craig's basement, to a space I know well. And maybe it's that or maybe it's riding high on being chosen in the crowd that makes it easier to let go. To let him walk me back to my bed with his lips on mine.

It isn't until I feel the zipper of my jeans slowly opening that I realize he hadn't been toying with the button but opening it, and instinctively I trap his hands. Immediately, the kissing stops, and he pulls away with a frown.

"I'm not . . . ready for that," I say, trying for confidence, though it comes out a mumble. "Can we go back to just kissing?"

He rolls his eyes. The asshole *rolls his eyes.* "I thought you were up for some actual fun."

"Some actual fun like getting naked with a guy I just met?" I nearly choke on my tongue. "What the hell would make you think that?"

"Oh come on, everyone knows you pulled some weird bullshit with your application to get into Rumson and room with Archie Buchanan like some creepy stalker. Figured you'd be grateful someone still wanted you after he rejected you, but." Lucas shrugs and braces his hands on his thighs to stand. "So much for that."

"You *must* be joking." I really might throw up on his shoes. I don't think I'd even be embarrassed if I did; he deserves it. "*I* did everything right. It's the *school* that screwed up, and—"

"Evie, chill."

"My name is *Everett*," I snap, because while my name may be the original root of all this trouble, a guy who came back to my room under gross pretenses and tried to push me to go further than I wanted to does not get to use my nickname. "Might want to let all your loser friends who insist on calling me 'Rumson Girl' know."

I expect him to storm out, to yell something back, but instead, he says, "Everett," with a confusing amount of calm.

Assuming there's an apology coming, I take a deep breath and force myself to chill. "What?"

"You're not gonna tell anyone about this, right? It *was* fun for a minute, but I'm kind of with someone, and—"

"Oh my *God*." How does this keep getting worse? "*No*, I'm not gonna tell anyone; why the hell would I want anyone to know about this? And you're *with* someone? What does that even—"

All of a sudden, my brain flashes back to the first time I spotted him, to my assuming—before his flirting with me made the clear implication he was single—that he was maybe, potentially involved with the girl at his side.

The girl with the French braid.

"*Heather?* Please tell me it's not Heather. Please tell me I did not just make out with the boyfriend of one of the nicest people I have ever met." Please tell me I did not just potentially hurt someone *exactly* the way my sister hurt me, sending me here in the first place. Even though I had no way of knowing, the very thought makes me sick to my stomach.

"You're not going to tell her." I can't tell if it's an ask or a demand, and I don't know how to reply. I'd rather die than tell Heather. But she's also a really fucking nice person, unlike the inhabitants of this room, and doesn't she have a right to know who she's getting into bed with, literally and figuratively speaking?

Apparently, my silence is unbearable, because he snaps. "You're *not* going to tell her." This time, it's definitely a demand, but I'm too frozen in shock and disgust to acknowledge it. The whole reason I don't have a best friend anymore is because mine didn't see fit to tell me when my boyfriend was screwing around on me, and while Lucas and I only kissed, he sure as hell *tried* to do more.

He must read into my silence that he needs to try a different approach, because his face softens into something resembling friendliness. "Everett. Heather is a really sweet girl. You wouldn't want to hurt her, would you?"

God, I don't know who I'm sadder for—Heather, for having a boyfriend this two-faced, or me, for being stupid enough to bring this guy back to my room. But I think about how Heather's eyes shone as she told me and Sabrina how much she loves it here, and I can't be the person to take that away from her.

"You're right, I don't, but that means you have to keep your mouth shut too. If I hear a single word about your having seen the inside of Rumson Girl's room—"

"You won't," he says, hand over his heart. "You have my word."

"Like that means shit," I shoot back, walking toward the door and holding it wide open. "You can see yourself out, I'm sure."

I wait until he's long gone, and then I get in the shower and sit on the floor with a hand wrapped around the safety rail, watching my tears mingle with the spraying water and roll down the drain.

I give myself time to cycle through All the Emotions, but eventually, I have to peel myself off the floor, partly so I don't use all the hot water, but mostly because this hair cannot go to bed wet or untamed. At least the lavender scent of my shampoo and conditioner is calming. I've moved on to drying it as best I can when my phone rings, and I see "Dad" flashing on the screen.

It's not a surprise that my parents are checking in to see how my first day was, but I pause before answering anyway; I still haven't quite forgiven the fact that I had to trudge up here and deal with this whole dorm mess alone. But it's not like I can just not pick up, so I take one more second to make sure I feel fully composed, drop my microfiber towel on the sink, and take the call.

"Hey, Dad."

"Hey, kiddo." His voice sounds a little distant, almost grainy, like his phone is on speaker. Which is confirmed a moment later when my mom's voice says, "How'd your first day go?"

"We heard there was a little mix-up with the dorms," Dad adds. "Everything okay now?"

Everything okay now? That's it? That's all they have to say about their daughter being placed in the wrong dorm and living with all boys? I'm tempted to fire something back, but it strikes me how *tired* they sound. Just straight-up exhausted, like making this phone call took the last bit of energy they had left. I don't know if it's Sierra or the fact that we're fighting or that they're working harder given my coming here was a surprise expense they hadn't budgeted for, but the fire in me dies out as quickly as it sparked.

Plus, in fairness, all *I* want to believe for the rest of the night is that everything is okay now, so I can't blame them for wanting the same.

"Yeah, everything's okay. I ended up with my own room and bathroom, so, can't complain."

"Oh, that's great, honey," says Mom, clearly stifling a yawn. "I'm sorry we couldn't come see it today, but we'll be there for Parents' Weekend."

Ah, yes, Parents' Weekend. In two months. "Sure, Mom. Sounds good."

"How's the food?" Always my dad's first question.

"So far, so good. Can't go wrong with a baked-potato bar."

"You truly cannot," he says with a smile in his voice. "And how are the people? Have you found a card buddy—"

A crash in the background on their side, followed by a stream of profanity, cuts him off, and I wince at the realization that Sierra's there. Of course she found a way to disrupt even this thirty-second conversation. "Your sister's here," Mom says weakly, as if forgetting that I can hear everything through the speaker. "Do you want to say hi?"

My parents know that something between Craig and Sierra was the biggest reason I wanted to leave, but I wasn't about to tell them that I caught their precious oldest child bare-ass naked in bed with my boyfriend. Of course, without knowing that, they think it's just silly drama between us, like one too many sweaters borrowed without asking, and that this is more about my needing space and being dramatic than anything else. My mom assured me that I'd miss Sierra to death five minutes after I left, and I guess she's still convinced of that.

"I do not," I say as diplomatically as I can, "but it sounds like you guys have your hands full over there. I should go. I'll let you know how classes go tomorrow."

They don't seem to mind being shoved off the phone, and as soon as we hang up, I take one deep breath after another, trying to cool down the heat in my face.

Sierra steals my boyfriend, and no one cares.

Sierra curses a blue streak around my parents, and no one cares.

Sierra comes back from parties smelling like vodka and cigarette smoke, and no one cares.

I do everything right—barring tonight's stupidity with Lucas—and I end up being the one who has to run away.

What is even the *point* of being good when you get so much more out of being bad?

In a flash, it hits me. Maybe my fresh start didn't kick off exactly as I'd planned, but that's fine; I can learn from this. Because I knew what I was running away from when I came here, but I *didn't* know what it was I wanted to achieve here, and now I do.

Before I found out Lucas was a wild disappointment in every way, I *did* enjoy slipping out of orientation, breaking the rules, finally being the one to get away with something.

During move-in, when I channeled Sierra's take-charge attitude instead of rolling over and being polite, I actually finally got something done.

Today, I wasn't the good girl.

Maybe, here, I don't have to be.

And wouldn't you know, the perfect person to help me break out of my shell just happens to owe me a favor.

I open up one of my card decks and rub the two of spades for luck, then bound upstairs and look for the door right above mine, hoping to catch Matt before he commences any nightly activities I do not want to witness. Thankfully, I can see through the wide-open door that he's in there, grabbing a few things from his desk before he heads back out. Unfortunately, I forgot that his snarky roommate would be there too, but whatever; I've gotta do this while I still have the drive.

"So," I say, making both boys look up at the doorway. "Remember when you said you owe me one?"

Matt grins. "You mean a few hours ago?"

"Oh good, it's still fresh. Hold that thought." Okay, how do I phrase this? Especially in a way that won't have Salem mercilessly destroy me with mockery? "I . . . need some help."

"You need me to reach something for you?"

God, tall guys love being tall. "I need you to help me be a different person."

Salem wasn't even drinking anything, so I'm not sure what he starts choking on, but I hope it hurts.

Matt, meanwhile, takes my request in stride, as if he hears things like this on a weekly basis or so. "And what kind of person is that?"

I march into the room and sit myself down on Matt's bed. "Do you know that people are actually saying that I *begged* to live with Archibald Buchanan, of all people?"

Matt grins. "I've heard that, yeah. That's not true, is it? Because if it is, I'm gonna have to revise my assessment of your being a cool girl."

"Of course that's not true! It doesn't even make any sense!"

"Okay, phew—had to check. But yeah, people love to talk shit, and a girl in a boys' dorm is interesting. Plus, you happen to have tangled with the wrong kid today; Buchanan's a legacy, and he's got a bunch of annoying legacy friends. But tomorrow one of them will find a sale on boat shoes and they'll move on to a new topic. So who cares what they think?"

"I do," I say firmly. "I came here for a new start, and instead I'm goddamn 'Rumson Girl,' and I hate it. I want to be in control of how people see me. I definitely *don't* want to care about other people's stupid opinions, and I don't want to be 'the nice girl.'"

"We all heard you tear Barnett a new one at orientation," Salem points out, I guess referring to skid-mark guy. "Don't worry—no one thinks you're a nice girl."

"Well, I'm usually a nice girl," I snap. "That was an exception." I pause. "And so's this."

"Sounds to me like you're already doing a great job." Salem gives me jazz hands, and I wish I had something on me to throw at his smug face.

"Ease up, Grayson," says Matt, and I could hug him. "I think you're a nice girl, but I'm still not sure what it is you want from me. Are you coming on to me? Because usually I can tell when a girl wants to bone, but you're a bit of a conundrum, dormie."

A conundrum. That's already far more interesting than anything else I have ever been called. "I do not wanna bone," I say, nearly gagging on the words. "In fact, I specifically do not wanna bone, or date, or anything involving boys right now; this version of me has made way too many bad choices in that department. Also, if I'm gonna be on people's radar, let it be for something a lot cooler than having been Archibald Buchanan III's roommate for three minutes."

"And you think I can make you cool?"

"I think the kinds of girls who climb your rope ladder probably have a lot more fun and take a lot more risks than I do. And while I really do not have any interest in climbing your rope ladder in a literal *or* metaphorical sense, I *do* want to become the kind of girl who takes chances. Breaks rules. Makes her own reputation. Has actual *fun*." I cross my legs in a way I'm sure would be extremely seductive if I were not wearing plaid flannel pajama pants. "Teach me your mischievous ways, Matthew."

Out of the corner of my eye, I see Salem opening his mouth, and I immediately shut that down. "Not a word."

He shrugs and goes back to shoving his clothes in his drawers. It makes my hands itch to fold them, but bad girls don't fold other people's shirts. Boxers, *maybe*.

"Evie." Matt sits down on the edge of his desk with a sigh. "You do not need to be anyone else. And I do not want to be responsible for corrupting you in any way. You seem very . . ." He waves his hands as he tries to come up with the correct phrasing, and that's how I know it's going to hurt like a dagger to the soul. "Pure of heart."

"Says who?"

"Says the fact that you showed up at my door in flannel jammies asking for help getting into trouble because you literally don't know how to do it yourself," he says, the corners of his mouth lifting in a smile. "This campus does not need another me, and besides, I only have one vice. Unless you're interested in a very specific kind of lesson . . ." His lewd gestures do suggest expertise, but I shudder anyway. "Yeah." His smile turns into a full-fledged grin now. "That's what I thought. Catch ya later, dormie, roomie."

He puts a warm, brotherly hand on my shoulder on his way out, and I want to die.

"Okay, well," I mutter, "that was about as humiliating as a day can get." I turn to walk out, when suddenly I hear my name, and I cringe. I should've known Salem would get one last insult in before I go.

I whirl around. "If you tell anyone about this, I will murder you in cold blood."

"Is that part of being a bad girl?"

"Oh, shut up," I snap. "Did you just want to tell me that I'm pathetic?"

"No, not that. I mean, yes, also that." He tries three times to shut his overstuffed drawer, and finally gives up and stands. "But I'll help you anyway."

"You." I lean against the doorframe. "Why on earth would you help me?"

"Because I am dying to see what it looks like when a girl whose head is literally a ball of sunshine goes rogue."

My hand immediately flies to my puffy bun of curls. "What is it with you Graysons and my hair?"

He drops onto his bed and picks up a lighter from his bedside table, tossing it from hand to hand as he ignores my question. "I will, however, need something in return."

"Oh?"

"Obviously I don't need your help to become a total stud, but Matt tells me you signed on to keep his dirty little secrets, and I'm gonna need in on that action."

"You don't strike me as the lady-killer type," I say bluntly. "At least not in the metaphorical sense."

He snorts and flicks the lighter like it's a child's toy. "No? Guess I'll have to stick to the usual weed and truancy then."

"I'm not peeing in a cup for you, if that's where this is going," I inform him, staunchly keeping my eyes away from the flame, feeling for reasons I can't begin to understand as if it's a challenge.

"I wouldn't dare ask, but only because I've heard they can tell it's a girl." He tosses the lighter aside, picks up one of those minibasketballs, and starts spinning it with his fingers. "That said, I'm sure there'll be plenty of other opportunities to cover for me, and Matt's right—if you need to ask how to get yourself in trouble, you've definitely got exactly the never-touched-weed, four-point-oh kind of vibe I need." He's right on both counts, but I don't like how he says it. "My parents are really fucking pissed about me getting tossed out of my last school, and if it happens again, the next one is *not* gonna be a castle-looking joint with a waffle bar. So you help keep me here, and I'll help you . . ." He waves a hand in my general direction, as if my entire situation is just too dire for words.

It's only the second-most insulted I've been today, but it still feels like too much to let slide. "I have a better idea," I say, holding up my hand for the ball, which he tosses in my direction. It lands with a satisfying smack against my palm, and I toss it back. "How about instead of covering for you while you continue to be a parent-displeasing stoner slacker waste of space, I just . . . help you not to be?"

His smirk is so annoying, I wish it were physically possible to rip it from his face. "So I can be more like you, the super-dork who somehow landed herself in an all-boys dorm?"

"Hey." Again, tough to argue that point, but he doesn't have to say it.

"*You're* the one who showed up here begging to be taught how to be cool," he reminds me, tossing the ball back and forth between his hands. I can't help watching the ball roll off the tips of his long, thin, surprisingly elegant fingers, like a kitten mesmerized by a yo-yo. "And I can't argue with you needing it, because that was literally the most uncool thing I have ever seen in my entire life."

"Yeah, well, at least I *chose* to come to Camden," I snap, because it's literally all I've got. Anyway, it doesn't matter; he's right that I'm here to change, and I *will* change. "Whatever, are you in or not? You teach me how to be bad, and I'll teach you how to be good. Deal?"

"Guess so." And then he sends the ball flying back like a boomerang, and of course, my reflexes can't keep up and it bounces right off my face. But I guess that's something we can work on, too. I ignore his quiet laughter, grab it from the floor, and toss it at him, making for the door. "Your first lesson is free—fold your damn clothes. We'll start on the rest tomorrow." I *do* love a project.

"You're a peach, you know that?"

"No," I say, yanking open the door and flashing my most charming smile over my shoulder as I make my exit. "I *was* a peach. Now I'm a bad apple."

Chapter Four

NOW THAT SALEM AND I are—well, not *friends,* but partners in a pact, at least, I decide we're tight enough for me to sit with him at breakfast. "By the way, I met your sister yesterday," I tell him as I plunk my tray down next to his, my stack of waffles with a dollop of whipped cream a heaping contrast to his omnipresent sad green apple.

"I know." He pulls a paper clip from his pocket and twists it out of shape with his free hand. I know before it even touches the table that he's going to use it to scratch his name into the tabletop. I don't know where her never-ending supply of paper clips came from, but Sierra used to do that all the time.

"You know? I didn't think you and your sister talked."

He gives me a quick side-eye before returning to his task. "She's my sister. I talk to her every day, whether I like it or not. Do you not have siblings?"

Well, that's a loaded question. And oh, how I love the idea

of Sierra not existing in this new world of mine. But still, it feels like too big a lie. And anyway, I can't imagine Salem will care to do too much digging. "One. And we do not, in fact, talk every day. Or at all."

"Oh."

"You didn't tell Sabrina about our . . . arrangement, did you?"

He rolls his eyes. "Yeah, like I'm dying to share that you slipped a note under my door this morning outlining a basic hygiene regimen."

I was actually particularly proud of my first contribution, and he can pretend his nails aren't cleaner this morning than they were yesterday, but I know better. Still, I keep my smugness to myself so I can scout the room while he goes back to his rabbit food. I know it's inevitable that I'll see Heather and Lucas together at some point, but I'd like to push it off for as long as humanly possible.

Thankfully, when Sabrina rolls in a few minutes later, she's sans roommate, buying me at least a little more time before I have to face the very nice girl whose boyfriend I accidentally-ish made out with. I wave to get her attention so she knows we have a seat for her, and she joins us a couple of minutes later with a heaping bowl of cereal as rainbow bright as her all-black ensemble is . . . not.

"Hark, the goth princess has awoken." Salem flicks a bright pink O off the top of her breakfast as she forcefully nudges his tray aside to make room for hers. "Does your vampire clan know you're up before nine A.M.?"

"Does your face know it's hideous?" she returns without

so much as a glance in his direction as she shoves a spoonful of sugar in her mouth.

"Do your faces know they're the same?" I ask, and receive disgusted looks in return.

"Guess you both survived your first night in Rumson," Sabrina says wryly, tugging on one of her Wednesday Addams braids. "I'd say you deserve a cookie, but you wouldn't eat it"—she nods toward Salem's green apple—"and you . . . have already got plenty going on there." She eyes the heaping pile of whipped cream on my waffles.

"Tell me you are not judging *my* sugar intake when you're eating a bowl of cavity seeds for breakfast."

Salem gives his virtuous apple breakfast an extra-large smug chomp, self-righteousness dribbling down his chin as he grins while scrolling on his phone.

"Don't mind him," says Sabrina with a wave of her hand. "He's always been annoying, always will be annoying."

"Noted," I say with an official nod. "And how was your first night at Lockwood? Was it one big massive slumber party full of snacks and rom-com watching and everyone doing each other's nails?"

"I can't actually tell if you're kidding."

"Neither can I," I admit in a grumble, stabbing into a waffle and dragging it through the melting whipped cream, "but I bet whatever you did, it was better than having a bunch of guys play the penis game in front of your door while you were trying to sleep."

"Sorry, the what now?" she asks, blinking slowly.

"You know—people take turns saying 'penis' louder than

the person before until everyone's screaming it? Do you not have this game in . . . where are you guys from? Romania?"

"Yep, nailed it," Salem says coolly.

"And we do," Sabrina adds, scooping up another colorful bite as she too checks something on her phone. "I just wanted to hear you describe it."

I stuff a piece of waffle into my mouth and chew. "I don't think I like either one of you, now that I think about it."

They fist-bump without lifting their gazes from their respective screens.

Note to self: Make new friends. I finish my waffles as quickly as I can and declare that I'm heading to my first-period English class. Turns out, Salem's in the same one, so we head over to the charmingly nicknamed "Sac" (a.k.a. Student Academic Center) together, which is helpful, since I have no recollection of where the classroom is inside its network of hallways.

"Skeevy—" There's a yank on the back of my shirt, and I just miss banging into a beefy guy about twice my height when Salem pulls me out of the path of hallway traffic. "We're in here."

I'm too flustered over nearly going the wrong way to shoot dagger eyes at Salem for the noxious new nickname. And it doesn't make me feel better that Salem's just as new as I am, but he's not tripping all over himself getting lost in these new-to-us hallways.

"It helps if you actually move," Salem says with a snort, dropping awfully heavily into a seat for someone who probably weighs eighty pounds soaking wet.

I stick out my tongue like the sophisticated young woman I am and slide into the seat next to him. At least his obnoxiousness is a decent distraction from the hell of my brain.

Spoke too soon. While Salem may be a soul-sucking void, I catch a now-familiar blond head walking past me as I pull out my preferred pens. Apparently, I don't get even one single period of freedom before I have to stare my newest bad choice in the face.

Well, metaphorically speaking; I'm still two rows behind him. But I hate it all the same.

Before I can come up with a good reason I must switch sections immediately, a birdlike woman marches right up to the whiteboard and stabs "Mrs. Frank" on it with a firm hand of black dry-erase marker. She's wearing an absolutely pristine white shirt with a gray flannel skirt and the most severe loafers I've ever seen on someone who wasn't playing a prison guard in a movie.

"Alton, Kayla?"

Well, no pleasantries, then.

I crane my neck for a glimpse of the girl saying "Here," eager to put faces with names so this place can stop feeling so alien. Apparently, I'm not the only one with that idea, and I feel bad when all the prying eyes make her shrink a little in her seat, hiding her cheeks with a curtain of box braids.

"Burke, Lucas?"

"Yes, ma'am. It's a pleasure."

Ugh, truly, he can go fuck himself. I never used to think in swear words, but two days at Camden and I've already learned that sometimes, you just need them. It's truly annoying that his accent and dimples are as cute as they are; Sierra would call him a-fucking-dorable. And she'd say it in the same tone she used to use about Craig, like he was a sweet child who probably looked like a Ken doll under his jeans.

Maybe that's why she just had *to sleep with him.* I stifle a snort, not realizing I'm scratching a groove into the desk with my pen until I'm staring the blue ink straight in the face. *She had to know if he was all doll parts.*

I lay the pen quietly on the wood and focus on the whiteboard, letting the names of my classmates drift around me and trying to recenter myself. I've played Why Did Sierra Do It? at least once a day for the last four months, and it's a stupid and pointless game. Sierra slept with my boyfriend for the same reason she did everything: because she wanted to.

Which brings me back to the question of the day: What do *I* want to do to kick off my year of badassery?

I hazard a glance at Salem, who barks "Here!" as soon as "Grayson" is called, drowning out what must be his real first name before letting her know he prefers to be called Salem. He's a little mystery wrapped in an enigma, that one. He pretends to be annoyed by his sister, but he goes by the nickname that ties them together. And he pretends not to care about self-improvement, but he smells much better today, like clean flannel and leather, a hint of pine.

He's kind of a jerk, kind of a mess, and definitely needs some etiquette lessons, but if I'm going to pull this miserable year out of the depths, he might be my only hope.

Thankfully, Lucas isn't in chem with me second period. (Though the delightful Archibald Buchanan is, and can you believe he didn't want to be lab partners?) I don't glimpse him while traipsing through the Sac lobby at snack time for a freshly baked chocolate chip cookie, either. (I have no idea if that's a regular thing, but I do know it's officially my new favorite part of boarding school.) We're seated alphabetically in APUSH, which puts us all the way across the room from each other, and in the biggest blessing of all, we don't even have the same lunch period.

At least someone in the universe is on my side.

Still, a whole three more years of this sounds like a nightmare.

"What's the face? Are you not a fan of frittatas?" Salem pronounces the word in the absolute most annoying way possible, with extra emphasis on every *t* and a few he definitely made up.

"I'm surprised you're deigning to eat with me again today," I say before smiling at the server and receiving my eggs with hash browns on the side. "Really, don't feel the need to take pity on me. In fact, perhaps now would be the right time for you to discover the lost 'good boy' art of eating alone."

"No can do," he says ruefully as he gets a plate filled with way more food than could possibly fit in his string bean of a body. "See, my roommate keeps trying to take me under his wing, and he happens to be in this lunch period. So unless I want him trying to sit me with a table full of jock bros, I need a diversion."

"Jock bros?"

He rolls his eyes. "You know what I mean."

I do, but more than that, I don't have anyone else to sit with. Sabrina and Heather don't have lunch this period either, and the only person I recognize thus far is Kayla Alton, who's wearing headphones while she works on something, clearly not looking to mingle.

And so, it is with a heavy sigh that I follow half a step behind Salem to get drinks and then snag an empty table, where I slide my tray down next to his.

It doesn't go unnoticed. "What's with you?" He reaches into his bag and pulls out a sandwich, ignoring the huge heap of eggs and hash browns on his plate. "I feel like you're usually . . . bouncier."

"Again, you're thinking of my hair," I tell him, digging into my lunch. I'm not sure I've ever actually had a frittata, but it basically just looks like a fluffy egg pie, and that cannot possibly be bad. If I were at GHS right now, I'd probably be poking at a soggy slice of pizza or a mound of beef stew that resembled neither beef nor stew.

Camden's menu is a clear upgrade, but for the briefest of moments my heart aches anyway, because I'd also be feeling Craig's ankle hooked around mine, and hearing Claire quiz herself with her trademark flash cards between bites of a bagel with cream cheese and cucumber cut into fourths.

Well, once upon a time I would have, anyway.

I watch as he takes a bite of the sandwich, which looks to be peanut butter and jelly on whole wheat. "You brought your own sandwich to lunch?"

He shrugs. "So?"

"You . . ." I gesture at his egg mountain. "What was the point of—"

"Hey, roomie." Before I can finish my sentence, a huge hand claps Salem's shoulder so hard he almost coughs out his sandwich. "Mind if I join you?" Matt doesn't wait for an answer before taking a seat. "And Evie! I hope I'm not interrupting anything."

The innuendo in his tone has me nearly choking on a piece of fried potato. "So much," I say, my eyes watering as I take a sip of water. "Salem and I were about to bang on this table."

"She wishes."

"Hey, I told you," says Matt, grabbing Salem's fork and helping himself to the hash browns he's clearly not eating. "If you've got a lady—or anyone else; you do you—in the room, just hang a sock on the door."

"I did that. Last night. You came in anyway."

"Yeah, but I covered my eyes, didn't I?"

I narrow my eyes at Salem. "*You* had a girl in your room last night?" For a brief moment, I have to wonder what it could possibly look like for Salem to lay on the charm enough to convince a girl to hook up with him, and I simply cannot. She'd have to be the type *very* easily seduced by a bit of swagger and a pair of gorgeous eyes. Not that *I* have thoughts about Salem's eyes; I'm just saying—

"No, I just wanted the place to myself." He swallows the last bite of his sandwich and stands up. "Well, this has been real, but I gotta go be not here." He slings his messenger bag over his shoulder and starts to stand, but Matt pushes him back down.

"You're being rude to the lady."

I nod. "Your roommate is not the friendliest, I'm finding."

"Eh, he'll warm up," Matt says confidently. "You gonna come cheer for him on Thursday night?"

"I haven't made a single plan for this week further than attending the club fair after classes today." I glance at Salem, who seems to be trying to laser-beam an exit portal into the tabletop using the power of his stare. "What's Thursday night?"

"Nothing," he mutters.

"And I thought *I* was a bad liar." I take a noisy sip of my fountain Coke and turn to Matt. "What's Thursday night?"

"My parents are making me try out for the basketball team, okay?" Salem spits. "Now shut up, both of you."

I try not to laugh. I really do. But the image of the skinny goth boy next to me ambling slowly up the court in a jersey and shorts is way too much.

"Oh, fuck you." Salem starts to gather up his stuff again, but this time I push him back down.

"I'm sorry, I'm sorry." I use my free hand to dig my nails into my thigh, which finally helps me stop laughing. "Anyway, isn't basketball a winter sport? Why are there tryouts already?"

"It's for the intramural team, technically," Matt explains. "We play Tuesday and Thursday nights. But Coach basically handpicks players from it to make varsity in November and uses those games as preseason training. He's not supposed to, but." He gives a big, showy shrug. "Anyway, your boy here's just lucky to have a roommate who knows the ins and outs and convinced him of the importance of showing up."

"Strategic thinking," I say, tapping my temple. "I dig it." I turn to Salem. "For what it's worth, I think it's awesome that you're trying out, and I will definitely come cheer you on."

"Please don't."

"He doesn't mean that," Matt assures me.

"Oh, I know. What time are tryouts?"

"After your bedtime," says Salem at the same time Matt says, "Seven."

"Great!" I smile toothily at Salem, whose eyes are absolutely brimming with murder. "Oh, and I'll bring Sabrina! I bet she'd love to cheer on her bro."

"I will kill you in your sleep."

"Thursday night, seven o'clock," I confirm, taking another huge bite of eggs. "Can. Not. Wait."

At GHS, the extracurricular offerings were pretty standard, and since I didn't have the athletic ability to do volleyball like Sierra, or the musical talent to do marching band like Claire, I resigned myself to afternoons of studying, crappy TV, watching Craig and his friends play video games in his basement, or playing poker, when I could get a decent game together. (And before people got sick of me taking their money.)

At Camden, extracurriculars—well, cocurriculars, technically—are mandatory from four to five every weekday afternoon, and judging by the club fair, there's plenty to fill the time. Who needs tennis or debate when you've got baking and board games? (Yes, I obviously sign up for both of these.)

I'm trying to size up both the Book Club and Quiz Bowl tables at once when I realize I know the pair standing in front of the Business Investors League booth. Sure enough, there's a French braid grazing the sign-up sheet as Heather bends over to scrawl her name, and next to her, Lucas's deep dimples are in high relief as he chats with the besuited upperclassman rep.

I immediately head in the opposite direction, but I don't get far before I hear my name being called, and slowly turn to find Heather smiling and waving me over. I have no choice but to drag myself to the Business Investors League table. "Hey, Heather. I didn't take you for the investor type."

"I'm not—yet," she says with a hint of the warm smile that seems permanently affixed to her face. "But it seems like something I could stand to learn. My mom's always saying she wishes she knew more about the stock market, so I figured I could learn for us both."

"Love that," I say, and the way Lucas is looking at her, it seems like he loves that too.

Or maybe he's simply trying to avoid eye contact.

And then, because the bile in my stomach hasn't come all the way up yet, her smile widens and she says, "Evie, have you met Lucas?"

"Met" is just such an interesting word for what I've done with Lucas, and when I meet his eyes, I expect to see them widen in fear or prayer or *something*. But there's no reaction, like either he's so confident I'll play along, or he's already forgotten who I am.

Either way, fuck that guy.

"He's in my English class."

He swallows, nods, jerks his thumb toward the table. "You joining up too?"

"Not my type of gambling, personally. But I expect to make a mean cinnamon bun by the end of a semester of Baking Club."

"Definitely a worthy choice," he drawls, as if I care about his approval. Heather's already checked out of this conversation, eagerly flipping through different binders and pamphlets laid out on the table, and I take that as a sign that I've put in enough time.

I glance around for a smooth exit strategy, my eyes lighting on a familiar face on the row of athletic booths. "Speaking of worthy," I say, infusing my voice with as much "unlike my present company" as I can, "I see a friend I've got to say hi to. Good to see you, Heather." And then I turn my back on Lucas Burke to sail right over to Matt Haley, and I can feel him watching me every step of the way.

"Dormie!" Matt throws his arms wide when he sees me walking up to the basketball booth, where he sits next to a hot Asian dude whose jaw could cut glass. His teammate is staring at his phone as if it holds the secrets of the universe, but every ten seconds or so, he glances up at the absolutely stunning girl standing across from them, looking like he wishes he could literally drown himself in her strawberry-blond waves. "You coming to join the team? I *knew* you were a Cougar at heart."

"Yes, Matthew. I've decided to join the boys' basketball team to add further confusion and ensure I will never get out of Rumson. I thought you guys would really benefit from my extra height."

The girl gives me a toothy smile, and even though I am reasonably certain I am heterosexual, I also feel like I would give her all my earthly possessions if she'd smile at me like that again someday. "Oh, I like you. You're the Rumson Girl?"

I resist the urge to grimace. "Evie."

"Isabel McEvoy." There's a brief moment where I feel like everyone's waiting to see if that means anything to me, but it's over so quickly that I must've imagined it. "Matty and I go way back." Before I can respond to that, she tips her head to the side, her gorgeous hair flowing over her shoulder. "Hey, what did you sign up for on Friday afternoons?"

"Nothing yet, I don't think." I glance down at the haphazard schedule I've been jotting down in my Notes app. "So far I've got Book Club, Baking Club, and Board Games Club, so I guess I need something else with a *B*? *Not* basketball," I clarify to Matt before he can get any ideas.

"Well, 'community service' starts with a *C*," says Isabel, "but we do collect *bottles* for recycling sometimes? And *bring* food to the elderly?"

I nod. "That counts." Not exactly the Friday night of my dreams, but it's not like I have any plans, and anyway, how does one say no to community service? Or to Isabel McEvoy? "Where do I sign up?"

"Oh, I got it. Don't worry," she says with another smile that has undoubtedly brought at least 50 percent of the student body to its knees. "I won't forget you."

She says it like I'm memorable, like I'm somebody, like I'm not just a campus punch line or a warm body or a gateway to somebody else, and in that moment, she is my favorite person at Camden.

"You know," she adds, "I thought you'd take a little more convincing."

"Do I not look like someone who would service my community?" I bite my lips as even Matt's teammate looks up from his phone at that one. "Hold on, I hear how that sounds."

"No judgment from me," Matt says with a shrug. "I am all for servicing the community. I know that's what I'll be doing on Friday night."

"Let me guess—there may even be bottles involved?"

"Probably not bringing food to the elderly," he admits, his mouth widening into the cocky grin I'm coming to know very well, "unless you count—"

"Do not finish that sentence," Isabel and I say simultaneously.

"You're both no fun," Matt says, but the smile on his face doesn't fade in the slightest. "And speaking of people who are no fun! Grayson! Come over here!"

I turn to see Salem not-so-subtly looking for an out, but finding none, he trudges over to the basketball table, hands jammed in the pockets of his hoodie. "I already told you, I'm coming on Thursday. You can chill on the hard sell."

"Can't a guy just say hi to his roommate?"

"And a girl say hi to her bestie?" I can't resist adding.

His answering scowl does not disappoint, but you can see the exact moment he spots Isabel standing behind me, because he stands up a little straighter, adding inches to his height in an instant, and adjusts the strap on his messenger bag as if it'll make him look even 5 percent less like he just rolled out of bed. The urge to tease him is so strong, I have to change the subject in order to stop myself.

Of course, what comes out of my mouth is "I'm going to service the community on Friday night."

Well, at least that drops the scowl from his face, though his smirk isn't any more welcome. "Thanks for the advance warning. I'll make sure to wear earplugs."

Oh, I am going to cheer extra loud at tryouts.

Extra, extra loud.

Chapter Five

SEVEN O'CLOCK FALLS RIGHT IN the middle of the study-hour block, but as I learn by Thursday night, no one really cares where you are in the evenings if you're on campus and your homework's getting done at some point. By ten minutes to, my homework is long complete, and I'm wearing the closest thing to a cheerleader outfit I could find, partly because it'll annoy the hell out of Salem and partly because it was the best costume choice I could think of for the current mission: encourage Salem to make the team (a thing his parents clearly think of as good). Aaaand if it maybe helps some of the other guys on the team think I'm hot, that's maybe not the worst thing as far as my new reputation goes.

Sabrina's door cracks open a few seconds after I knock, and her dark gray eyes look me up and down, taking in my cropped sweater and pleated skirt. "Did you seriously dress up like a slutty cheerleader?"

Sabrina's wearing a tight black skirt to go with black tights and a black top whose shape I cannot begin to understand. "Did you bring an extra blood bag in case you get thirsty?"

"I'm sure I can find some on the court after a few minutes of Salem going up against the Camden basketball team." She swipes on a coat of black cherry lip gloss and yanks the door closed behind her. "Why are we doing this again?"

"Because he's your brother and you love and support him," I remind her as we head toward the gym.

"So why are *you* doing this again?"

"Because he's your brother and I loathe him and want to watch him fall on his ass."

"Got it."

Tryouts are already in full swing by the time we arrive, but Salem immediately spots us anyway, his groan audible. Sabrina and I both wave and flash back huge smiles, and I even shake imaginary pom-poms. "I burned incense for luck!" Sabrina calls to him, and watching him attempt to melt into the floor is really gratifying. I'm positive he's going to accidentally let a basketball go flying out of his fingers and directly toward our faces, but then a guy who must be the coach barks his name and off he goes.

"Why exactly are your parents making him do this?" I ask Sabrina as we make ourselves comfortable in the bleachers with a few other scattered spectators.

"Are they?" She snorts. "Probably trying to make him more social. They tried the same thing on me with the tennis team in junior high."

"Did it work?"

One of her thin eyebrows arches delicately. "Do you think it worked?"

"I do not."

"And that is why you are in honors classes." Suddenly, her eyebrows crash down to earth. "Uh, is it just me, or is Salem not horrifically bad?"

Honestly, I hadn't really been paying much attention, but now that I am, I'm borderline horrified to see that Salem is . . . pretty damn good. He ambles around the court like he has nowhere in particular to be, but his ballhandling is surprisingly artful, thanks to those long fingers, and when he gets a clear shot, he's got some killer aim. Plus, he's like six foot thirty, so he gets some blocks in by default.

I'd planned to obnoxiously cheer Salem on through every dribble off his foot and wild airball, but as usual, he simply refuses to cooperate. Instead, Sabrina and I watch in stunned silence as Salem makes not one but two NBA-worthy steals, then crushes all the other guys in a free throw competition. "What the fuck?" she whispers, taking the words right out of my mouth. Just the fact of Salem having biceps is confusing and strange.

The only thing making his competence slightly more bearable is that Lucas is *also* trying out, and Salem is absolutely destroying him.

Finally, the coach blows the whistle and sends them for a water break. As a sweat-drenched Salem chugs an entire Nalgene's worth in one go, I'm pretty sure he's smirking at us.

I stomp down the bleachers until I'm sitting a couple of feet away. "Well aren't you the little jock in hiding?"

He waggles his eyebrows and continues to drink, his gaze flickering over my cheerleading outfit without betraying a single emotion.

"Seriously, Salem, what the fuck?" Sabrina demands. "When did you learn how to shoot like that?"

He finally tears himself away from the water and wipes his face on his shirt. "When Mom and Dad said they'd add two hundred bucks to my car fund if I made the team."

"Fucker!" Sabrina's mouth drops open. "God, they're not even hiding that you're the favorite."

"How could anyone possibly hide that I'm the favorite?"

Matt walks up and holds up his hand for a high five, which I'm pretty sure Salem only gives him to drown out Sabrina's retort. "Way to go, Gray. There's still one more round of guys, but Coach is already glowing about you."

Salem just nods, his eyes on the floor, but he's so obviously beaming on the inside, biting his usual pout so it won't blossom into a proud smile. It would almost be cute, if it weren't . . . Salem.

"So what's next, brother dear?" Sabrina asks. "Gonna surprise us all with a hot cheerleader girlfriend?"

"Careful," Matt warns, gesturing toward me. "You don't wanna make this one jealous."

God, so predictably annoying. "But . . . but I thought I was *your* girlfriend!" I say to Matt with just the right amount of lip wobble. "Are you telling me our love has been in my head this whole time?"

"See? I'm telling you," Matt says knowingly to Salem. "Trouble."

Salem rolls his eyes. "Aren't you late for an unprotected orgy under the bleachers?"

Matt starts to reply, and is immediately cut off by a stunning blonde who bounces right up to him and kisses him full on the mouth. "Matty, you promised to . . ." She trails off and whispers the rest in his ear, for which I am extremely grateful. Next thing I know, she's leading him—where else?—under the bleachers.

"Not unprotected!" he calls back. "Never unprotected."

"Gross," Salem and Sabrina say simultaneously, but before I can respond, the door flies open and in walks Isabel with three similarly stunning friends. They promptly take up residence in the back row of the bleachers, as if hoping not to draw attention, but there isn't an eye in the room that isn't sparing them at least one lingering glance.

Well, other than Salem's. He's pretending to be immune, but I've already seen him preening in front of Isabel, and when he excuses himself back to the court, he is definitely puffing out his chest a little. I can't really blame him—they do look like one of those *Vanity Fair* spreads on Young Hollywood—but I wish he'd just own it.

And then I realize: This is the perfect thing for me to deliver on for our pact. Good grades, making the team, and cleaning up your act are all well and good, but what says "parent pleaser" like a respectable girlfriend?

I shoot glances at Isabel for the next fifteen minutes until I finally catch her eye, then wave, just enough to remind her that she knows me. I'm relieved when recognition does in fact dawn on her angelic face.

I'm going to make this real for Salem, and if it *happens* that I get myself inducted into the school's hot-girl clique at the same time, an undeniable cool-girl move, well. That's just good planning.

I spend half of English on Friday trying to think up how to get my plan in motion at community service tonight, and half of it wanting to take the pen Salem will not stop clicking next to me and jam it through his brain.

"Must you?" I whisper fiercely as he taps his thigh with it in no pattern I can possibly discern. "I'm like three seconds away from luring you down to a cellar with a cask of amontillado myself."

"Aw, look at you, doing the reading." Salem uses his makeshift instrument of torture to tap the cover of the Poe anthology we're studying this month.

"Clearly you did too, if you get the reference," I point out.

"Touché. I do love me some Gothic literature."

"A jock *and* an academic. Why Salem Grayson, you do contain multitudes."

A faint smile tugs at his mouth—entirely against his will, I'm sure. "So," I whisper while I have him in a good mood. "What's with all the nervous pen flicking?"

"Who says I'm nervous?"

"Mr. Grayson? Ms. Riley? Something you'd like to share with the class?"

Salem and I immediately straighten up in our seats as Mrs.

Frank draws the entire room's attention to us. "No, ma'am," we say simultaneously.

"Good." She returns to the lesson, and I return to staring Salem down until he sighs.

"Just waiting for the tryout results to be posted, if you must know," he mutters after a minute.

"I must," I confirm with a grin. "So you're really serious about this, huh? I'm so glad I got to see you in action."

"Oh, shut up."

"No, seriously. You're really good, Salem." Hey, we're partners in crime, or at least in this pact. I can be generous. "I have literally zero doubt you made the team."

He doesn't say anything, just sketches something I can't see in the margin of his Poe anthology, but the corner of his mouth curves up.

We stay well behaved for the rest of class, but before long I'm just as antsy as Salem to see his standing made official. As soon as the bell rings, I jump out of my seat, expecting Salem to be right behind me. But despite all that pen clicking, he's taking his sweet time.

"Aren't you dying to find the list?" I demand.

His face pinches slightly into an inscrutable expression. "It's not a big deal."

"What are you talking about? You were just . . ." I trail off as I realize. "Okay, you can't act excited about this or whatever. But I can." Before he can get out a word, I dash into the hallway, where the list has indeed been posted.

Salem Grayson is right at the top.

"Dude!" I double back to find him and give his shoulders an excited squeeze. "You made it. And I think we can both agree this is entirely due to my cheerleading. I'll have to make it a regular thing."

"You really do not," he says dryly, but right now even he can't suppress the tiny smile playing at his lips.

"We need to celebrate. How do we celebrate?" I lower my voice as we fall into step on our way to the science wing. "If you were still acting on your worst behavior, which of course you are not, how would you celebrate such a win?"

"You wanna get high with me on the roof?" he asks, eyebrow in the air. "Because that's what my friends and I would do at home."

"Tempting, but no. I've already decided my reign of terror will not include drugs."

"Your reign of terror? Is that what you're calling your planned badass phase?"

"You don't like it?"

We stop in front of my chem class. "I'd say 'never change,' but I wouldn't mean it."

"Right back atcha."

Salem starts to continue on, then seems to realize I'm not entering the classroom. "Isn't this where you have chem?"

"Yeah, I just." I shudder. "Ugh. My original roomie is in this class, so it's where the guys are the most annoying. There's always someone—usually Duncan Barnett—with a Rumson Girl joke the second I walk in, and I need a minute to brace myself so I don't scratch his eyes out."

"You're shitting me." Salem narrows his eyes, then seems to come to the conclusion I am not, in fact, shitting him. "Come on. I'll walk you in. He won't fuck with me."

"Much as I appreciate the chivalry, I'm pretty sure it's not gonna stop unless I stop it for myself. I just haven't figured out how to do that quite yet." I tip my head to the side, looking up at Salem. "Any ideas, my bad-boy guru?"

"One idea is that you never, ever call me that again."

"Turns you on, doesn't it?"

"On second thought, I'm just gonna leave you to the wolves," says Salem, turning to go.

"No, come on." I grab Salem by the back of his shirt. "We have a deal."

He sighs, but relents. "Make him uncomfortable. Guys like him can't stand it. If you just stay quiet or roll your eyes or whatever you're doing now, he's gonna keep doing it. So make him sorry he ever tried. I believe in you, Skeevy. You make me sorry I ever tried every single day."

Just then, the bell rings, and Salem swears and twists out of my grip to head to class, while I turn in to mine.

"Rumson Girl!" Duncan says right on cue. As one of Archie's best friends, he's consistently the most annoying about it, and definitely the guy behind the rumor that I specifically manipulated my way into rooming with the heir to Buchanan Imports. "Is it true you make everyone in the dorm sandwiches every day? Or am I misunderstanding what I've heard about you and Rumson sandwiches . . ."

Uncomfortable. I can definitely do uncomfortable. And I can do it with a big smile on my face, too.

"First of all, if this is you asking for a three-way with me and Hoffman, I've already told you a hundred times, absolutely not. If this is you asking for *another* three-way with me and Archiekins, I already told you, that was a onetime thing. But if you're just looking for tips, my professional opinion is that you're beyond help, and no surgeon in the world is going to be able to fix that"—I glance pointedly at his special place—"particular issue."

"Ha ha," he retorts, but it's mostly drowned out by everyone laughing at him. They might be laughing at me, too, but at least I know my face isn't turning beet red like his is.

Dr. Bock calls everyone to order, which means the end of that, and I take my seat, but not before glancing back at the door. It could just be my imagination, but I swear I catch a glimpse of Salem smirking behind the small window before he disappears.

I try to keep my own smile under control as I pull out my notebook, my eyes on my desk.

I don't know that it'll shut Duncan up tomorrow, but it's nice to have hope.

Pact, 1; rich tools, 0.

The Community Service Club meets by the main parking lot every Friday afternoon, since it's pretty much always being shuttled to one spot or another. Today it's the local soup kitchen, and in addition to Isabel and her three stunning friends, the van that takes us there also contains Mrs. Dodd, the faculty advisor; Kayla Alton from my English class; a senior couple who at no point tear their eyes or mouths off each other; two freshman boys who are clearly there to stare at Isabel and Co.; and, as I probably should've guessed, Heather, who cheerfully sits down next to me and tells me all about the people I'm going to meet, because of course she did community service all of last year as well.

The van pulls up just as she's telling me about "Bobby, who's hilarious and always wears this hat with a frog on it." At no point has there been an opportune moment to ask her whether she knows her boyfriend is a scumbag. Which means I could be forgiven for letting the entire ride go by without telling her, right?

"Hey! Evie!" A hand lands on my arm, and I'm shaken out of my upset by Isabel McEvoy's glossy smile. "So glad you made it."

"Happy to serve my new community," I reply, acutely aware of both her friends and Heather watching us. "Have you met Heather?"

"Yeah, we—" Heather starts, right as Isabel says, "No, I don't think so!" She holds out a hand toward Heather, who pastes on a smile as she shakes it. "And this is Jenna, Ashleigh, and Priya." She turns to me. "Girls, this is Evie."

They all chorus friendly hellos, and it's clear Isabel's mentioned me, which is just . . . so confusing. They're all unreasonably and dauntingly gorgeous—Jenna's a study in contrasts, with pale white skin, dark hair, and otherworldly blue eyes; Ashleigh looks exactly as I imagine Tyra Banks did at sixteen; and Priya's one of the few South Asian students

I've seen at Camden, with warm brown skin, strikingly long-lashed dark eyes, and a wide smile that could stop traffic. I don't know how stunning people somehow seem to get along simply by virtue of being stunning, but I do know I do not fit in with them.

Thankfully, I don't have time to think about it before we're ushered inside by the organizer, who introduces herself as Brenda and launches into a speech she clearly gives every visit.

"Welcome to the Pinebrook Community Center's soup kitchen," she greets us, pushing the sleeves of her chunky mauve sweater up to her elbows. "How many of you have volunteered at a soup kitchen before?" Heather, Kayla, and Isabel raise their hands. "Great, so you guys are old pros. The most important thing to remember is that these are simply people in need, and they deserve the same respect you'd give anyone else. Smile. Call them 'sir' and 'ma'am.' A little kindness goes a long way.

"Another thing we take very seriously is hygiene. We're working with food, so we want to be extra careful." She hands a cardboard box to Mrs. Dodd. "Your teacher is going to pass around latex gloves. Please take a pair."

"Do we need to wear hairnets?" asks the female half of the couple that was sucking face in the van.

Brenda smiles. "No, just keep your hair tied back and out of your face and you should be fine," she replies, looking around at us. Her gaze lands on me, and she frowns. "Except you. You should wear a hairnet."

Of course.

I do my best to ignore the stupid freshman boys taking pictures of me in my hairnet, and anyway, they mercifully stop when Isabel puts on her own. "If one of mine gets in the food, everyone will know it was me," she says with a grin, tweaking a strand of her strawberry hair before twisting it all up into an elegant knot.

My heart warms at the solidarity, and while I don't understand why Isabel is being so nice to me, I *do* wish Claire could see me and how I'm making *real* friends. I would've traded a hundred Dunkin' runs and ice-cream-filled sleepovers to have her stick up for me when it counted. And here, a girl I barely even know—a girl who clearly doesn't need any more friends than the ones she's already got—is letting herself look like a dork for me.

Well, okay, she doesn't look remotely like a dork, because it's just not possible, but. The sentiment is there.

I get assigned to peas and carrots, right next to Heather, who's charged with distributing corn bread. Not the most exciting offerings, but I try to take my cues from the Nicest Girl in the World and prepare myself to serve every scoop with a smile.

"So how do you know Isabel?" she asks, the smile never leaving her face as she arranges the yellow squares neatly in the shallow rectangular basket. Her tone is casual, but I realize that this has probably been bugging her since I first introduced them. I pretended not to hear, but I caught her saying that she and Isabel have met before, and it makes sense—if they were both on community service last year, they've probably done this together already.

Is it wrong that the idea I might've somehow stumbled into a slightly higher social stratum than the girl whose boyfriend used me and threw me away feels pretty damn good? Yeah, it's wrong. But I *never* get to be this girl. The sister of Sierra Riley never gets to be this girl. I just need, like, three seconds to enjoy it.

"Oh, we met at the club fair. Mutual friend." And here's my chance. "Speaking of people we met at the club fair, what's the deal with you and Lucas? Are you guys, like, a thing?"

Her face lights up. "Yeah, I guess we're official now. We hung out a lot last year, became really good friends, and then we just kinda started flirting and realized we liked each other. Right before the summer we said we'd see how things were when we got back, and then we talked, like, every day. So right at orientation, he asked me to be his girlfriend, and that was that."

Cool. I want to hurl everywhere. The fact that he asked her "at orientation," whether that means shortly before or right after he and I hooked up, is so gross. She seems so convinced of his greatness despite all evidence to the contrary, and it reminds me of, well, me. I deserved so much better, and so does Heather. But I just say, "Cool."

"Yeah," she says, her voice growing a little dreamy, making me incredibly sorry I ever opened this line of conversation. "We met at the parents' luncheon at orientation last year and ended up sitting together. My mom's from the Midwest, so she was excited to meet his parents. Honestly, it all feels very fated."

"Cool," I say again, because I've forgotten every other word in my vocabulary.

When she opens her mouth again, I'm already dreading whatever's about to come out, but thankfully, it's "Mr. Lambert! So nice to see you again!" I realize the time for food service has come, and the room has filled with hungry people patiently waiting for us to fill their trays with corn bread, chili, and, at the less exciting end of the table, my peas and carrots.

I tear my eyes off of the Nicest Girl in the World and get to work.

Chapter Six

THE NIGHT IS STILL YOUNG by the time the van drops us off at Camden, and I know exactly how I'm spending it. I bypass my room and head up the stairs instead to knock on Salem's door. When there's no response, I prepare to bang even harder, but then the door opens and Salem fills the frame, shaggy hair sticking out in all directions. "Skeevy? What has you darkening my door?"

"God, you stink." The smell of weed emanates from his every pore. "How do you not get in trouble when you're being that obvious?"

"For one thing, I don't usually have girls standing in my doorway, loudly declaring that I've been smoking."

"Well normally, this is when a gentleman would invite a lady inside."

He snorts. "I'm not a gentleman, and you are definitely not a lady."

"You're not a gentleman *yet*," I correct him. "But we are going to fix that. And we are going to take our first big step tonight."

"Which means?"

"Which *means* you're going to crawl out of your room and join me at one of the many fine options available to us." I walk across the hallway and scan the list hanging on the second floor's communal bulletin board. "How about movie night?" I ask as I shoulder past him into his room, slipping off my shoes and making myself comfortable on his soft flannel sheets.

"Movie night sounds like—"

"A great idea? I know, I think so too. But you should shower first; you smell like bong water. And let's introduce you to a comb. Also, this music is abysmal. Can we work on that too?"

He exhales sharply, rustling his damp shaggy bangs and proving my point. "This is Phish!"

"I don't know what that means." I curl my legs under my butt and take in my surroundings. Matt's side of the room is pristine, like he makes sure to keep it in perfect condition in case a female visitor should come by. "Where's he?"

He glances at his wrist, as if there were a watch there. "Hmm, it's Friday, so . . . I believe that means Kylie."

"At least he's efficient?"

"That he is." Salem crosses his arms behind his head and leans against the wall. "Now, can we get back to your wanting to give me a makeover? Or actually, maybe we should never, ever get back to that."

"It's not a *makeover*. This is going to be your first time

doing an actual social thing. I'm just helping you present yourself decently to the world. This is why you have me. I'm gonna clean you up, hook you up with the hot girls, and impress your parents so hard they'll lose their minds."

Do I know how I'm going to do any of that? I do not. But up until my friends betrayed me and I had a little breakdown, I was *excellent* at parent-pleasing. Craig's parents certainly loved me. I wonder how they feel about seeing my sister slip into my shoes.

Or maybe they never had to see it, because she probably dropped him as soon as I left and the game stopped being fun.

"And how exactly does this fit into *your* reign of terror?" he asks as I hop up and start digging through his closet, pushing aside flannel after grungy hoodie after flannel.

"We'll get to that," I promise, "but right now, we're focusing on you. And you can't pretend you have no vested interest in learning how to become a chick magnet."

"Did you just—"

"I'll use whatever terminology I want to use," I say, cutting him off. "And if you think I haven't noticed you checking out a certain long-legged redhead, you are dead wrong."

There's no smart-ass response, which I take to mean I've hit the right nerve. And, almost simultaneously, I hit the right shirt. "Here," I say, sliding the black button-up off the hanger and tossing it in his direction. "It appears to be your only shirt that doesn't have a band logo on it."

"You know I packed that shirt strictly for Parents' Weekend, right?" He throws it back at me. "I'm not wearing that to watch a shitty rom-com in a room reeking of fake butter."

We compromise on a zip-up hoodie that looks slightly nicer than the others and a pair of well-worn jeans. Then he kicks me out so he can get dressed, and I tell him to pick me up from my room.

"You do not need me to pick you up," he says, already sounding tired. "This isn't an actual date."

"No, but you need to learn how to take a girl on one, so get practicing. I'll see you in fifteen minutes. *Showered.*" I let myself out, and only then does the panic set in, because I may have helped dress Salem, but who's going to help dress me? Yes, most of the point of tonight is to get Salem noticed, looking like an actual human, but a tiny part *is* about people seeing *me* out and about with an actual boy, rather than fifty ~lovers~ they've made up in their minds.

Salem is only a couple of minutes late, but he looks fresh and clean, and the jeans are, admittedly, excellent-ass jeans, literally. His hair isn't *neat,* but it looks more rock-star disheveled than stoner mess. All in all, I'd give the cleanup a seven out of ten on the "Am I taking this seriously or just humoring the annoying girl downstairs" scale.

"Are you ready?" he asks on a sigh that sounds way too exasperated for the fact that our night is only just beginning.

No, I am not ready. I'd put on my black jeans and a silky green top and I realize now I look way too overdressed for a freaking on-campus movie night. But I was already running late and I had to apply eyeliner three times before I got it right, and how am I still a disaster? "One sec—I just need to change my shirt."

His gaze flickers over me. "You look fine, Skeevy."

"Just gimme one minute. You can wait inside. I'll change in the bathroom." I grab a T-shirt that's admittedly plain but has a very flattering (read: low) neckline and hang it on the grab bar by the toilet while I remove the fancier top.

"Where's all your stuff?" Salem calls. "You seem like someone who'd have pictures all over the place."

I make a mental note to hang up some random garbage so people will stop asking me that. The thing is, he's not wrong; I was that person, once. My room at home was full of silly portraits done by Claire and my mom's favorite inspirational sayings in shades of purple and silver. My bookcases were packed with candy-colored romance novels, and there were cute little cactus candles dotting the shelves and strings of fairy lights brightening my walls with a soft glow.

But it was in that soft glow that I used to make out with the boyfriend my sister stole. And all the best-friend magic of those paintings faded the moment I came crying to Claire and she admitted she'd known for a while. My parents bought me those candles and sayings, and I didn't need to bring any reminders of the people who responded to every shitty thing Sierra did with some variation of "She's just acting out; move on." As if breaking into all my social media accounts and posting a picture of me in my underwear in response to my making the debate team as a freshman when she didn't is equivalent to a toddler drawing on the wall in crayon.

So no, I don't put pictures all over the place anymore, or anything else I used to do back when I was "Sierra Riley's little sister." Having bare walls is a small price to pay for finally being allowed to put up any walls at all.

"I'm a minimalist," I lie as I slide on the T-shirt and fluff out my hair before emerging from the bathroom. "Better?"

"Also fine."

"You're supposed to be helping," I remind him.

"How is this any less than you did by telling me to change and smell less bad?"

I take a dramatic sniff of him and note that the stench of weed has been replaced by something pleasantly woodsy instead, a little stronger than the pine-scented soap the other day. Like he might actually have ventured into the world of cologne. "That's two tips! And you took both!"

"Okay, well, you already smell fine, so I have no other advice."

"Nothing? I look boring, Salem! A T-shirt and jeans screams 'nice girl.'"

"So add a leather jacket," he says, rolling his eyes.

"Do I look like I own a leather jacket?" I ask, and as I'm saying it, I realize. "*You* look like you own a leather jacket. Lend it to me?"

"What if I don't have one?"

"You do."

Another deep sigh, and then he slogs up to his room and brings it down. It's too long, and the sleeves are *definitely* too long, but with the addition of a couple of long necklaces, I actually kind of love this look. "What do you think now?"

"I think we should go before the movie ends and you made me get dressed for nothing."

"I'll take it." I swipe on some lip gloss and off we go to

make our debuts as the Sociable Athlete and the Tough Hot Girl.

Salem completely ignores me on the walk to the Student Center, opting instead to listen to music so loudly I can make out lyrics through his headphones. But when we arrive, he seems to remember that he's supposed to be picking up some chivalrous skills, and he holds the door open for me.

Of course, he sweeps into a low bow and says "Milady" in a dry British accent as he does it, but it's a start.

"Why thank you." We follow signs to the auditorium, where they're showing the movie, and I could swear I feel a couple of eyes on us as we pass. It's exactly what I need to turn to Salem and say, "Remember when you asked how this fits in for me?"

"I do."

"Great! Hold my hand."

"I'm sorry, hold your what now?"

I hold out my hand. "Take it. Obviously we're not going to let people think we're really dating, but it's good for us both if people see us as the kind of people who *can* get dates. We just want people talking."

"I literally do not ever want people talking. I'm perfectly happy with the entire world shutting the fuck up, always."

I should've known he'd be impossible about this. "Fine. Let's just go."

Salem sighs. "I am going to remind you that all of this stupid planning was your idea, okay? Remember that before I do this."

Curiosity officially piqued, I promise.

Before I can even process what's happening, a surprisingly muscular arm wraps around my shoulders, that deliciously woodsy scent fills my nostrils, and I realize Salem is steering me toward a romantic seat in the back with a casually possessive arm that draws a surprising number of gazes. Even Isabel and her friends, lounging in the corner of the room, drink us in with curious eyes.

It's perplexing and, I have to admit, weirdly thrilling.

I don't even care when I realize Lucas and Heather are right in front of us, and it's highly unlikely they missed our entrance.

"So you won't hold my hand," I whisper with a smirk, "but—"

"Shut it. Holding hands wasn't the right move. That was. Trust me."

Weirdly enough, I do.

A chill settles over my shoulders as Salem takes his arm back, or maybe I'm just missing its warmth. Either way, the instinct to curl into him is strong, and for the first time since that awful night with Lucas, I wonder if maybe I *should* try to find another guy. . . .

No. I make bad choices with boys. Craig was a bad choice, and Lucas was a bad choice, and if I'm going to make good choices in the future, I need to hold a lot more power than

I currently do. *Eyes on the prize, Evie,* I tell myself, as if I'll know the prize when I see it.

I can only hope that I do.

I glance at Salem, but his eyes are firmly on the screen, and I catch the light flickering on his sharp jawline instead. If it weren't for the slight tic indicating he was clenching it, I'd almost think he was actually enjoying the movie we just entered ten minutes late.

Tomorrow, I'll make this up to him, I vow. I may not be able to deliver Isabel yet, but a weed-free study session to help his slacker ass? That I can definitely do.

Salem can't wait to bolt when the movie's done, and I have no reason to linger, so we leave the second the closing credits roll, and promptly bump into Matt. He's got an arm around a girl I don't know while deep in conversation with a couple of guys I recognize from basketball tryouts, and he lights up when he sees us. "Roomie! Dormie!" he says cheerfully, holding up his free hand for Salem to reluctantly slap and me to much more enthusiastically follow up. He gives me a once-over, complete with a slow whistle. "Looking good, Riley."

I'm not yet at the point where I'm cool enough not to blush at that, but I try to cover it up with a joking hair flip anyway.

"Me and these guys were just gonna go shoot around in the gym for a while. You in?" Matt asks Salem.

We both know Salem's gonna turn down the offer before

he even opens his mouth, but I refuse to let him. If this is what the basketball players do, then he's gonna follow their lead, and he's gonna like it. "Go ahead," I tell him, as if I'm what'd be standing in his way, and not his general misanthropy and loathing of all things recreational that can't be smoked or blasted from speakers. "I'm gonna go see what your sister's up to."

Those stormy gray eyes narrow, but I just squeeze his arm and whisper, "Good boys are joiners who practice their sports." Then I say my goodbyes and am pleasantly surprised to see that Salem doesn't put up any further fight about being dragged off to the gym.

The campus is unusually quiet as I walk through the quad alone, with most of the students either still lingering around the Student Center after the movie, or at game night in the library, or, like Matt and Salem, throwing balls at things in the gym. There are a few kids scattered on the grass, though, tossing Frisbees and picnicking on blankets, and there's something about the serenity of it all that overwhelms me. I close my eyes, inhale the scent of grass and pine, and let the evening breeze ruffle my curls.

In this moment, I am so, so glad I came to Camden.

And then I remember that while I may be heading to Lockwood, what awaits me at the end of the night is a solo room in a building full of boys who, with a few exceptions beyond Matt and Salem, either glare at me, leer at me, or pretend I don't exist.

As I enter the girls' dorm, I'm not sure whether I hope Heather is already back or still out of sight—both seem like bad options—but I do hope that Sabrina, at least, is in their room. Sure enough, I hear the faint drifting of music down the hall as soon as I enter, and only one person on the first floor of Lockwood listens to emo covers of sea shanties.

"Sabrina Grayson!" I rap on her door, loudly enough to be heard over wailing about whaling. "Hang out with me!"

The door flies open, revealing my favorite goth in black sweatpants and a matching long-sleeved tee, an undeniable smirk on her face as she registers my presence. "I thought you were at the movie. On a date. With my brother. Which I cannot even begin to fathom."

"God, how fast does gossip travel around here? You haven't even left your room." I let myself in and am relieved that Heather hasn't somehow beaten me here. "And obviously we were not actually on a date."

"Okay, well if you're here to pick my brain for how to turn hanging out with my brother into something more, I have zero advice for you except to fully equip me with barf bags any time you two plan to be in my presence." Then her expression twists into something more serious. "For real, though. I really, really hate to be lied to."

"I'm not lying!"

"You're literally wearing his jacket, Evie."

Oh, right. It was so surprisingly comfortable, I'd forgotten I even had it on. "I asked to borrow it," I admit. "I needed something to make my outfit more interesting."

She looks like she wants to say something else, but thankfully, she thinks better of it and slides back down onto the fluffy pink rug instead. "Well, how was the movie?"

"Stupid. Mostly." I close the door behind me and join her on the floor, where a pile of tarot cards sits next to a can of Dr Pepper and a laptop. "Do you read these?"

"I'm learning." She gestures at the computer screen, and I see it's open to a page on card readings. "Want me to read for you?"

Do I? I'm not in the best state of mind to hear I have a bleak future ahead, but given I'm here to turn my life around, I *am* impatient to know what the cards hold for me. "Please! But if it's bad, can you lie to me a little? I have not had the best luck with, uh, this entire year."

The best thing about both Grayson twins is knowing you can say something like that and neither one will express even the tiniest bit of interest in digging any further. Sabrina just nods and shuffles the cards.

I don't know why I hold my breath when she draws the first one; it's not like I know the first thing about tarot, or what any of the cards suggest. But when she places it down in front of me, I wanna gag.

The Lovers. Fantastic.

Sabrina, meanwhile, is delighted. "The Lovers! This card represents relationships, connections. This bodes well for you partnering up, if you're so inclined."

Orrrr it knows I already partnered up and it was a terrible idea. The pair on the tarot card looks like Adam and Eve—the ultimate couple of mass destruction. That sounds about right. "Next."

She rolls her eyes, but puts down the second card. "Ooh,

the Nine of Wands. This means you'll have to work hard to get with this lover—"

"Stop saying 'lover.'"

"To get with this lover," she repeats, louder, "will require much self-improvement, sacrifice."

Oh, I sacrificed. And I'm working on self-improvement. But I would not like to return to any of my past "lovers" anytime soon, thank you. "Is there a 'win the lottery' card in there somewhere? I'd like to hear something good."

"This isn't about bad or good," says Sabrina, tapping the deck. "We're just gaining some insight into your life, maybe helping guide your choices for the future. And you're not even old enough to play the lottery, smart-ass."

She flips over the third card and breaks into a huge smile. "The Knight of Cups. This card symbolizes creativity, romance, maybe a slow burn . . . man, this deck really wants you to get laid, ideally by an artist."

"This deck needs to mind its own business and gets its own social life." I fold my arms behind my head and lie back on the floor, suddenly feeling exhausted. "Boy drama is such bullshit."

"Yep."

There's a note in her voice that suggests I've struck a nerve, and I rise up on an elbow. "Got some experience in that department, do you?"

"Literally none, in fact."

"Come on, do you really never have any? Like truly *any*?"

"Never," she says flatly, and I get the feeling even my

question is somehow disappointing her. I'm so wrapped up in my own ridiculousness that it takes me a minute of awkward silence to figure it out.

"You don't like boys, do you."

"Nope," she replies, just loud enough to be heard over the shuffling of the cards.

"You've had some girl drama, haven't you."

"Yep." The *p* pops like a verbal gunshot. She turns to put away the cards, and I take the moment to try to decipher whether to keep asking questions or just change the subject.

The ping of an incoming text spares us both, and she scoops up her phone and snorts.

"Your brother?" I just *know* he's checking in to make sure I'm behaving myself.

"He's such a moron."

"And a loser," I chime in, even though right at this moment, I feel slightly, mildly, a tiny bit friendly toward him. But Sabrina doesn't need to know that.

"Hey—only I get to call my brother a loser," Sabrina says as she taps back a text, but the corner of her mouth is curved up enough for me to know she's only half-serious.

"Well tell the loser I said hi, then."

She does, and thirty seconds later, she says, "He says this is a very sad idea of a cool night, and that you've downgraded Graysons. Hey! I think I'm offended."

"Tell him I said to bite me."

"With pleasure."

She sends off a text, and the reply comes quickly and

makes her snort. "I will spare you his reply. But also, I have got to get out of this room; I can't look at these walls anymore. You wanna go up to the lounge? There's gotta be something to do there."

I shrug and together we head up to the third floor, which houses the dorm mom Mrs. Fletcher's apartment, a computer room with exactly one desktop and printer, and a cozy lounge area full of couches arranged around a large coffee table and facing a TV. One wall holds a kitchenette, which is really just a long counter, a fridge crammed full of labeled food, a sink, and a microwave. There's also a bookcase with a few scattered titles people have dumped here after reading, a couple of old board games, and a little gold-tone statue of a Camden cougar.

"God, this is so much cleaner than the Rumson lounge," I observe as I walk over to the kitchenette and start opening up the cabinets, suddenly ravenous for the microwave popcorn I didn't get to have at the Student Center tonight. "Boys are disgusting."

"Don't need to tell me twice."

"Ah, got it!" I spot the box of popcorn and grab a plastic-wrapped packet. "So, as long as I'm staying, how about you tell me more about your girl drama."

She rolls her eyes. "There's nothing to tell. We broke up. Now Molly's still at our old school with her new girlfriend, and I'm here with my brother."

"And me," I remind her with a sunny smile, unwrapping the popcorn and putting it in the microwave. "Don't forget me."

"I could never," she says dryly.

"So is Molly why you came to Camden?"

Sabrina screws up her face into an expression that narrows her cool gray eyes to slivers. "No. Yes. Maybe." She exhales sharply. "Salem was coming here, and my parents are very big on things between us being even, so they said if they were paying for him to go to boarding school, they were going to make the same offer to me. The idea of boarding school had never even crossed my mind, but at that moment, the idea of getting the hell away from Molly just sounded so damn good. And I figured if Salem could handle it, so could I."

"And what was Salem doing here? He didn't actually tell me why he got kicked out of your old school. Though 'weed and truancy' were mentioned."

"Oh, if only it were that basic. No, my brother is a fucking moron, who was not only smoking *on* school property, but in the principal's office. Which he broke into. On a Saturday."

"Yikes."

"Yup. I don't know if one of his loser friends dared him or what, but there's really no apologizing your way back from that one. I don't even know if you could *buy* your way back from that one, not that we have 'buy your way out of a principal-embarrassing drug scandal' money. And before you ask, no, we don't have 'send two kids to boarding school' money, either. Camden was the only school that gave us enough financial aid, and that's *with* the help from the grandma my parents absolutely hate to ask for help."

"For what it's worth, we don't have boarding school money

either." It's a fact that still makes my guilt about begging to come here sit like a stone in my belly. Camden's generous financial aid was definitely a factor in it being the ultimate choice, but if I don't maintain the terms of my academic scholarship, I'm definitely screwed. "But wow, that's obnoxiously stupid, even for Salem."

"I know, right?"

The microwave beeps, and I get to work putting the popcorn into a bowl while Sabrina flips through the channels to try to find something on Camden's limited cable selection that doesn't suck. "So what about you?" she calls as I do a final shake for the kernel remnants. "What brought you here?"

"Honestly, same kind of thing," I admit as I join her on the couch and hold out the bowl. "As you, not Salem." It's both weird to open up and nice to feel like I've finally found someone I can share with. The hardest thing about Sierra and Craig wasn't even that they broke my heart—it was easy enough from the outside to see that Craig wasn't worth it—but that the only person in the world I trusted enough to share my feelings about it with wasn't even on my side.

Well, the hardest thing was my own sister stabbing me in the back, but at least it was consistent with her personality. Claire turned so fast, I'd swear Sierra had something on her, if Claire had ever actually done anything interesting.

Anyway, talking about it again feels nerve-racking, but I'm sure talking about Molly isn't one of Sabrina's favorite pastimes either, so fair is fair. "The boy was sort of the least of it, but we definitely did break up. After I found out he was hooking up with my sister. And my best friend knew about it."

Sabrina's hand freezes in the bowl of warm popcorn. "Oh. Shit."

"Yeah."

"Dude, your sister sucks."

"Yuuup. In so many ways, but that was just the final straw. I couldn't imagine going back to school with all of them after that. So here I am." I drop onto the couch next to Sabrina and dig my hand into the bowl for a fistful of popcorn.

"So what's it like between you and your sister now?"

I think of the simultaneously satisfying and empty feeling of finally blocking her email address, partly because I didn't want to give her a way to get in touch with me and partly because I didn't want to feel worse if she never even tried. At least this way, I'll never know. "It's nothing. Nonexistent."

She nods slowly, and I can tell she wants to choose her next words carefully. "That must be really hard. I mean, Salem sucks, but I also don't know that I could be here without him." She narrows her eyes. "Don't you dare ever tell him I said that."

I mime locking up my lips and tossing away the key, even though I have a feeling he feels the same way about her. Meanwhile, I can't even imagine what Sierra would say if you asked her how she feels about me.

Probably something like "Evie who?"

Sabrina returns to flipping through channels, but turns out Friday-night pickings are exceedingly slim. "Cooking show?"

"Cooking show," I affirm with a nod, because nothing

says comfort TV like watching people make cupcakes flavored like chicken and waffles with maple buttercream.

As we lie back and demolish the popcorn while debating which sounds worse, avocado cream filling or honey barbecue frosting, I feel one of the thousand cracks in my heart seal itself shut.

Chapter Seven

DESPITE THE LATE NIGHT, I wake up relatively early the next morning—in time to catch breakfast at the Beast, which is so empty it feels like offering it on Saturday mornings is basically a formality. I've always been an earlier riser; just feels like there's too much to do with the day to sleep through it. Once I've eaten my weight in waffles and disposed of my tray, I start to head out and am surprised to see not just Isabel but all three of her besties enter the cafeteria.

"Evie!" I love how Isabel always sounds so utterly delighted to see me. "Come sit with us."

I realize with my tray already gone, there's no way for them to know I already ate, so I grab a little fruit salad and fancy myself looking dainty and ladylike with it. "We were just talking about you," Isabel tells me once we've taken seats. "I didn't realize you were *with* that boy."

Once again, it's time to figure out how to play this—would it be a good thing, or a bad thing?

Before I can even try, Ashleigh chimes in. "That's Salem Grayson, right? Landon says he thinks once they whip him into shape, he's gonna be a serious star on the team."

"He's certainly got the height," Isabel adds.

"And the hands," Priya says with a giggle, her long, thick black hair bouncing.

The other girls smirk and I suddenly feel very young and out of my element. "I . . . yeah. I mean, we're not. We're friends. Dormmates, too. But yeah, just friends."

Judging by the glances they exchange, it feels like that was the right answer, but I couldn't for the life of me tell you why.

"He lives with Matt, too, right?" Priya asks. "Have you ridden *that* train yet?"

I have to steel my jaw in place to stop it from dropping at the idea, only to realize Matt still would've been better than the station stop I actually *did* make the first week of school. Even a train that stops at every station is more appealing than one that . . . Okay, I'm losing this metaphor, but the point is, Matt's cool and Lucas sucks.

"Don't be embarrassed if you have," Ashleigh adds knowingly. "Everyone's gone through a Matt phase. Well, except me."

"That's Ash's way of segueing into the fact that she's been with Landon since the dawn of time." Only when I hear Jenna's wry voice does it strike me it's the first time that I've ever heard her speak; she's usually a quiet, somewhat unsettling ice-blue-eyed force. "We know, Ash. We all have our wisteria bridesmaid dresses picked out."

"Periwinkle!" Ashleigh corrects her with a note of panic, as if these dresses have already been designed and ordered. Then she catches herself. "I mean, they're not the same."

Next to me, I sense a movement in Isabel's hands, and realize she's digging her nails into her palms. A quick glance at her face confirms she's trying not to laugh.

"Of course, Izzy here insists she's never had a Matt phase either." Priya's voice and smile are both sugar-sweet, a lovely pairing with her candy-floss sweater and matching dagger-sharp nails, but the waggling of her enviably thick eyebrows suggests she doesn't believe it. To me, Matt and Isabel give off a brother-sister vibe, but then, what I don't know about sex could fill the Beast, so.

"So?" Ashleigh asks. "Are you into Matt?"

Talking to these girls is dizzying, and I'm having trouble keeping track of the impressions I'm trying to be giving. If I want to be a cool girl, a hot girl, a badass girl—these are the girls I need to impress, which means my answers need to be right.

"I'm still scouting my options," I say in a breezy voice I don't think I've ever used in my entire life.

I'm convinced they'll be able to see right through me, but thankfully, Priya claps. "My kind of girl. Now let me think who's got potential . . ."

"Ooh, what about Nick?" Ashleigh offers.

"Ontiveros or Brenner?" Isabel asks.

"Ontiveros, obviously," Jenna says, at exactly the same time Priya says, "Brenner, definitely."

I glance back and forth between them, and get the feeling I'm being caught in a very weird standoff. "Two options sounds good to me," I say cheerfully, hoping to defuse some of the tension I still don't really understand.

"Like I said." Priya smiles smugly. "My kind of girl."

"And what are you up to today, Evie?" Jenna asks, swirling a spoon through a bowl of berry-studded yogurt.

They all turn their eyes on me, and I have no idea what exciting things I could possibly pretend I have lined up. "Not sure yet," I say slowly, trying to remember the suggested options for Saturday afternoons. Most of them are nature-y—rafting and hiking and climbing—the kinds of things my parents would drag me and Sierra to on weekends in the Before Times that I'm not ready to revisit. The rest are sort of blurring at the moment.

"Good," says Isabel, booping my nose like I'm a child. "You're coming shopping with us."

Shopping? With the four most perfect-looking humans to grace the entirety of the Camden campus? I am so, so out of my league here.

And yet, there's only one possible response, despite the fact that I definitely cannot afford to shop wherever these girls do: "When do we leave?"

It's hard to say what's the most surreal about what follows from there.

It could be getting into the back seat of Ashleigh Cartwright's

Land Rover, where I squeeze between Priya and Isabel for a ride to the mall and pray I'm wearing a sufficient amount of deodorant and my legs aren't stubbly.

It could be the way a single question about my hair somehow leads to a whirlwind makeover, complete with hair straightening and a makeup tutorial.

It's very potentially the fact that the four coolest girls in school are giving me fashion advice and picking out clothing for me like I'm some sort of project, which sounds terrible except that I was badly in need of both advice and fashion sense and now I have new stuff that looks amazing.

But mostly, it's just surreal how interested they are in *me*.

"So what's it like, living in a boys' dorm?" Priya asks as she pokes at her skin in a magnifying mirror.

"Anyone look surprisingly hot in a towel?" Ashleigh wants to know.

"Most importantly, who's dropping by your room after hours?" Isabel wonders aloud, her eyes twinkling as she lifts one scent after another to her nose.

"What makes you think *anyone's* dropping by my room after hours?" I ask as my face is blushed and contoured and highlighted. I keep my tone playful, as if there were even a snowball's chance in hell that I might have a gentleman caller, but at this point, there's no one I can even imagine getting with, especially at Rumson.

Though Archie and I sure would have a great meet-cute to share with our kids.

"Oh, come on." Jenna points a coal-black eye pencil in my direction. "You have your own room, you don't have to head back after curfew, and you live below a guy who keeps a rope ladder swinging from his window to yours at all times. Don't tell me you're staying squeaky clean. We're meeting up with Matt and the other guys in half an hour, and he's going to tell us whether you've been naughty or nice."

The other girls look at me knowingly and I don't even know what to say. I haven't stayed *entirely* squeaky clean, but they sound seductive and worldly when they talk about guys, and I'm . . . not that. But if I do tell them I made out with someone, they might try prying for who, and that is *not* something I'll be sharing.

Is it better if they think I'm a boring prude who can't even get a guy when she's constantly surrounded by them, though?

"You know what you need?" Isabel asks, spritzing the inside of her wrist and lifting it to her nose. "Bellas."

"Bellas!" Priya and Ashleigh cheer.

"What are Bellas?" Why am I always the last to know everything?

"Come on," Jenna says authoritatively, and everyone puts back the makeup they were holding. I try to get up to join them, but she stops me. "Wait. First, you need to get that eyeliner."

I'm about to argue—I'm already seriously overdoing the spending today, and my parents are going to kill me when they see the bill I've rung up on my "emergency" credit card—when I realize that buying one of the items used in my makeover is a requirement. Crap. Another twenty bucks I don't really have.

"Gimme," Isabel says, holding out her hand. "I'll throw it in with my stuff."

She says it so casually I can't bring myself to argue, and less than five minutes later, I'm the proud owner of a fancy new eyeliner and on my way to find out exactly what "Bellas" are.

I've learned so many things today, like how to contour my face, how to extend the life of a blowout, and how much designer underwear can cost. (Turns out "Bellas" are an obscenely expensive brand of underwear, the official brand of the Camden Hot Girl Clique.) And right now in the food court, I'm learning how many soft pretzels Matt Haley can stuff in his face, which is, frankly, too many.

"I can't get used to you with straight hair." Matt cocks his head as he polishes off the last of what must be his third. "Feels wrong."

"What he *means* to say," Isabel says with an elbow to his side, "is that you look nice, and it's fun to try new things."

Cool, now I'm feeling even more self-conscious. I'm searching for something, anything, to change the conversation away from my appearance, but thankfully, Landon promptly does just that. "You look nice too, baby," he says to Ashleigh, nuzzling her soft curls, which he can easily access because she's perched on his lap. "You should wear your hair like this every day."

"I do wear my hair like this every day," she says, grinning while everyone else makes retching motions. It *is* a little nauseating how perfect they are, like it's too much to even aspire to. He looks like he should be in a sneaker ad, dark skin glistening with sweat while he artfully skyrockets to the hoop.

"So, Matt, how's the new roster?" Priya asks gleefully, tweaking the straw in her smoothie.

Isabel rolls her eyes. "She doesn't mean basketball, in case you couldn't crack that code."

"Don't worry, I always know where Priya's head's at," Matt says with a wink, and I immediately have a feeling I know whose designer wardrobe will flash by as it scales the rope ladder tonight. "So far, the 'one girl per dorm' quest is moving along *very* smoothly."

I know what Jenna's gonna say before the twinkle in her eye and smug tilt to her smile even herald it. "Does that include Rumson?"

Heat rises in my cheeks at everyone's smothered laughter, but Matt takes it in stride. "Would you believe the one girl in Rumson has been totally resistant to my charms so far? It's like she doesn't even know who I am."

God, he really might be my new best friend. "Or maybe it's like she knows exactly who you are," I say sweetly, dragging a spoon through my frozen yogurt.

Now everyone laughs for real while Matt puts on a pout, and I take a bite of my melting vanilla with rainbow sprinkles.

"You know, Evie won't tell us a thing about living there," Isabel tells him. "We might need to pay a visit to see for ourselves."

Oh good, just what I need—for these ridiculously well-put-together people to see my weird prison-cell-like room.

And then suddenly, the perfect idea for both recouping

the money I didn't actually have to spend today and bringing everyone to Rumson without making my room the centerpiece of the visit comes to mind.

"You should. Matt's a great host, and I was just thinking that we haven't had a decent poker night yet."

"Ooh, poker party sounds like fun," says Matt, flashing a wicked grin as his waggles his eyebrows at Isabel. "Remember that game—"

Isabel cuts him off immediately. "I don't think the girl meant strip poker, Matty."

"No, I definitely did not."

"Well, nevertheless, sure, let's do it," he says casually. "I'll invite some guys from the floor. Does this mean you play, dormie?"

"I do." I take another bite of fro yo to hide my smile. "I used to play a lot with friends back home."

"Shouldn't you ask your roommate if he's on board before inviting a whole bunch of people over?" Isabel suggests, examining her perfect peach nails.

"I'll take care of that," I say, and instantly regret it when everyone's gazes swivel to me. "I mean. We're friends. It'll be fine."

I do not want to attempt to decipher the look exchanged between Matt and Isabel at that point. It feels like it's at my expense somehow, but Matt just says, "I'm sure it will be," and the conversation easily flows from Salem back to the basketball team, the first thing to take Landon's attention off Ashleigh's mouth in at least five minutes.

Having nothing to contribute, I finish my fro yo in silence, and try not to think about how much Salem is absolutely going to kill me.

The rest of the group splits up for various activities when we get back to campus, but I head straight to Rumson and dash up the stairs to bang on Salem's door.

"What do you want, Skeevy?" he calls without opening it.

"How do you even know it's me?"

"Because you always fucking knock like you're in a horror movie and you just came upon a lone cabin in the wilderness." He swings the door open, and I'm gratified to see his eyes widen at my makeover. "Where the hell have *you* been?"

"Oh, just the mall with some friends," I say casually, possibly stepping on his foot a little as I let myself inside and drop onto Matt's bed, knowing he's currently meeting up with his designated Ewing Hall conquest. "The blowout was Jenna's idea. Priya picked the outfit. And Isabel treated me to the eyeliner so I could get a free makeover. Isn't that sweet?"

"Is it?" He's still staring at me, but like I'm a strange, unfamiliar animal, rather than a hot girl who got a spectacular makeover, and it's really killing my buzz. What is it about these guys and an aversion to a change in hairstyle?

Whatever, it doesn't matter; it's not like I'm trying to impress either of them. "It is. And you might like to know that you came up several times on this outing. Of course, they thought we might be a thing after seeing us at the movie together last night, but don't worry, I let them know you're single and ready to mingle."

"I can't help feeling like I absolutely do not want you meddling in my love life. Ever." He scowls as he shoves aside the mass of flannel blanket on his bed and sits down on the edge.

"Okay, well, that might be a problem, because I've already made us plans for tonight, and they involve a party in your room that includes four of the hottest girls at Camden, three of whom are single."

"Evie, what the fuck. You invited them *here*? Why?"

"Matt thought it would be fun to have a poker night," I tell him, patting Matt's pillow in lieu of indicating his actual roommate. "Tonight, Salem Grayson, we are going to raise your social profile and introduce you to some hotties."

"Has anyone used the word 'hotties' in the last twenty years?"

"Salem." I walk and sit at his feet, taking his lightly callused fingers in mine. "This is as well-adjusted as you're ever gonna get. You know what helps parents get over being expelled for smoking weed in the principal's office, of all the stupid, godforsaken places? Showing them that you are really and truly changing into a normal human being."

He pulls his hands away and braces them on the thighs of his basketball shorts. "Sabrina told you why I got expelled?"

Whoops. It honestly hadn't occurred to me that it was a secret. "What's the big deal? It's not like it's news that you have a . . . penchant for cannabis."

"You know you can just say I like weed, right?"

"Heard that, too."

He exhales a frustrated breath, and I cock my head, taking in his pinched expression. "Seriously, Salem. It was a stupid thing to do, but I'm willing to bet a lot of us are here for stupid reasons. I know I am, even if it wasn't my fault."

"Can you all just stay the hell out of my business, please?"

"After tonight, yes," I promise, though we both know I'm lying. "But the girls are already coming, and Matt invited a couple of guys, too. It's just gonna be a few people, playing poker. That's it."

"Why poker?"

Okay, well, at least his curiosity is beating out his anger. That's a positive sign. We'll see how that holds when I tell him the truth.

"Um, because I spent a ton of money I don't actually have today at the mall, and I need to win it back."

He snorts. "You know poker's not, like, an automatic win, right? What if you lose even more money you don't have?"

"I won't."

Silvery-gray eyes narrow to slivers. "Do you cheat?"

"I don't have to," I say honestly, because I have exactly one useful skill in the world and this is it. "I'm just really, really good."

He cocks his head and sizes me up, clearly trying to decide if I'm being serious, and finally, he blows out a breath. "Okay. Fine. You can have your stupid party here," Salem concedes, "but only because this is something I absolutely have to see."

"You won't regret it," I say sweetly. "Well, unless you try playing against me."

"Trash talk! From the little Barbie literally kneeling at my feet! I'm terrified."

"You should be." But I do get up and dust myself off, heading to the door. "Wear something decent. Jeans, at least, and the cologne you were wearing on Friday. Do not be barefoot. No weed. And clean up. If you want a girl to even *think* about getting into that bed, you need to make the damn bed."

"Weren't you leaving?"

"Try not to miss me too much." But when I'm just about to step out the door, I hear Salem's voice again, so quiet I'm almost not sure whether I was intended to hear it.

"I liked the unbraidable hair."

My breath hitches, and for this of all things, I don't have a comeback. So I simply pretend I did not, in fact, hear it, and leave.

I shuffle my favorite deck for the fifteenth time that hour, feeling a fizzing in my blood at the thought of getting to play tonight. I love pretty much all card games, and they love me back, though the people who play with me generally don't. Sierra hasn't been willing to play with me since I shot the moon in a family game of hearts without her realizing it when we were eight and nine. Claire used to like to watch me play solitaire and FreeCell—said she found it soothing—but hated anything that had even the tiniest tinge of competition. Even my parents gradually shifted from indulging me in games of rummy or spit to giving me Concerned Parent Talks about gambling addictions.

My love of competitive card playing is something I've mostly tried to shut off here, because the money-making games in particular bring out a more aggressive side of me than I need anyone seeing. But if I'm not trying to be Nice Evie, or Good Evie, then who cares?

Let them all see how badass I can be, without any help from Salem.

Ordinarily I'd wear sweatpants and a T-shirt to go upstairs, but with my hair in rare straightened form, my eyebrows newly shaped, and my cheekbones beautifully highlighted, I feel like I have to do my look justice. I don't want to overdress, but I put on one of my nicer T-shirts with my best jeans, throw on a cute cardigan, and painstakingly refresh my makeup while trying to recall all the instructions from the woman at the makeup counter.

I even contemplate changing my underwear to the expensive Bellas Isabel and Co. insisted I buy in a signature color, just as they each have. (They assigned me "virginal pink," ha ha.) But it's not like anyone will be seeing it tonight. By the time I'm done, I barely recognize the girl looking back at me in the mirror. But that's a good thing, right? I wanted to be someone new. I wanted to be someone who makes you look twice. I wanted to be someone who looks like she regularly stays up past nine on a school night.

And I definitely do, finally, look like a girl who knows how to have fun.

Now, off to have it.

I practically skip upstairs to Salem's room, visions of royal flushes dancing in my head.

Chapter Eight

A RUMSON HALL DORM ROOM DOESN'T quite possess the necessary décor for a festive poker evening, but somehow, Salem and Matt have made do, tracking down a round table that'll work well enough for our purposes and, improbably, a case of poker chips. "Buddy of mine at MCC lent it to me," Matt said proudly, referring to the nearby community college.

Jason Hammond and Brent Cage from across the hall are already in the room when I arrive, but as we get ourselves situated and start passing around snacks, more and more people show up. Landon and another guy from the basketball team whose name I don't catch. I meet Nick Ontiveros, whom Jenna'd suggested to set me up with, and wonder if that's somehow her doing. Even Archie shows up, immediately gracing me with a scowl as he takes a seat across from me at the table. (Duncan, unfortunately, is nowhere to be found, which is a shame—I would've loved taking his money, even now that he keeps his mouth shut around me.)

We're already three hands deep into Texas Hold'em by the time the girls show up and make themselves at home on Matt's and Salem's beds, and, in Ashleigh's case, on Landon's lap. None of them feign an interest in playing, but Isabel does perch over me and go, "Ooh, is having five aces good?"—which I can tell would piss the crap out of Archie if he weren't torn between his annoyance at the joke and his gratitude for the view down her shirt.

Meanwhile, I'm keeping things low-key as I pick up everyone's tells, because this is *not* a sophisticated group. Archie straight-up smiles and frowns, and tries to hide it quickly. Salem's foot taps when he can't wait to make his next move, but if he knows it's going nowhere, he starts scratching his name into the table with his thumbnail, as if he's already checked out of this hand. Landon compulsively checks his hole cards—there's always someone who does, and depending on at what point they do it, it's a dead giveaway—but even if he didn't, Ash can't stop herself from smiling when he has an obviously good hand. Brent can't remember all the rules, so if he looks confused, he either doesn't have anything or might have a flush but forgets that's a thing. Matt always reaches for his chips too early when he's got a good hand—rookie mistake. Jason's the only one who's halfway decent at bluffing, but unfortunately for him, he keeps tilting his cards so they reflect perfectly in his glasses.

I take the fourth hand with three jacks, then bluff my way to a win for the fifth.

"What'd you have?" Archie asks, trying and failing to keep his voice casual as I rake in the pile of chips, including a sizable contribution from him that makes me wonder what he was holding before he panicked after my second raise.

I stack up my winnings. "Your mom."

"Real mature. Did it beat a straight?"

"Did you seriously *fold* with a straight?"

He curses under his breath, and it makes the win that much sweeter, especially when Salem says, "Damn, Skeevy." We ante up and Matt deals again, and as soon as I see the two and three of spades, I have a good feeling. I never lose a hand when I have the two of spades, which is why I used to wear a Claire-crafted bead version around my neck. I'd even thought about putting it on tonight, because much as I wanted to, I couldn't bring myself to leave it behind in Greentree. But I figured it probably no longer carried the luck it used to.

Clearly I don't need Claire and her jewelry, because I end up with a flush. I raise steadily, but Archie's already decided that I'm constantly bluffing, so he jacks up the pot, and I'm only too happy to keep going.

"How do you know how to do this?" Priya asks, fascinated.

"My dad and I used to play a lot." True, but I don't mention how frequently we used to play with cousins at family gatherings, using jelly beans or Jolly Ranchers as currency. Or the poker nights I used to have with some friends at Greentree I haven't spoken to in months. Or the fact that I'm ranked in the top three hundred of my favorite poker app.

No one does better at poker than a girl being underestimated by a table of guys. Ask me how I know.

Finally, Archie calls, and curses under his breath when I display my row of spades.

"Damn, she took you, Buchanan." Jason laughs, and the other guys whoop and cheer as I rake in his chips. Even Salem cracks a grin.

"Might've been worth being nicer to me that first day," I say sweetly, and Archie's scowl is a thing of beauty.

Everyone needs a break after that, so I grab a handful of chips and a can of Coke, then open up the window between Matt's and Salem's beds for some fresh air. The cool breeze feels glorious on my skin as I sink onto Salem's (neatly made!) bed and take a drink of the lukewarm soda, the perfect antidote to the adrenaline coursing through my veins. I've already made enough money to cover my spending at the mall, and it feels so good to see Archie choke.

"You better not spill that in my bed," Salem commands, but the corner of his mouth is quirked up.

"Come on," I say as he sits down next to me, taking my can and helping himself to a sip without so much as wiping it off. "That's not all you have to say to me, is it?"

He fixes me with those mysterious gray eyes, as if I'm offering up a riddle and the answer can be found plainly on my face, if you just search hard enough. Finally, he concedes. "I will never underestimate you again, Everett Riley."

Satisfied, I smile smugly and take back my Coke for another long drink, burying my sock-covered toes under his warm thigh. "Took you long enough. But you know I'm not giving your money back, right?"

"Wouldn't even dream of asking."

And, you know, I believe him.

We're not really a God family, so it's hard to explain why my first thought when I wake up on Sunday morning is *I should go to church.*

Maybe I feel a *little* bad about taking all that money off my classmates.

But only a little. Certainly, the devilish feelings don't stop me from putting together another cute outfit and donning some makeup again. Plus, my bonus winnings from last night are burning a hole in my pocket with all sorts of thoughts on how I could spend them.

I decide to pass on church, especially since I'm starving, so I bring my remaining homework to the Beast and sit in the corner, stuffing pancakes slathered in whipped cream and berries in my mouth while I tackle geometry. People slowly trickle in while I work, but between day students being home for the weekend, the actually devout being at chapel, and everyone else doing a Sunday morning sleep-in, the room might be even calmer than yesterday. The only real sounds are the hissing of the coffee maker and the slamming of a stapler nailing new weekly announcements to the bulletin board, all of which are going to be emailed to us anyway.

The math is relatively easy, and without the distractions

of text messages or tablemates, I sail through both it and my breakfast. But I have no other plans today anyway, so I decide to stick around and nurse a glass of OJ while I move on to English.

As if just thinking about Mrs. Frank conjures him up, I hear the familiar thud of Salem dropping into the chair next to me, followed by the heavy thump of his ratty messenger bag landing on the table. Even if I hadn't recognized the bag, "Looking so studious over there, Skeevy" would've given him away immediately. "Studying how to take even more of Archie's money?"

"Would that I could. I'm surprised you managed to roll out of bed at this hour, though it's pretty clear you did exactly that," I say, indicating his faded black Soundgarden T-shirt and pants that have somehow been worn to colorlessness. "I see you're also on the study-while-you-eat plan."

"AP Psych quiz," he confirms. "Envy me."

I do, not that he realizes. Of course he got into the class I'd most wanted to take, which was already full by the time I enrolled at Camden. Taking a minimum of two AP classes this year was part of the deal with my parents for coming here, and chem and APUSH were two of the only ones available to sophomores. Annoyingly, Salem is in the latter with me, too, and I don't understand it, considering this is the first time I've ever seen him study. "So brilliant," I mutter, pointedly turning my focus to the thick book in front of me. "What story are you doing for English?"

"'Masque of the Red Death.' Haven't started writing yet, though. I figure that'll be Thursday night's problem."

"Salem." I shut the book as quickly as I've opened it and fix him with a serious Look. "My part of the deal will not allow me to let you put off a huge assignment until the last minute. Come on—we can outline together."

"Hard pass, Skeevy. I'm just here for breakfast and a quick chapter review."

"I thought you weren't a breakfast person."

"I'm a black-coffee-on-Sunday-mornings person," he says, and then he goes and gets himself some, leaving me inexplicably tempted to go through the bag he left behind. I wrinkle my nose when he returns and the bitter scent hits me. "I guess coffee is not your thing."

"Not even a little," I confirm. "Aren't you, like, thirty years too young to be drinking that?"

"I'm an old soul." He purses his lips and blows at the cloud of steam that wafts from the cup. "Is your talent gonna be nagging people to death or what?"

"Talent?"

He nods toward the bulletin board. "Talent show. You haven't seen the fifty thousand flyers already pasted up all over campus this morning?"

"I have not. Will you be showing us how to roll fifty joints in under a minute?"

"Ha ha. I am now . . ." He starts ticking off on his fingers, then loses count immediately. "Nearing forty-eight hours completely sober, thank you very much. But oh, right, we already got to see your talent last night. I assume you'll be whooping some poker ass onstage for everyone's viewing pleasure?"

"Lemme guess," I say, putting my fingers to my temples like a psychic. "*You'll* be doing some incredibly emo performance on an acoustic guitar whose name is . . . Jenny. *No,* Betty. Yes, your guitar's name is definitely Betty."

"Since when do I have a guitar?" His lips twitch as he brings the coffee back up to them for a sip.

"Oh, come on. You are the stereotype to end all stereotypes. Of course you have a guitar. And if I knew anything about the music you listen to, I'd tell you exactly what you'll be playing."

"If you want a crash course in music that doesn't suck, all you have to do is ask, you know."

"Oh, do you know someone who could give it?" I ask sweetly.

He just rolls his eyes and goes back to his cup o' bitterness, and I turn back to my homework. I expect him to do the same, but instead he whips out a worn paperback from his bag—I immediately guess it's going to be Kerouac or Vonnegut and am sorely disappointed but also relieved when it turns out to be Colson Whitehead—and we sit in strangely companionable silence for a while. But it isn't long before the gears in my brain start turning again as I think about how I can use the talent show to my advantage.

I don't have any talents other than cards; that's just an unfortunate fact. But if watching old teen movies on sick days has taught me anything, it's that you don't need a genuine talent if you just show off hotness, and amazingly enough, I think that's a thing I'm learning how to do.

If the talent show is a regular thing at Camden, I'm willing to bet Isabel, Jenna, Priya, and Ashleigh have some sort of routine at the ready, and what could possibly make me look cooler *or* hotter than joining them? Maybe it's a long shot, but they've already taken me shopping and picked out my freaking underwear; is it really so beyond to think they might be willing to include me in this too?

"What's going through your head right now?"

Salem's question startles me out of my plotting, and I look over to see him watching me suspiciously over the edge of *The Nickel Boys*. "Nothing to worry your pretty head over."

"Why does that feel like the most dangerous thing you could possibly say?"

Dangerous. That's certainly a word no one's ever used about me.

Looks like I'm making some progress.

With my homework behind me, I dedicate the afternoon to figuring out how to approach Isabel about the talent show while also thinking about what I could possibly offer. Then, of course, there's the task of actually tracking her and her friends down, but turns out I didn't need to worry about that; they find me first—or at least, one of them does—thanks to Camden's all-day Sunday dorm-intervisitation policy.

"So this is your Rumson lair." It takes me a minute to

realize that the person speaking those words is standing in my doorway and talking to me. I left my door open because I've become accustomed to the background noises of squeaky sneakers and trash talking, even when I'm playing solitaire. I certainly never expected to find Jenna London in front of it.

Of the four girls, Jenna is definitely the scariest. I don't know if it's the black hair / ice-blue eyes combo or the fact that she smiles like she's about to sink her teeth into your neck, but I physically have to push my tongue against my teeth a few times to loosen it up enough to respond. "Home sweet home," I finally choke out.

She doesn't enter, just lets her gaze travel over the room like she's giving the world's most hideous outfit a once-over. "Maybe you should use some of last night's winnings to hire a decorator."

I'm pretty sure it's a joke. I'm not sure if I'm supposed to laugh.

I settle on a wry smile, but she seems to be over me anyway. There's a light tapping on my doorjamb and she moves on, leaving me no clue what she was doing here in the first place, or where she's off to next.

Okay, not the most promising start to getting myself included in their talent-show shenanigans. Or finding out if those shenanigans exist to begin with. Frankly, it's impossible for me to imagine Jenna doing anything that requires looking like she cares about something. The only thing I've ever seen bring her joy is making fun of her friends.

Come to think of it, that's the first time I've seen Jenna

without Ashleigh, Priya, and Isabel. Maybe that's what was so unsettling about her presence here.

I don't have any more time to think about it before my phone rings, and I give it a quick glance only to freeze when I see the word "Home" light up my screen.

I've only spoken to my parents a couple of times since I got here, but those calls were always from cell phones—a quick dutiful check-in from my mom on her way home from work, or my dad letting me know he's thinking of me while mixing up a stir-fry. They almost never use the landline, and I can't help thinking it's because it's not them at all, but Sierra trying to weasel her way into reaching me.

I let it go to voicemail, even though I would kill to hear "Hey, kiddo" in my dad's voice right now.

My mom and Sierra have always had this *bond.* They both love going out to have parts of their bodies polished and waxed and sugared and whatever. They have the same dark, wavy hair that makes them look positively unrelated to me and has left me watching enviously while one braided the other's hair on many a rainy afternoon. And my mom *loved* how Sierra had so many boys to talk about—the guy she sat next to in French and the stranger she flirted with at the pharmacy and the line of them asking her to prom every year. It may be stupid, but part of the excitement about finally getting a boyfriend was being able to have silly conversations with my mom about Craig over cups of hot chocolate, just like Sierra did.

But of course, my sister took that too.

My dad, though . . . We may not have as much in common

as Mom and Sierra do, but he always had the time and patience to teach me card games and tricks, and even a little cardistry—his favorite hobby. Every skill in my arsenal, from poker to canasta, comes from him. And even now, when I'm so happy to be an hour away from them all, I wish he and I could just squeeze in one game of gin rummy.

God, I hate how many things Sierra took away from me. It's like every day, I discover a new one.

I wait for the notification that a voicemail has been left, but my phone remains silent for the rest of the afternoon.

The talent show proves to be a surprisingly popular topic of conversation at Camden. Apparently, it's some kind of institution, and it's one of the few nonmandatory events that every single student attends. At dinner that night, Heather, Kayla, and Kayla's roommate Maya are more than happy to give Sabrina and me a rundown.

"Mr. Hoffman emcees it every year, and every year he messes up half of his jokes. Still unclear whether *that's* some sort of meta joke or if he's taken one too many footballs to the brain." Kayla pauses to sweep her braids behind her shoulder and take a delicate bite of her Bolognese, which is apparently *also* a Camden institution for Sunday-night dinner. "There used to be this awesome band that always closed down the show, but they graduated last year, and supposedly they got a contract at an indie label, but no one knows if that's really true or not."

"I heard that fell through," says Maya, "but there are plenty of people who perform every year and are epic."

"It's really fun," adds Heather, neatly wrapping spaghetti around her fork. "You guys should think about performing. I was too nervous to do it as a freshman, but I'm definitely gonna do it this year."

Salem's not listening to a single word—he's parked himself next to me with earbuds in his ears and a book open in front of him—but Sabrina and I listen with rapt attention as Maya tells us more acts we can expect to see, including a senior who sings opera, a freshman who's rumored to be a speed-painter (no idea what that is, but assuming it's as advertised), an impeccable hip-hop routine from the Dance Club that Kayla assures us will star Ashleigh front and center, and, incredibly, a junior ventriloquist.

"This all makes me feel very talentless," Sabrina jokes, and I'm glad someone else said what I was thinking, but one thing I will not be doing is making myself sound subpar. I may not have a talent for the show yet, but I will come up with one. And this seems like the perfect opportunity to dig into whether Isabel and her friends have anything I can somehow glom on to.

"Does anyone else do dance routines?" I ask casually. "Or, like, a lip-syncing kinda thing?" Yes, I Googled "talent show ideas for people without talent." Lip-syncing is shockingly popular. And also not a thing I am good at. But I figure if there's anything I can pick up in a couple of weeks, that's a solid one.

"God, that's the cheesiest," Sabrina cuts in, dragging her

fork through the sauce on the plate. "When did we start pretending that required multiple brain cells?"

Well, so much for that.

"Oh, the way my cousin does it is definitely a real talent," Heather says earnestly, turning to Kayla. "Remember those videos I showed you? She's so good."

Kayla nods and smiles, and all I can think is that there exists a girl so pure of heart, she proudly shows off her cousin's lip-syncing videos, and I made out with her boyfriend.

Yeah, I'm once again the Girl Who Wasn't Chosen, but once upon a time, I was also a Nice Girl—maybe not Heather level, but nice. Sweet. And we're both living proof that sweet is not enough. Even if it gets the guy, it doesn't *keep* the guy. Because the guy will always eventually get lured away by shameless flirting and sexy clothes and, above all, a willingness to do what the sweet girl won't.

Even if the girls are sisters.

Ask me how I know.

"A freshman did tap last year," says Maya. "She slipped and fell on her butt in the middle. It was not pretty. Let's just say she does not go here anymore."

Okay, so maybe I'd been so fixated on how I could look impressive that I had forgotten that I could even more easily make a complete ass of myself. Whoops. "Yikes," I say with a goofy swipe of my forehead before remembering that I am being uncool and I need to shift the attention elsewhere immediately. "So what are you guys thinking of doing?"

"I'm thinking about singing," Kayla says with a hint of bashfulness in her voice. "Or maybe doing a monologue."

"Ooh, I was thinking the same!" Heather's warm brown eyes light up, and I watch as she, Kayla, and Maya spin off into a conversation about how much they love drama and music and theatre and lights and camera and action. (Well, maybe not action.) If I didn't feel like an outsider before, I certainly do now.

"Do you know what you're gonna be doing, Evie?"

I blink at the sound of my name; apparently, I've been watching them without really listening. But now Kayla's just asked me a question and Heather and Maya—and Salem and Sabrina, who definitely think I don't notice them peeking over like the little weasels they are—are looking at me with curious interest, and I have no idea what to say, other than that I do not want to concede that I am wildly unimpressive in front of these people.

"I may do something with some friends" comes out of my mouth before I can stop it, and I regret it immediately. Faster, if possible. Because I can see them all trying to figure out who exactly my friends are who are not seated at this table, and frankly, that is a very good question.

The silence that drags out after that is almost worse than if they'd actually just asked, and I'm trying to recall everything I know about physics to see if I can make myself melt into the floor when Salem finally says, "Just warning you that if it's baton twirling, I've heard Hoffman likes to jump in and relive his high school glory days."

"Noted," I say with a grin as everyone else jumps in with jokes and guesses about what various staff talents would be. It's tremendously gratifying when I make everyone, including Salem, crack up with the mental image of Mrs. Frank break-dancing, to the point where I almost forget that now I really have to go and beg Isabel to do something with me.

Almost.

Chapter Nine

EVEN IF I DIDN'T KNOW Isabel lived in Hillman House, I would've known she lived in Hillman House. Tucked away in a lush green corner of the campus that is going to be next-level stunning when the leaves change, it's a stately Victorian with a glorious wraparound porch and room for only twelve girls. Of course, it costs twice as much as living in Lockwood or Ewing, so it wasn't even on my radar of possibilities, but there's still enough competition for it that they have to host a lottery for residency.

How incredibly lucky that somehow Isabel, Jenna, Ashleigh, and Priya have managed to win spots every year for three years. What are the odds, et cetera et cetera.

Unsurprisingly, the inside is as beautiful as the outside, and as soon as I enter I'm hit with the scents of fresh flowers and lemony wood polish. I could not feel farther right now from the locker-room smell of Rumson. The bedroom doors also don't have the same whiteboards that hang on the doors of every other dorm—presumably so they won't destroy the painted wood—so I have to check the polished brass boxes in the mail room to find that Isabel's single is upstairs, room 204.

At least the dorm doesn't *sound* any different from Lockwood—roaring blow-dryers competing with Beyoncé and Harry Styles—and I use that to center myself as I take a deep breath and knock.

The door swings open almost immediately, as if Isabel had been on her way out at the same time, but if I've interrupted something, it doesn't show in the broad smile that sweeps across her face. "Evie! What are you doing here?"

"I wanted to ask you about something." God, I *hear* the nervousness in my voice, and it's so pathetic. We may not be besties, but we definitely count as friends, right? I mean, she took me to the mall so recently that my hair's still straight.

"Ooh, I'm intrigued." She steps aside to let me in, and I take a few more breaths as I enter, trying to remind myself for the millionth time that this is not Greentree, I am not "Sierra's little sister" or "Craig's girlfriend" or "the weird girl who hangs out with that other weird girl who draws all the time," and all my good-girl spinelessness should be as far in my rearview as the life I left behind.

By the time I turn around, my gaze is steady and firm, and I settle into the cozy armchair in the corner as if I've been there a thousand times. "Do you guys have any plans for the talent show that might need an extremely charming fifth person?" I flutter my newly mascaraed lashes.

Isabel breaks out into a hearty laugh, and instantly I know

I've made a mistake. "You think this is like one of those old rom-coms where the hot girls have a hot routine they break out at every talent show?"

Do not shrink. Do not shrink. Do not shrink. I shrug casually, as if my ridiculous naivete is whatever, and try to think of an answer that wouldn't make Salem roll his eyes. "Well, a girl can hope."

Isabel drops onto her bed and folds her legs seamlessly into a lotus position on her pastel bedspread without even using her hands. "Unfortunately, I am utterly devoid of talent. Ashleigh does hip-hop with her team, Priya has the voice of an angel, and Jenna—well, Jenna is a classically trained pianist, but she'd enter a talent show over her dead body. Sorry to disappoint."

"No worries," I say as brightly as I can, which ends up coming out way too brightly. *Dial it down, Skeevy,* I hear in Salem's obnoxious voice. "I, too, am utterly devoid of talent. Just thought it might be fun to do something."

"You're not utterly devoid of talent, though," Isabel says with a wicked grin. "I watched you slay at that poker night."

"Yeah, I don't think that's a 'talent show' kind of talent."

"Okay, but do you have any other talents with cards? Something that *could* be a talent-show talent?"

"I mean, I do card tricks, some really basic cardistry—"

"Perfect!" Isabel lights up. "Who cares if it's basic? You can be a magician and I can be your assistant. It'll be fun."

"I don't actually do any tricks other than card tricks."

"So? You'll brand yourself as a card magician. I mean, if you really wanna do something."

"I do," I say firmly.

She snorts. "Did you lose a bet or something?"

"Ha, not exactly." *How to put this . . .* "I'd like for some people to know me as something other than the Rumson Girl, even if it's the Talent Show Dork."

"Ah. Well. Don't you worry about that," she says, sashaying over to her closet to pull out a sleek black pantsuit that would probably be perfect if Isabel wasn't at least half a foot taller than me. "We're going to make you the hottest magician Camden has ever seen."

I smile and put the pantsuit in front of me to get an idea of the general look, and yeah, I could make something in the right size look good. "I'm counting on it."

With my next phase of planning in the works, I spend a couple of days pondering exactly how to make being a card-trick expert look cool. Unfortunately, my partner in crime does not seem to realize that when you enter into a pact with someone, you are expected to be at their beck and call at all times for brainstorm sessions, which is how I end up banging on Salem's door on Tuesday evening.

I'd let myself in, but I have already twice learned my lesson in Rumson about barging into a room of boys without first alerting them. Then again, Salem's already plenty alert to my presence, which I know because, well, the sound of a shoe hitting the door is pretty distinct.

"I'm *studying*, Skeeveball!" His voice is just loud enough over his omnipresent blasting music to penetrate through the door that he still has yet to open. "You know, like you reminded me to do fifteen times today? I'm being good. You should be proud."

"I'd be prouder if you opened your damn door like a gentleman." Finally, I decide it's time to drop my ticket in. "Plus, I come bearing baked goods."

There's a beat of silence, and then finally, "You may enter."

Inside, the music is twice as loud but every bit as incomprehensible as it was on the other side of the door. "What *is* this," I ask, gesturing to where his phone is hooked up to a speaker, "and how the hell are you studying with it on?"

"It's Rage Against the Machine, and it is extremely on topic for studying revolutions, thank you very much." Still, he turns it down a little. "Anyway, I was promised baked goods?"

"Actually, all I said was that I *had* baked goods," I correct, just to be annoying. Still, I hand over a couple of chocolate chip cookies I made in my first meeting of Baking Club the day before, keeping one for myself. "Now, I *am* very proud of you for studying, but we also need to work on these music choices. There is no way this does not make your parents cringe themselves into the ground, and there's *also* no way any girl in her right mind would wanna come back here and make out to this."

He takes a bite of his cookie and silently says "I have made out to this song a million times" with his arched eyebrow.

"Liar," I mutter as I take a seat at his desk, and he just

shrugs, which is extra annoying because there is no way Salem has actually ever tolerated someone's presence (and vice versa) long enough to make out with them, let alone to this soundtrack. I can't even physically *imagine* him kissing someone. Like, where would he put his hands? Everywhere seems too gentle and intimate for someone who uses pocket knives as fidget spinners and listens to metal loud enough to wake the dead, though I admit he is pretty dexterous with a basketball, and— Wait, *why* am I imagining Salem's lips and hands exploring anyone, anyway?

I take a sanity-preserving bite of cookie before continuing my thought. "Anyway, only listening to old music makes you seem like you're not open to new things and experiences. There's something so dreary about acting like nothing new can be cool. You don't wanna be that guy."

"I am absolutely happy to be that guy."

"Hey, you asked for my help," I can't resist reminding him, even though he's clearly been sorry about that fact every single minute of every single day since.

"Stick with providing sustenance." He swallows down the last chocolatey bite. "I might need to join Baking Club."

Okay, that might be even harder to picture than—

Nope, still harder to picture Salem with his tongue in a girl's mouth.

Again, *not* picturing Salem with his tongue in a girl's mouth.

What was I here to talk about again?

Oh right. Me.

"Anyway, no thanks to you, I locked in a talent-show idea

I think you're going to like very much." At least if Isabel wears the kind of outfit she's planning to. "But it's kind of cheesy and I need you to help me make it cool."

"I'm really starting to think there's not one thing I could do to make you cool. Where did you even get the idea that being in the talent show was somehow a badass thing to do?"

"I had a different initial vision," I admit, "but it went off the rails kind of quickly when I was talking to Isabel. Who, by the way, will be my partner for this, so you may actually want to be nice to me."

"You know you entirely invented my interest in her, right?"

I roll my eyes. "Yeah, okay. Like you don't literally improve your posture in her presence."

"It's instinct!"

"I'll bet it is. Anyway, you're supposed to *want* to help me, the way I want to help you. I'm starting to think I've gotten the rotten end of this deal."

"*You?*" He snorts. "I'm the one who has my phone going off fifty times a day with reminders to brush my teeth or call home."

"Yeah, and your breath smells better and your mom is happier!"

"My breath smelled fine before!"

It did—he pops Tic Tacs pretty constantly, I suspect to annoy people with the noise—but that isn't the point. "Well, I bet your dental hygiene is better now, and you're welcome for that."

"You also took my weed and lighter, didn't you."

I did in fact sneak it out of his room on Saturday night;

I've been wondering how long it would take him to figure that out. "I'm doing you a favor—now you can't smoke *and* you won't accidentally burn down the entire dorm because you were bored one night."

I can't make out any words in his grumbling of a response, but given there's no fight about it, he seems to agree.

Or has more stashed somewhere.

"You can't make me sound like some uptight pain in the ass when you asked for this," I remind him firmly.

"Technically, *I* asked for someone to cover for me to keep me out of trouble. It was *your* idea to just . . . keep me out of trouble. And it's making things very boring."

"Boring is good when your idea of exciting is getting high in your principal's office," I counter as I hop up from the chair and head to the door, "but you don't want my help? That's fine. Something tells me I'll be just fine without yours." The whole idea was stupid anyway. It might've worked with Matt, but Salem was never gonna care about anyone other than himself.

Seems I suck just as much as ever at figuring out who actually deserves my cookies.

To his credit, the next morning, Salem seems to realize he's being a dick. *Fine*, says the note that lands on my desk in English. *I'll help you.*

Shortly after, a follow-up lands. *Do you know how to do laundry?*

I flash back to that first moment of Rumson orientation, that dickbag Duncan implying I was there to clean up after his loser ass. *Do your own fucking laundry,* I write in firm block letters before tossing it back.

He snorts, loudly enough that a couple of kids in front of us turn around, and then there's the sound of a new paper tearing and a scratching as he ekes out another barely legible note.

I'm not asking you to do my laundry. I'm asking you to teach me how to do laundry.

I glance up to see him watching for my response, and raise an eyebrow.

More tearing. More scrawling. Even with him bent over the paper I can see his lips curving up as he writes and then tosses the paper on my desk like a Frisbee. *Teach me how to be good, Peach.*

Mrs. Frank calls on Salem then, and while I would've been completely lost, he, annoyingly, gets the answer right and earns a nod of approval. As soon as she's moved on, he starts writing another note. *Teach me laundry and you get to go shopping in my stuff.*

Okay, that actually is a pretty decent deal, even with Salem being a foot taller than me. There's plenty I could do to crop one of his T-shirts, which on him look grungy but on me would look cute AF and definitely edgier than anything I own, and I do love that leather jacket . . .

I turn the last note over and pick up my pen. *Deal. Be ready for me after dinner on Friday. I'll be the one knocking like a banshee.*

* * *

I would've chosen a card-game club if there'd been one, but since there wasn't, I figured I could probably like other games as much if I gave them a chance. It was true for Board Games Club, where I played Codenames with a bunch of other sophomores and had a solid time despite losing miserably, but as I stare at the collection of black and white plastic pieces in front of me, I fear both my partner and I have sorely miscalculated.

"Do *you* know how to play chess?" Sabrina whispers to me from across the board.

"No clue," I admit as I glance around, watching other people set up their pieces in a way that suggests there is very much a right way and a wrong way. "Do you?"

"I know the queen has the most power," she says, touching a chipped black fingertip to the top of a crowned piece I assume is the royalty in question. "But it's killing the king that wins the game."

"Okay, yes, I know the king part. But I kind of thought they'd be teaching us how to play." I glance around at the duos who've already begun their games, and am more than a little disappointed that we don't get those clock things to press when our turns are over. "Or that it'd be easy to figure out."

"You thought chess would be easy to figure out."

"Well why are *you* here, if you knew you wouldn't know what you're doing?"

"I signed up for the GSA on Wednesdays, but apparently

I was the only one, so they shuttered it for lack of interest," she says with a tinge of annoyance. "There weren't a lot of choices left by then, so I just picked something chill where no one would bug me for an hour."

"That sucks," I say, and I mean it. "Is it open to allies? I am *such* a good friend that I would totally bail on chess if it'll help get the group started."

"I think that ship has sailed, but—"

"Ladies, do you two need help?"

We look up to see Brian, who can't be more than a couple years older than we are but is trying his hardest to project Elderly Grandfather with his wardrobe, standing over us. The eyes of the club admin are displeased but trying to stay mild behind their wire-framed glasses. Judging by the book in his hand currently bookmarked by his index finger, he was hoping to be able to simply ignore us for the entire hour, and we are now a disruption of that plan.

Here's where Old Evie would've made herself small and polite and pretended she didn't need anything so he could get back to *Elbow Patches for Dummies*, or whatever he was reading.

But I am not Old Evie, and I'm pretty sure he *is* supposed to be providing instruction to those of us who need it. And chess may not be a "cool girl" game, but I've always wanted to learn. "Yes, actually!" I say sunnily, even as Sabrina kicks me under the table. "Could you teach us how to play?"

"You . . . want me to teach you how to play chess?" He pushes his glasses farther up on his nose. "Right now? Like, from the beginning?"

"That'd be a great place to start!"

He stares at me for a few more seconds, as if he's trying to confirm I'm not kidding, and then he sighs, pulls up a seat, and shows us how to arrange the pieces, ending with the line of pawns in front. He's starting to explain how they all move when someone else calls for his attention—a chess emergency, I guess—and he tells us to look up the rest on our phones.

"I don't have my phone here, do you?" Sabrina asks me.

"Nope." We're not supposed to have our phones on us until after cocurrics, and I haven't quite broken all my rule-following habits just yet.

"So I suppose we can just guess?" Sabrina picks up her queen and places it in the center of the board. "I feel like she should be able to do whatever she wants, including skipping over these loser pawns."

"Agreed." I consider my own pieces. "Bishop probably can't go anywhere, being a very serious man of the cloth, right? But look at this little horsey! He can definitely jump over pieces and probably go anywhere on the board." I pick up the horse and place it right in front of the pawn blocking the king.

"So, your whole skilled-with-games thing, that's specifically a card thing, huh?"

"A hundred percent." I glance up at Brian, who's moderating an argument between two guys who clearly do know chess. "Think he'd mind if I whipped out a deck of cards?"

"Do you *have* a deck of cards?"

"Literally always. But he *did* just teach us half the game, so I feel like we should play." In my head I can hear Salem mocking me for being a softie, but I can also see myself giving him the finger, so I feel like it all evens out.

"Fine, then. I'm gonna take one of your pawns with my queen."

"That's fair," I say with a nod as Sabrina sweeps her queen across the board and knocks off one of my defenseless little guys. "And I'm gonna do the same with my horsey." I take off the pawn in the adjacent square and move in my piece, just as a girl from the table next to us says, "It's called a *knight*. And it moves in an L shape *only*."

I'm about to open my mouth to thank her for the information, even if she's being a little B about how she imparts it, when Sabrina says, "Not in our version."

The other girl rolls her eyes but returns to her game to mind her own business, and I make a mental note that maybe I'm channeling the wrong Grayson twin in my endeavors.

And also to stop calling it a "horsey," maybe.

We settle into our game, making up rules as we go along and talking about our other cocurricular choices. I hadn't even known there's a tarot club on Mondays, or that Sabrina's signed up for Book Club tomorrow, same as I am. "Guess we're going to spend the entire first meeting fighting about what book to read," she says as she takes another of my pawns with her queen. She's done that every move so far, leaving me with one left.

"Can't wait." I actually kind of can't. I used to only read books with happy romances and happier endings, but these days I feel like I could stand to be introduced to books with revenge and murder. Or at least dragons.

But speaking of happy romances and happier endings, it occurs to me that I know very, very little about Sabrina's once-happy romance and its very unhappy ending. I know it isn't any of my business, per se, but, well, I'm trying to get my shit together so I can have a normal relationship someday, and maybe Sabrina would like to come along for that ride.

"Can I ask you an incredibly invasive question?"

"What better time is there to be incredibly invasive than over a chessboard?"

"That's shockingly open of you," I say as I jump my other knight around on the board, taking him on a little sightseeing tour of the black and white squares.

She shrugs. "If it's none of your business, I'll tell you it's none of your business."

"Oh, I already know it's none of my business."

"Great, then you're prepared for my answer. But I'm warning you that if your question is anything like 'How can two girls *do* that?' I'm going to be extremely graphic." She takes my last pawn with a flourish.

"Jesus, no, obviously not." I survey the board, and decide that a king can definitely move as many squares as he wants. I move it toward the queen, but I'm not sure whether he can take her; Sabrina *did* say the queen was the most powerful piece. "I was just wondering about Molly. Why the two of you broke up, I mean. And whether you think you're ready to date again. Or is it one of those things where it's not really over?"

"No, it's definitely over," she says flatly. "She thought we were getting too serious, and wanted to date other people. I can't even hate her, because sure, it's valid. But I *was* serious, and it came out of nowhere, and it just really fucked with me. How one person can think things are literally perfect while the other one is writing a breakup speech."

"Makes you feel like you can't trust anything, including your own instincts," I mutter. "*Especially* your own instincts. And how can you not hate the person that now permanently makes you doubt yourself?"

I'd kind of forgotten I was speaking aloud until Sabrina says, "*Yes*, exactly. That's exactly it. Everything feels shaky now."

"Yeah."

Sabrina and I stare at the board, and then she uses her queen to kick my king in the nuts.

Or where I assume his nuts would be if he were not a piece of plastic with a cross on top.

"I think I won," she says with the faintest of smiles. "Start again?"

Chapter Ten

AFTER ANOTHER ROUSING COMMUNITY SERVICE effort (recycling!) on Friday afternoon followed by a quick dinner and shower, I roll into Matt and Salem's room with my own hamper in tow, because I haven't exactly been on top of my laundry situation either. I imagine most of the students at Camden take advantage of the optional laundry service, but that is decidedly not in the Riley family budget.

I do, however, know how to do it myself, which I guess puts me a step above Salem . . . or maybe three steps, considering that when he opens the door to let me in that night, I see piles of dirty clothes all over the place. "Whaaaat is happening here?" I ask, dropping my hamper and surveying the black cotton landscape.

"I know there's something about lights and darks, but I don't really wear much light," he says, scratching his head as he returns to the mess. "So I thought maybe the light*er* stuff?" He holds up a pair of jeans.

"Okay, no." I rescue the jeans from his hands and flip them inside out before tossing them into his now-empty laundry bag. "Colors get washed in cold water, and that definitely includes jeans, unless you want them to shrink into doll clothes. Washing them inside out helps keep the color. White stuff gets washed in warm or hot water, but you can just throw everything in cold; that way you only need one machine for everything, and . . . I literally do not see a single white article of clothing here anyway. Now come on, get all this stuff back in the bag."

While he scoops his pants, shirts, and shorts back into his big black laundry bag, I realize something. "Why don't I hate this music?" I ask.

He grins. "*Someone* told me to try new things. This is Måneskin—one of Sabs's favorites. She has a massive crush on their bassist."

"Finally, someone in the Grayson family with taste."

"Are you referring to the music or the bassist?" he asks with a waggle of his brows, and I roll my eyes even though I am definitely going to Google her later. But the music really is catchy, and as Salem walks around the room, yanking stray socks and boxers off the floor and stuffing them into his laundry bag, I can't resist moving a little to the beat. It *could* be a fun song to do some cardistry to . . .

"It's not terrible," he concedes, "but I stand by my personal taste being supreme. Have you ever even listened to Nirvana? Or Garbage? Or the Pixies?"

"I think you already know the answer."

"Yeah, well, you should try, at least."

I roll my eyes again and he goes back to picking up his clothes while I start taking notes on my phone of which tricks I wanna do now that I've heard potential musical accompaniment. But I'm not typing long before the door swings open and Matt stands in the doorway, surveying the scene in front of him. "This is adorably domestic," he observes, earning himself a scowl from Salem. "I could definitely use a hand with my laundry, if you're offering. I couldn't tell you what that stain is on the pants I wore last night, or, well, I could, but—"

"You're on your own," Salem and I tell him simultaneously, then exchange a glance before Salem stuffs in the last pair of shorts. "Come on, Skeevy."

"Uh, you may wanna wash those sheets, bro," Matt tells him with a nod at the bed. "And that gnarly towel of yours."

"Okay, yes, you should definitely wash those," I confirm. "Where are your towels?"

"I have one towel. It's hanging on a hook in the bathroom, and it's wet."

"Good news—it's going to stay wet in the wash, so you can go ahead and get it. I'll even strip your bed for you." I immediately throw a glare Matt's way. "No stripping jokes."

He holds up his hands innocently. "It was too easy anyway."

"I thought 'too easy' was exactly how you like it," I shoot back as Salem heads to the communal bathroom and I yank his sheet from the mattress.

"That's my girl," Matt says with a grin.

It strikes me then that I am in the presence of the one person who is the genuine male equivalent of what everyone *thinks* I am, and he doesn't seem to give a shit about his reputation one bit. Matt could probably give me some decent tips for how to handle it, and for all he loves to joke around about everything, I also know he'll take me seriously.

"Hey, can I ask you for some advice?" I glance at the door. "Later, I guess."

"My door is always open to you, dormie. And yeah, later's good; I've gotta go meet my study group at the library now anyway."

"Is that a euphemism?"

"I wish." He stuffs a few books in his bag. "That sounds a lot more fun than AP Bio."

"You're in *AP Bio*?" I immediately feel bad for how incredulous I sound, but the way he smirks, he's clearly used to it.

"Me and pretty much all the other kids planning to go premed." He says it casually, as if the guy best known at Camden for his bedroom skills planning to become a doctor is no big deal. And, technically, I guess it isn't. I mean, he certainly knows human anatomy. "I'll see you later, Skeevy."

"Oh my God, don't you dare start calling me that!" I yell after him, his laughter carrying over his shoulder as he heads out to campus.

Shaking my head, I return to the task of Salem's sheets, pulling off his top pillowcase and then the bottom one. As I pick up the latter, I see something black underneath, and I pinch it between two fingers, figuring it's another piece of Salem's laundry left behind.

But unless Salem's got a hobby I don't know about, that is definitely not his underwear.

In fact, I *know* that underwear, or at least that brand; I've got a pair in the very laundry at my feet.

My pair, however, is pink.

Because the person who wears black?

Is Jenna London.

"Hey." Salem peeks his head inside and I immediately shove the underwear in with the pile of sheets. "Got my towel. You ready?"

I think I nod. I know I stand. But am I ready to have a casual conversation about detergents and water temperatures with Salem when I just found out he's hooking up with Jenna London?

Not so much.

* * *

Being unable to leave Rumson for the next two hours until my laundry was done ended up being the perfect excuse to avoid the world while I turned this newfound information over and over in my head, especially when Salem got a text and bailed. He promised that if I just moved his clothes over, he'd be back to grab them from the dryer, but I had no desire to see him when he returned from his booty call; I said I'd handle it all. And though he may have been suspicious of my sudden act of kindness, he clearly knew it was better to just take me up on the offer than waste time asking questions. Which left me entirely alone.

I text Sabrina.

Evie

Are you doing anything? I'm doing laundry and I'm bored.

Her reply comes a few minutes later.

Sabrina

Sorry, @ services @ Jewish Students' Club. Promised mom we'd go for her mother's yahrzeit.

Huh. So that's where Salem is, I guess. I mentally apologize for the booty-call assumption.

Evie

I didn't know you guys were Jewish.

Sabrina

Surprise! *jazz hands*

I start to ask what a yahrzeit is, and then I remember that Google is free.

Evie

Ah, well, happy deathiversary to your grandma

Sabrina

Thx, I'll pass that along

I don't know what else to do with my night. I'm not going to a movie by myself, especially if Heather and Lucas might be there. I don't wanna go upstairs to the lounge, in case some of the more dickish Rumson guys are there, the ones who like to either loudly remind me that the communal bathrooms are off-limits to me or invite me to join them inside. I have no interest in the open gym or open art room or even the open kitchen; if I bake something, it'll just mean getting stuck waiting in the Student Center after I've already been stuck waiting in the laundry room.

With a sigh, I open up the laptop I'd tossed on top of my hamper and get started on the APUSH reading. I more than anyone can't leave my laundry behind; God only knows where my underwear would end up if I left it unattended in here for even a minute.

Studying: just what all the cool girls do on Friday nights.

I read until the washing machines cease their rumbling and then I move everything over into the dryers and sit and wait again. I'd assumed there'd be at least a few people in and out of the laundry room tonight, but no, turns out no one else is uncool enough to spend their Friday night doing laundry.

I wonder what Isabel and her friends are doing, especially if Jenna's not as otherwise occupied as I thought she was. Probably something totally beyond me, like taking Ashleigh's car into town and going to a bar or whatever. Even though we have plans to get together tomorrow to talk about our talent-show routine, I still don't feel like Izzy and I are at the point where I can just text her and say *yo what up*.

(*You will never be at the point where you should be tex-*

ting anyone and saying "yo what up," Salem would tell me, I know.)

Then again, would a cool girl be second-guessing whether it's uncool to text a friend and see what she's up to? No, a cool girl would not. A badass *definitely* would not. I'm still not sure which of those things I aspire to be, because in my mind, they go hand in hand, but either way, it's a status I have not achieved.

Yet.

Deep breath. Find Isabel McEvoy in contacts. Type words. Go.

Evie

We still on for tomorrow?

Five minutes of no response later, I've just about given up when suddenly, incoming text.

Isabel

Yep! But can we make it 11?

I'm def gonna need to sleep in.

Ah, yes, I too will require recovery time from this night of debauchery.

Evie

Sounds good!

So much for that.

People always want to know why I love playing cards so much, and the reason I always give is that it's something my dad and I did a ton when I was a kid. And it's true—that is definitely the number one reason. When Sierra and my mom would go out and do the special mother-daughter things that mothers and daughters who actually have things in common do, my dad and I would kick back with cans of fruity seltzer and play.

When I was little, it was war and go fish, then spit and casino. Gin rummy came next, while I learned the very basics of blackjack and poker. On the rare occasions we played as a family, hearts or spades often came out, or Pres, which Sierra gleefully told me was actually called Asshole. As I got older, I learned everything I could—bridge, canasta, even whist. But in truth, my favorite thing about cards is that solitaire is and always has been a perfectly legit solo activity, and it's kept me company on more occasions than I can count.

It sounds pathetic when I put it that way, which is why I never do. But it's also why I carry a deck in my pocket the way other people carry fidgets or pens. And I guess this is the perfect time to put it to good use.

I play solitaire until the buzzer goes off, and then I empty both dryers, and text Salem to let him know his hamper is waiting in the laundry room. After, I bring my stuff upstairs, get ready for bed, and lie staring at the ceiling for far, far too many hours until sleep finally comes.

"Do it slower," Isabel insists, her big green eyes like saucers as I finish the same card trick—my favorite one—for the third time in a row. "I'm going to figure it out."

"If you can figure it out, it's not going to be a very impressive talent-show display," I point out as I intertwine my fingers and flip my hands inside out to stretch them. "The point is to dazzle everyone with my skills."

"Well, your skills and my legs," she says with a grin, holding the bodysuit she'll be wearing as my assistant up against her torso again. I don't know why she owns such a thing, but then again, if I had her body, I'd probably have it in twelve colors.

She showed me the outfit the minute I showed up in her room for practice, after a morning spent over waffles and math homework, and suggested I wear something similar. But even the new and improved version of me can't fathom wearing something *quite* so . . . so. Seeing as I'll be playing the role of magician, I figure I can just put together an all-black outfit that works.

"I also had a thought about music," I tell her, searching for the song in my phone I listened to in Salem's room yesterday. "Thought it might be fun to have this in the background. What do you think?"

She listens while I put on Måneskin's cover (Salem made sure I knew this) of "Beggin'," and when her body starts moving to the music after the first ten seconds or so, I know I've got her, and I'm strangely proud. "I like this," she says with a smile. "Yeah, let's do this. Where'd you hear it?"

I'm certainly not telling Jenna London's best friend that I heard it from Salem, so I tell her someone was blasting it in Rumson.

"God, I still can't believe you *live* there. What's it like?"

"Loud." I shuffle the cards once, twice, three times. "Guys yell a *lot* of shit to each other. And they stink. They come back from sports and smell rancid, and then they take showers and smell like too much body spray. They leave their shit all over the place. I wish I could tell you it's as glamorous as it sounds, but it's mostly just gross."

"Oh, I believe it," says Isabel. "But I don't mean the boys. What's it like for you, having no girls around?"

My hands freeze on the cards. "You know, you're the first person to ask me that. Everyone always just wants to know stuff like whether Matt wears boxers or briefs."

"I'd put money on boxers."

"You'd be correct. And it's hard, not having girls around." I exhale slowly, my fingers starting to flip through the cards again. "I had a best friend at home. And a sister. And the girls I sat with at lunch or hung out with after school"—mostly girlfriends of Craig's friends, which seems sad now that I think about it—"and I was really looking forward to having a roommate. I know most people love their privacy, but. I don't know. I didn't even realize how much I was looking forward to it until I opened my door and saw my roommate was Archibald freaking Buchanan."

"Well, then I'm glad you have me," she says with a grin, wrapping an arm around my neck.

"I am too," I say, and I mean it. I don't know why on earth Isabel McEvoy chose me for a friend, but I am extremely grateful every day that she did.

"And what about Matt's roommate? You guys seem tight."

"Do we?" I snort, knowing that Salem would probably mime an act of violence on himself at the very thought. "Don't tell him that."

Her mouth curves into a smile. "Why's that?"

"There are prickly jerks, and then there's Salem Grayson—an entire other level. I don't think there's a single person on earth he likes as much as he likes dead musicians."

"So you guys have never . . ."

"Never . . . ?" Then the meaning of her question hits, and I laugh for real. "God no. Me and *Salem*? In what world?"

"I had to ask!" She twirls her long strawberry hair into a bun on top of her head and stretches out her limbs. "I suspected we were doing this routine to impress someone, and I was afraid it might be him."

"It's not," I assure her. "But wait, why 'afraid'?" All at once, everything registers. "You know." It's not a question.

"Evie—"

I jump up from where I've been sitting on the floor. "You know about Salem and Jenna. You've always known. And you're trying to get dirt for her." I think back to the day at the mall, and how they teased me about him then, too. At the time, it'd felt like an induction into their glorious group, but now I see it for what it was: a fact-finding mission. "God, I should've known."

"Evie, no, come on. You're making it sound like this evil plot. We *are* friends—"

"Really, Isabel? Because using me to make sure I'm not

getting in the way of the guy your friend wants is not what friends do. Making me a stepping stone to someone else—getting an invite from me to his room . . ." I can't even continue. It's all so pathetic. I am right back where I was a few months ago, a tool in the quest for two people to find each other while I lose everything.

How am I back here?

"I gotta go." I stumble out of her room to the sound of her calling my name, the cards fluttering from my hands to the plush carpet below.

It's a relief to make it to Rumson without bumping into anyone, and when I get back to my room, I do something I never do and lock the door. There isn't a soul on earth I want to see right now, or for the rest of the day. All I can think about is who's using me, and am I *ever* going to be someone who just gets to have a life and friends and a boyfriend without there being an asterisk on it all?

Okay, you're going to make yourself crazy. I can't be alone with my thoughts. I need some noise to drown them out. I flip open my laptop and open up a music app.

I'm about to put on one of my usual comfort choices like Taylor Swift when I decide I need a change of pace. What were those bands Salem mentioned again? After all, he gave newer music a shot when I suggested it; it seems only fair that I try his.

I look up Nirvana, thinking of the shirt he wore on the first day, and he's right: a lot of this isn't bad. From there, I follow "If you like this, you may like that" suggestions that take me from Hole to Veruca Salt to Letters to Cleo. I explore Foo Fighters and Soundgarden and Mad Season. I take a quick break to pick up food from the Beast and bring it back to my room so I can listen some more.

Some of the music is good. Some of it is awful. Some of it reminds me of sitting in Craig's basement and watching him maneuver soldiers and elves through virtual battlefields while barely acknowledging my existence. Some of it makes me think of Sierra for no reason at all other than that it feels like her vibe and apparently my brain and this shit with Isabel are determined to pull me back into the past.

And finally, after I don't even know how many songs have passed, I do the thing I've been determined not to do.

I go online to look up all the people I left behind, starting with my sister.

Sierra's pictures always make it look like she's having the best time in the room, and if any part of me had thought maybe that would change in my absence, that's now squashed. It's just like it's always been for her—cracking up at a party, clutching the arms of her usual partners in crime, Jace and Levi. Lying out on the grass and lifting her face to the sun. Showing off an outfit in shades of neon, her fingers raised in a peace sign. Not one thing about her life has changed.

Including the fact that Craig and Claire are nowhere to be found.

So they didn't end up managing to worm their way into her orbit for real, then. He slept with his girlfriend's sister, and she kept their secret, and for what?

Craig's only social media use is limited to stuff like gamer Discords, so I don't bother with that; instead, I click over to Claire, expecting the usual brightly colored squares of her art. She's never been big on posting pictures of her face, and she absolutely hates all photographs of her body.

Or at least she used to.

It's only been a couple of weeks since I left Greentree, and a few months since I've seen or spoken to Claire, but I swear I don't know who this person is smiling hugely with her arm around two girls with similarly dark-brown skin, her meticulous braids dip-dyed lilac. I have never seen the camo-print romper she's wearing in this picture at the Dunkin' Donuts we used to go to every Sunday morning, cheesing around the hot pink straw emerging from her iced matcha latte. (At least her usual order hasn't changed.) And there is no way that the girl wearing a bathing suit—a *bathing suit*—in this picture clearly taken at the town pool is my old best friend ClaireBear.

And even though there's no sign of Craig, or Sierra, or . . . any of our old friends, actually, in any of these pictures, it's too much.

I turn off my phone, throw it on my bed, and turn the music all the way up.

* * *

The last morning of the world's most depressing weekend, I get myself to the library bright and early. I've developed an affinity for a particular seat, and showing up while everyone else is still chowing down on bagels in the Beast is the best way to get it, even if I do miss Sunday Dunkin' runs with Claire now more than ever.

I didn't get a thing done last night except make playlists of the songs I actually liked and have one quick catch-up phone call with my parents, during which we told each other approximately nothing and pretended we were looking forward to Parents' Weekend next month. Once they confirmed grades, food, and room were good, I set them free to watch whatever show about international spies they were currently fixated on and treated myself to a luxuriously long shower.

But today . . . today is lab report and math homework and APUSH reading and story writing and studying for my Spanish quiz.

And it starts now.

I start with chem—my least favorite—and spread out my stuff, taking advantage of the library being nearly empty. But of course, I'm all of ten seconds into my lab report when someone else gets the same idea.

And I know without even looking up exactly who that someone else is.

"What are you doing here?"

"Listening to you hum 'Heart-Shaped Box,' apparently." Salem's voice drips with smugness as he slides his stuff onto the table next to mine. "I thought I heard some good stuff coming up through the floor last night. Glad to see you took my advice."

He sounds uncharacteristically friendly and cheerful, and when I finally look up at him, I see it's more than just his voice. He looks . . . happy. Together. Some might even say "good." He's wearing the jeans he wore to the movies the night he went as my "date," and he's managed to scrounge up a T-shirt that doesn't have a shredded collar. He looks way cleaner and more clear-eyed than he did a week ago, and he smells like he just came out of the shower.

He looks like a well-adjusted basketball player with a hot girlfriend and a 5.0 GPA and in that moment I absolutely hate him.

Doesn't he know that he wasn't supposed to succeed so well while I failed so hard?

Which I can't say, so I just grunt, hoping he'll take the hint.

Of course, for the first time in his life, Salem doesn't take advantage of an excuse to leave. Instead, he starts grilling me on what I listened to and what I liked as if we were two fangirls bonding over our favorite ship. Under other circumstances, it might've been fun, but right now I just want Salem to go the hell away—back into the arms of his perfect girlfriend, maybe.

"Okaaay, I see you're not in a chitchat mood," he finally observes. "Well then, do you wanna split up the history reading?"

"I'm working on chem."

"Doesn't have to be right now," he says, unbothered. Why,

today of all days, is Salem just . . . chill? And like in an "I have all the patience in the world for you" kind of way, as opposed to a "none of this shit matters" kind of way?

Oh, right, he probably woke up under Jenna London. That'd put most guys in a great mood, I imagine.

"I can do my own reading, thank you," I spit. "I'm not a child."

Well, that seems to do it. "What the fuck, Evie? Is this just PMS or did I do something to you?"

"Yes, please, add a spoonful of misogyny," I growl. "That'll help your cause."

"I don't have a fucking cause; I *thought* I was sitting down with a friend and working together, like we've done, oh, I don't know, about fifty times since we got here. But I didn't even see you yesterday, so I really don't know what the hell I could've done between hanging out in my room on Friday and now." Salem's eyes flash what in warm brown eyes might've been fire, but in his cool gray is just plain lightning. "Is this about the laundry? You said it was fine, and Sabrina said she told you where I was."

"She did."

"Well then did I get a red sock into your whites or something?"

"Do you even own a red sock?"

"No, I don't, which makes this even more confusing."

Sitting down with a friend. It's the first time he's ever called me that, and it'd probably warm my heart a little if not for all the strings that seem attached to it right now. Which is why I have to ask. "*Are* we friends, Salem? Or were you always using me to get to Jenna?"

"What?" If the library were busier, the entire room would probably break into angry shushes right now, but as it is, there are only three other students milling about, and no staff, so we get only a few shushes. Still, Salem lowers his voice to regular volume. "We started hanging out before Jenna came into the picture. She doesn't have anything to do with anything."

"Then why did you lie about her?"

"I didn't lie," he says, though the defiant set his jaw gets when he believes what he's saying a hundred percent is conspicuously lacking. "I just didn't mention it."

"*Why?* Why not tell me you were hooking up?"

He flutters his ungodly long lashes. "A gentleman doesn't kiss and tell?"

"I cannot begin to tell you the number of things wrong with that sentence coming out of your mouth." Starting with the fact that it's a confirmation. I didn't even know a part of me was holding on to the thought that he might tell me this was a total misunderstanding and it was actually Matt she was fooling around with, or the underwear under his pillow was some weird prank. But there it is. Confirmed.

Okay then. That's fine. I'm fine. What's there not to be fine about? Salem is hooking up with Jenna, and he's happy, and they're happy, and Salem and I aren't as close as I thought. Cool cool cool.

"What do you want me to say, Skeevy? I gave Matt shit

for being a slut and now here I am, doing the same thing. It's embarrassing."

"You have to know hooking up with a single girl doesn't make you a slut, but even if you were, so what?" I demand. "Matt's not hurting anybody. He's not pretending to be anything he isn't. He doesn't have a girlfriend, or an almost-girlfriend, and he isn't telling girls he loves them and then sleeping with their sisters. Every girl at this school who hooks up with Matt Haley knows what she's getting and she doesn't care, because she wants the same thing. There's nothing wrong with that."

"Those are some awfully specific examples."

God, of course he would pick up on that. "I'm just trying to make a point. There's nothing inherently slutty about hooking up, and there's nothing inherently evil in being slutty anyway, so maybe you could ease the hell up and realize your roommate is actually a pretty freaking nice guy." Frankly, I'd kill to have a roommate who cared as much about me as Matt clearly cares about Salem.

Salem narrows his eyes. "Please tell me you are not hooking up with Matt."

"*Jesus*, Salem, no, I'm not, and you are missing the point." I open my mouth to continue the tirade, but Salem holds up a hand.

"I know, I know. You're not wrong. He has been . . . nice," Salem admits grudgingly. "And relatively considerate, considering our room—or at least our window—is a revolving door."

"And?"

"And . . . you may have a point about the rest. I don't

know. I didn't exactly come here with a ton of experience." His eyes drop to the desk, an unfurled paper clip I hadn't even noticed in his hand scratching out an S in the scarred wood. "I might've been . . . jealous. A little. Of Matt."

My eyebrows shoot to the sky. "I'll be honest, I thought it would take at *least* six hours of physical torture to get that out of you."

"It should've," he mutters. "Anyway, feel better now?"

"No," I say honestly, because I still don't know how to trust him. Because I still couldn't trust Isabel. Because even if Jenna just tripped and fell into Salem's lap, I'm the one who brought her to his room for poker night, and I'm the room she stopped by on the way to his, I guess, and I'm the idiot who thought I was helping him with a hopeless crush on someone else entirely. But mostly, because I'm the one sitting here in clothes barely a step up from pajamas and hair a mess and no clue what I'm doing or whether I'll ever be able to trust my instincts with guys again, while he's turned himself around in no time at all. "Now if you'll excuse me, I need to get back to my lab report."

"You're kidding me."

I refuse to dignify that with even a meeting of the eyes, choosing instead to focus on the work he interrupted. "Nope. Why don't you head off and do something brilliant like break out a crack pipe in Headmaster Gibbons's office? Seems like you're losing your edge."

Okay, that might've taken things a bit far, and the angry sweep of his books back into his bag confirms it. I wait for the sound of him storming off, but instead, a shadow looms over me and cool, minty breath dances over my cheek. "You wanna know something true, Skeevy? Something secret?" he whispers dangerously. "I got caught on purpose so I could give Sabrina an out because I could see she was dying being around Molly. Feel free to yank that one from your bitchy insult box."

And *then* I get the storming off, but it's not remotely satisfying.

In fact, I can't even bring myself to let it stand. I jump up, leaving my books behind, and grab him by the wrist before he can leave the room, corded leather bracelets imprinting on my palm. "Wait, please. I'm sorry."

He turns, slowly, but his mouth quirks up in the tiniest of smugly edged smiles, the kind you might see on a cat who's spotted a mouse for dinner, and I know I'm forgiven. "Hold on, I wanna get that on a recording. Replay it a whole bunch of times on nights I'm having trouble sleeping."

"Oh, shut up and accept the apology."

The smile blooms into something slightly more whole, and he follows me to the table, spreading out his books. We work in much more (mostly) pleasant silence for a while, but by the time I finish my report, the feelings I buried for my apology have morphed into something that has me impatiently tapping my pen against the desk.

Finally, it clicks what I need. "I want a Bad Girl Day."

He blinks in my direction, biting his lip against a laugh. "Excuse me?"

"Look at you." I gesture at his cleaned-up appearance, his books splayed out in the library before 10:00 A.M. "You've already achieved Good Boy status. You've done the thing. You've got basketball and Jenna and you look and smell like an actual human. But I still feel like . . . me."

"Being you is not a bad thing, Skeevy," Salem says, more seriously than I expect.

"Yeah, it is, trust me." I can't bring myself to tell him that he might not have been using me, but the girls I thought were my friends sure were, and so were the ones before that. I don't want to be the girl people feel like they can do that to. I sure as hell don't wanna be a girl who cares if and when it happens. And right now, I still care way, way too much.

He sighs and puts down his pen. "Okay, so what does a 'Bad Girl Day' entail?"

"You tell me." I fold my arms on the table and rest my chin on them so I'm looking up at his pale face with its slashes of dark eyebrows, surrounded by equally dark hair that's starting to curl at the ends with overgrowth. It makes him look the tiniest bit softer, which I'm sure he'd hate to hear. "What kinds of things have you gotten in trouble for in the past? I wanna do those. Well, other than smoking in the headmaster's office; I'm not gonna do that. Or smoke at all, I don't think. I don't know. I'm still on the fence."

"What would you even smoke?" he asks, amused. "You don't have any weed."

"I have yours."

"Oh, no, you don't. I stole that back like five days ago." My jaw drops open, and he laughs. "Don't worry; I didn't smoke it. But I did give it to Jenna, so she and her friends have probably obliterated that by now."

The mention of Jenna and her friends twists something in my stomach, but I push past it. "Well, then, that answers that. What else?"

"Lots of destruction of property. You wanna destroy some property?" His eyes take on a twinkle that says he knows I won't, and if I hadn't seen it, he'd be right; I absolutely hate the idea of trashing someone else's hard work, especially if someone *else* has to clean it up. But that's Good Girl mentality, and this day's got a purpose.

"I wanna destroy some property," I say firmly. "Where do we begin?"

Chapter Eleven

"WHAT AM I EVEN SUPPOSED to write?" I ask Salem as I stand poised in front of the statue of Martha Camden, wife of Camden Academy founder William Henry Camden, whose pedestal is covered with black-inked names. "Everything here is, like, initials in hearts. Is this a couples' statue?"

"Supposedly," Salem concedes, and I both do and very much don't want to ask him if there's an SG+JL on here somewhere. "But I figured it was a good baby step, considering about a thousand people got here first."

"I don't need baby steps," I lie, putting my initials into a heart all on their own. Salem nods as if he believes me, then nods toward the accompanying Martha Camden bench and hands me his omnipresent uncurled paper clip. It takes me about ten minutes to carve a remotely satisfying SKEEVY into the polished wood, and while it is the worst nickname known to man, at least it's a slightly less dead giveaway of whose vandalism is on display.

"Nice job," he says with a nod as he takes back the clip and pulls out a lighter. "Wanna step it up?"

"I do not."

"Probably a good choice." He slips his lighter back into his pocket. "Cutting classes was another big one, but I guess a Sunday's not a great day for that. Oh, I once got a week of in-school suspension for streaking across the football field. You could try that?"

Over my dead body. "Maybe next week."

Salem drops onto the bench, kicking up his Vans as he considers other options. "Honestly, there's not a whole lot to be done on campus, especially if you're not up for smoking or arson. We might need to take a field trip. How would you feel about stealing a car?"

"Not great, especially since I don't have a license, and neither do you."

He swings his legs around and rests his elbows on his knees. "I mean. You *did* want to do things I've gotten in trouble for before . . ."

"Not things that could potentially get me a record," I clarify.

"Well, that doesn't leave a whole lot. But since it looks like we'll be taking the Camden shuttle, I think I know where we're going. First, though, a quick stop at Rumson."

"Okay, why?"

"Because it's my turn to teach you how to dress for the occasion."

"Candy store, candle shop, or Old Navy?"

My heart pounds in my chest as I consider my options. "Why just those three?" As if I want more. But I'm buying myself time.

"Because neither of us are interested in sporting goods and I thought the lingerie place would be awkward. Now, which one?"

The lingerie place certainly would be awkward, especially since it's where his girlfriend and I bought matching lacy underwear. Hard pass. "Candy store." Candy's small, cheap, and mass-produced; who *really* cares if I walk off with a little bit of it in the strategically placed pockets of the outfit Salem selected for this purpose?

"Good call. Let's go." He holds open the door for me—*now* those etiquette lessons come in handy?—and I slip inside, my eyes immediately flying to the pink-shirted staff.

Not one of them is looking at us. Not one of them looks like they give a shit about anything at all. They're probably just MCC kids, or even Pinebrook High students with weekend jobs. They don't care if a package of Starbursts finds its way up my sleeve. They don't. They absolutely don't.

"Are you *sweating*?"

"Shut up," I mutter.

"Jesus Christ, Skeevy. A pack of gum is like a dollar."

"It's still stealing!" I hiss, assessing the shelves for what I could most easily slip out of its colorful box. The glass jars on the central platform are out of the question, even though I'd kill for some gummy Coke bottles right about now, but there are cinnamints and Life Savers and a whole display of Airheads that looks promising. Or maybe the Tootsie Roll bins . . .

"It's not the fucking Louvre."

"Pardon me for not having cased the joint in advance."

"I will not pardon you for having used the phrase 'cased the joint' at all, in fact."

I accidentally step on Salem's foot. Twice.

"The longer you stay here browsing, the more familiar you'll look," Salem points out when he's done cursing me under his breath. "Your hair does not exactly blend into the scenery."

"I said I should wear a hat!"

"The only thing more conspicuous than your actual hair is your hair sticking out like a clown wig mashed down by a hat. Now pick something and let's go."

"*Okay.*" The loose saltwater taffies look easy enough, so I scoop up a couple and slide them into my T-shirt pocket, which is strategically hidden by the plaid button-up I'm wearing over it. I wait for a shout that never comes, and then add a couple of Bit-O-Honeys, which are, in my opinion, extremely underrated. Finally, a pack of gum makes its way into my bag too easily. Then I kick Salem in the sneaker and we head toward the exit while I try to keep my breathing under control.

And then, magically, we're outside. No alarm goes off. No one calls after us. We're just . . . free. And so is the candy.

We keep going down the hall and around the corner, and I finally let out the breath I've been holding since I picked up that first taffy.

"Holy shit," I manage, panting. "I did it. I shoplifted."

"You did!" Salem says with a proud smile. "How's it feel?"

I take a second to consider my answer. "Super shitty. I really do not like stealing. Did you do this a lot?"

"Nah, only a couple of times, with things I'm not old enough to buy legally—lighters and rolling papers, mostly. I did get my start at a candy store, though. Seemed pretty low stakes, and I can eat ten pounds of sour bears when I'm stoned."

"Wow, so marijuana really *is* a gateway drug."

Salem rolls his eyes. "Come on—what's next on the list?"

I can't bring myself to tell him. If anything else feels as bad as stealing does, it'll make it official that I am *not* cut out to be a bad girl.

He watches me for a minute before finally letting out a heavy sigh. "Gimme the candy, Skeevy."

"What? Why?"

"Just do it."

I reach into my pockets and put it all in Salem's hands. It feels good to be rid of it, but now I'm just afraid of Salem getting in trouble. He doesn't seem remotely bothered, though; he turns and heads back the way we came.

"Salem! Where are you going?"

"Where do you think?" he calls, and I watch him turn the corner.

I'm too afraid to follow him, and by the time he returns a few minutes later, my nails are bitten down to the quick. "Here you go," he says, holding up a little plastic bag.

I take it and open it up. Inside is all the stolen candy, a baggie of Coke-bottle gummies, and a clean white receipt. "You went back and paid for it? What did you tell them?"

"That my friend 'forgot' to pay. But you still get a treat for trying," he adds with a nod to the gummies. I don't know how he remembered they're my favorite, or when I even told him, but I tear into them like a mountain lion. "Classy," he observes with a grin.

I'm too hungry to even tell him to shut up.

Once I've ingested my weight in sugar, I let Salem in on my next thought. I've been thinking about it for a while, actually, and today seems like the perfect day. "We're going to the Ink Spot."

He's been following me in that direction, but now he stops in his tracks. "You want to get a *tattoo*? Skeevy, *no*."

"No?" A tattoo was not my actual plan, but I thought he'd find the idea hilarious. Instead, he looks straight-up horrified. "Are you telling me you don't have an entire sleeve of tattoos planned for someday?"

"I don't, actually—my mom's grandparents were Holocaust survivors and she made me swear on their graves I'd never get one—but that's not the point. This isn't like paying for stolen candy five minutes later, Peach. If you hate it, there's no magic eraser."

"What makes you so sure I'd hate it?"

He sighs. "What would you even get?"

"Hmm . . . I was thinking maybe your face, as a back piece. If I bend at the right angle, you can kiss my ass whenever I want," I say sweetly.

"Ha ha. Then what's really at the Ink Spot?"

"They have a piercing chair, too. I was thinking maybe a cute little stud, right here." I tap the outside of my right nostril. "What do you think?"

He tips his head. "I think . . . that'd look cool, actually. All right, come on."

We head down to the Ink Spot, trading ludicrous tattoo ideas as we go, and are greeted by a cute girl with pigtails the color of blue raspberry cotton candy and a double lip piercing that clearly captures Salem's attention. I can't help wondering if he's lusting after the piercing or the mouth it's attached to. She's definitely what I would've picked out as his type, and for the millionth time since my discovery on Friday night, I wonder how the hell he can be with Jenna London, of all people.

Unfortunately, Pigtails's coolness extends only so far as her own appearance; as soon as we tell her why we're here, she taps the sign next to her that says MINORS MUST BE ACCOMPANIED BY A PARENT OR LEGAL GUARDIAN.

"Oh, uhh, this is my dad?" I offer, indicating Salem.

"She'll be sent straight to her room after this," Salem confirms.

"Orrr I'm eighteen? Should I have gone with that?"

"Probably," Pigtails says with a shrug, "but only if you've got a good fake. We do check IDs."

"I do," Salem says, pulling out his wallet, but Pigtails stops him.

"You're a little late," she says, but at least she sounds a little sympathetic. "Come back at three when we change shifts. You have perfect eyebrows for a barbell."

"No one tells me I have perfect eyebrows for anything," I grumble as we walk away, the depleted bag of candy swinging between us.

"You have perfect eyebrows for scrunching up when you're pissed at me."

"That helps, thank you." We walk until we reach the central atrium, and I look over the banister at the shoppers below. As I watch them film each other on escalators and holding up hauls, I think about how today has been an incredible bust on my part . . . and then finally, I think of something even I can't screw up.

"I'm going shopping," I tell Salem.

"Yes, I did notice we are at the mall."

"Oh, shut up. I'm running into Azalea Commons—ten minutes, tops. You can go do whatever, and I'll meet you at the food court." If I'd been with Sabrina, or pretty much any female friend, I'd have dragged them into the cheap fast-fashion shop with me, but I can't bring myself to make Salem sit there while I try on outfits, looking for one daring piece to add to my wardrobe.

Sticking to the bargain bins, I find it easily—an aqua lace corset with lime-green ribbons that I change into in the bathroom immediately after checking out and cover with the button-up before stuffing my original tee into my bag.

Salem's sucking noisily from a cup of fountain soda when I arrive, five minutes later than I said I'd be. "Hey, you wanna share fries?" he asks when I walk up.

"Soon," I promise. "First, I need you to do a silly, embarrassing thing with me without making fun of me for it."

"Can I make fun of you for it *later*?"

"Sure. Come on." I yank him out into the parking lot and start unbuttoning my shirt.

"Whoa, Skeevy, this is not the place—"

"Do you seriously think I am flashing you in a parking lot?" My fingers fly over the buttons, and then I push the fabric off my shoulders. "It's just a different shirt."

"It . . . is definitely that." He sounds a little bit like he's choking on his tongue, and I imagine he's kindly swallowing down fifty shades of mockery. "You look—um." Am I imagining it, or are his cheeks flushing a little pink? "What's the plan here?"

"I just want some pictures," I tell him, handing over my phone set to camera mode. "I have nothing and no one to dress up—or down—for, and this is definitely not in Camden dress code, but I want just one little photo shoot of me looking like a rule breaker."

His lips curve into a little smile. "In that case, I have a prop for you." He reaches into his pocket and produces a case of candy cigarettes. "I picked these up when I was buying your stolen goods. Figured they might come in handy today."

It's so brilliant, I laugh as I grab one and slip it between my fingers. "Perfect!"

We do a full-on photo shoot, and I even convince him to take a selfie with me, cigarette gum hanging from both our lips as we loiter in front of a NO LOITERING sign. Then we play the penis game as loudly as we dare while we head back to the food court for those fries.

It's an absolutely ridiculous day, but damn if I don't feel a thousand times better when we hop off the shuttle back at Camden and then devour Sunday-night Bolognese at the Beast. Of course, we both still have a mountain of homework waiting for us after cutting our studying short this morning, so we trudge back to Rumson, passing the remaining gummy Coke bottles back and forth between us on the walk.

But in my room, other plans await.

"What are you doing here?"

Isabel rises from my bed, her gaze flicking to Salem and back to me. Even though she essentially broke into my room (not that it was locked, but still), somehow I'm left feeling guilty. "I wanted to talk. Didn't realize you were gonna have other company."

"She doesn't," Salem breaks in. "Just coming back from dinner and heading upstairs. Night, Skeevy. Iz."

Iz. I don't want to think about how much time Salem spends with Jenna's best friend that he calls her Iz.

"We're friends," I say firmly as soon as I hear Salem's footsteps grow fainter in the distance. "You don't need to come babysit on Jenna's behalf."

"You really think I just do Jenna's bidding all the time, huh?"

I don't have the eyebrow-arching powers of a Grayson twin, but I try my best. "Don't you?"

"No, you little wench," she says airily. "But I *am* a good friend to have, and considering you're using *me* for attention with your talent-show act, I think maybe we're even."

"I didn't make you do that," I insist, and I'm pretty sure about that.

"No, you didn't, but don't pretend that isn't why you came asking me specifically in the first place."

Okay, she has a point. "Fine, we're even. Friends?"

"Friends. *If* you teach me that card trick."

"Deal. *After* the talent show."

We go through my clothes, upon which she declares I don't have anything worthy of being a sexy magician. "These shorts, *maybe*," she says, holding the only high-waisted article of clothing I own, "if Priya will lend you her tuxedo blazer. You two are probably around the same size, give or take three cup sizes." She eyes my generous chest critically. "You'd need to leave it open, which means you need a sexy top underneath."

"Like this?" For the third time today, I unbutton my shirt, revealing the corset underneath, and Isabel claps approvingly.

"Yes, that'll work. God, that is so trashy, I love it. Why on earth are you wearing that?"

"Long story," I say, and it's only partly a lie. She definitely doesn't need to know I was with Salem when I bought it. We may be friends again, but the last thing I need is her misreading Salem's and my friendship and going running to Jenna about it.

"Okay, lady of mystery; you keep your weird secrets. Now let's practice."

We go through the routine again, which allows me to show off how much better I'm getting at my grips and fans, and Isabel applauds proudly when I finish the intro to the trick. She really is fun to do this with, and I'm just hoping that she means it when she says our friendship is real.

Friends are not the easiest for me to come by, and this time around, I want the ones I make to stick.

Chapter Twelve

I SHIFT THE PILE OF BOOKS higher up on my hip to keep them in place as I knock on Sabrina's door again. "Sabs! Come on! I know you're in there!"

I don't, actually, know that she's in there, but I find that works on Salem pretty often, so it's worth seeing if it's genetic.

"Sabrina!" I'm lifting my hand to knock again when suddenly I hear someone calling my name and turn to face the voice. It's Sabrina, making her way back from the bathroom, her face uncharacteristically scrubbed free of makeup.

"Has anyone ever told you that you are extremely loud?" she asks as she opens the door for us both.

"It's come up a couple of times."

"I'll bet. What's with the books?" she asks as she peers into the mirror on the inside of her door, examining her eyes closely to make sure she's cleaned off every last bit of liner.

"*Well.*" I drop onto the floor and spread out the pile. "I

thought about what you said, how you wanted to be in a GSA but there wasn't enough interest, so I thought we could start our own! I found this website that recommends different books, like you can find romances by trope or every YA with a pansexual main character, and it's all super gay. I picked out a bunch of them and figured you could pick one we should both read and then we can talk about it and stuff. And we can make way better choices than the official Book Club made last week." I pick up a pretty purple one. "Look, I even found a witchy one that looks like it has tarot cards on it."

Sabrina eyes the books suspiciously, then me suspiciously, before examining each one. "You thought I'd want to read a romance between a football player and a cheerleader?"

I shrug. "I mean. Lesbians."

She nods and sets it aside. "You do make a good point."

I wait while she goes through each one before finally settling on the one I thought looked the most depressing and right up her alley, but she declares she's going to try them all, just in case. We agree we'll take turns reading it over the next couple of weeks and discuss it afterward. "What refreshments would a GSA have for book-club discussion?" I ask. "I have to admit, I'm new to this."

She shrugs. "Rainbow cookies? Tequila? I don't know. We do not actually have to—"

"Yes, we do. We are going to do this right," I say firmly. "Now, what's the soundtrack for this meeting?"

"Janelle Monáe, Chappell Roan, and Billie Eilish," Sabrina says decisively, moving to put the music on her laptop, and it's gratifying to see her stoniness about this crack so quickly. Without even bringing snacks! She joins me on the floor and we open up the book, taking turns reading sections of it aloud to each other until the door opens and Sabrina tucks the cover flap into the pages to save our place.

"Hey, Evie." I immediately tense up at the sound of Heather's voice, concerned each time I see her that *this* time she's found out about me and Lucas, but she sounds as friendly and bouncy as always, and I relax. "What are you guys doing? Something for the talent show?"

"Nope, working on that with Isabel McEvoy. Are you performing?"

"Kayla and I are gonna do a scene from *Hamilton*." She slides off her sneakers and hops onto her bed, curling her legs up underneath her butt. "We were just with Lucas and Jesse, performing for each other."

Lucas? Performing? Ugh. Maybe I don't want to attend after all. "What are they doing?" I ask casually.

"It's amazing—they've completely and totally memorized stand-up routines. Lucas sounds *exactly* like John Mulaney when he does his."

Feels like stretching the word "talent" to its limit, but sure. I listen as Heather goes on about how Lucas and Jesse are so funny, and my heart aches as I think how easily I could bring that crashing down if I say or do the wrong thing. It'd be so much easier if Lucas were completely out of my social circle, but even if I wanted to ditch the Nicest Girl in the World, she'd still be Sabrina's roommate, and ditching Sabrina is not an option if I want to maintain my sanity in this place.

Still, I think about how much it hurt to find out Salem

had kept Jenna a secret, and this is so much worse. If that felt like a betrayal, this is . . . I don't know, but something uglier. And if Heather ever does find out, the domino effect of losing all my friends could be fast and furious.

Stop it. There's no reason to think you're gonna screw this up. You're doing fine. Everything's fine.

So why does it feel like a painful shift is inevitable?

One possible explanation arrives later that night, when I go to pee before bed. I am *always* more emotionally sensitive when I get my period, and with everything going on, I completely forgot to keep track of my cycle. Turns out even being regular can't help you if your brain is a mess.

But it takes me two minutes of frantic searching to realize the bigger problem: I forgot to pack pads and tampons. It all comes back to me in a rush that of course Sierra and I were on the same cycle, and of *course* she finished them, promised to pick up more before I left, and never did. And now it's been a month and I'm in an all-boys dorm after curfew, and I am so deeply screwed. Staining my sheets would be bad enough, but staining them and then having to use the washing machines at Rumson to clean them? Hell no.

It's fine. I'm just gonna stay awake all night. Or sleep in the shower. Sure, that makes sense. God, how I wish I had a tub.

Ugh, and Lockwood is *so* close. I bet it's *filled* with tampons and pads—nothing but period protection as far as the eye can see! But of course, it's locked at this hour, and so is Rumson, and am I seriously considering jumping out the window and running to Sabrina's so I can yell up for her to toss me down a tampon?

I think forlornly of the rope ladder, curled up and safely hidden in the confines of Matt and Salem's room. I could ask them to send it down, but I do *not* want to explain why, and ugh it doesn't matter because I have to change my underwear and go back to the bathroom anyway before I turn my pajamas into a crime scene.

I grab my phone and tap out a quick text to Sabrina, just in case she can somehow sneak out and save me, and am relieved when she immediately responds with a thumbs-up. I have no idea what she has planned, but I'm not wasting time having her answer my text questions when I need her here ASAP, so I just wad up some tissues and wait. Finally, I hear a tapping on the glass, but it doesn't sound like a pebble, more like—

"Aah!" I jump twenty feet in the air (I'm pretty sure) at the sight of Salem Grayson, standing on the rope ladder, a fist poised right by the window he'd rapped on. "No," I mutter. "No, she did not."

I push up the window, and am absolutely horrified when Salem unfurls his fist to reveal a couple of tampons and an overnight pad. "You're welcome," he says dryly when I just stare at his open palm, but gratitude has taken about a thousand back seats to wishing I could simply die, thoroughly and immediately.

"Is this what having one of those dreams where you go to school naked feels like? It must be. Oh my God."

He rolls his eyes. "Are you gonna take 'em, or should I just save it all for the next time I get a nosebleed?"

I snatch everything from his hand and immediately chuck it to the side, as if out of sight will put it out of his mind that he went on this recon mission. "I cannot *believe* she sent you for this."

"It's really not a big deal, Skeevy. She knew I had the ladder, and I *did* guess you were PMS'ing earlier, so I'm feeling pretty vindicated right now."

"Oh, shut up before I knock you off that rope and onto your ass."

"You wouldn't dare."

"I might." But I'm lying, because he just climbed out of his room after hours and brought me tampons and now he's here in front of my window, clinging to a rope ladder, looking surprisingly manly with his biceps glowing in the moonlight. Ever since I found out about Salem and Jenna, I've been wondering how exactly he landed her, and right now, for half a second, I get it.

"That's the cramps talking," he says with a grin, and once again, I wanna die. "G'night, Skeevy."

"G'night, Salem. And thanks for . . . this."

"I'd say 'anytime,' but I wouldn't mean it." And then he shimmies up the rope and is gone.

I don't even have the energy to yell at Sabrina right now, especially since I'd still have nothing without her, so I drag myself back to the bathroom and thank past me for at least remembering to pack painkillers. As I put myself to bed, wincing against the pain of cramps while I wait for the meds to kick in, I can't help thinking about the fact that Salem Grayson—*Salem fucking Grayson*—came to my menstrual rescue.

I am never gonna live this down.

And I have to get the hell out of this dorm.

No one in the housing office displays any semblance of caring for my newest petition to move to a girls' dorm, with the argument that I'm the only girl on campus without easy access to menstrual products—the girls' dorms have machines, plus everyone knows you can go to the dorm heads for them.

Even if Mr. Hoffman were the type to keep them on hand for transmasc Rumson residents and visiting girls—which he is absolutely not—I wouldn't ask him for water if I were dying of thirst.

They do, at least, compromise by giving me a bag of about a thousand tampons from Lockwood, and in my desperation, I accept. I really don't have any more time to fight, because we have Book Club tonight, and I'm still slogging through the pretentious nightmare that got voted our first pick.

It's a good excuse to avoid the Beast for lunch, anyway, and every other social activity. At Book Club, I sit with Sabrina, and we squeeze each other's hands every time someone talks about which scene made them cry or just, like, really made them want to live their lives to the fullest. On the way out, I tell her I need to avoid everyone possible, and she runs into the Beast and returns with takeout, which we eat picnic-style in my room. Afterward, we do our homework in the nice kind of silence, the one where you're not acknowledging each other's presence but you feel it like a hug all the same.

"This feels so much like hanging out with Claire," I say without thinking, and immediately wish I could take it back. It does, though—we were always doing things side by side, not really together. I would play online poker or give myself terrible pedicures while she beaded bracelets or made little charms out of clay to look like penguins or watermelon slices. It always felt nice, like we were close enough to do that, without it ever striking me as weird how much time we spent in silence or not wanting to do the same thing.

In reality, it probably fell somewhere in the middle, but the silent times only got more frequent the closer Craig and I got, because she made it clear from the get-go she wasn't interested in hearing about him, and I, admittedly, was way too interested in talking about him. Everything seemed interesting and special with him, and when he did nice things like bring me a soda at lunch without my having to ask for it, or brought over any handouts I missed when I was home sick, I was dying to talk about it with someone who understood how good that all felt. And that wasn't Claire.

Instead, I hung out more and more in Craig's basement, not just to watch him play games with his friends but to talk to the other girlfriends and hangers-on, to glow about this special thing or that, none of which were actually that special in retrospect. (God, imagining Craig bringing me a tampon is too impossible to even contemplate.) And of course, as soon as Craig ditched me for Sierra, those girls ditched me too; Alex Gaboury was the only one who even said she was sorry to hear about it.

So maybe . . . I was not the best friend either. I mean, not "hiding from my BFF that her boyfriend and sister are hooking up" level of bad, but, you know, not great.

"Have you spoken to her at all?" Sabrina asks, breaking into my thoughts. She's gotten the gist of the story over the past few weeks.

"Nope."

"Really?" Sabrina twirls her pen between her fingers at impressive speed. "I would've thought she'd have reached out by now. Seems like a pretty obvious thing to apologize for."

"The fight we had about it was . . . not great," I admit. "I yelled at her for being a traitor and she told me it was my fault for being so clueless, and it devolved from there. And I didn't exactly give her the biggest window to apologize before blocking her number and social media." It's also possible that I said some unkind things to her about being maybe a little boring or jealous or both that I didn't feel like apologizing for, either.

"Do you miss her?"

"Does it make me a jerk that I don't, really?" I don't make eye contact for that, concentrating my gaze on the cover of my Spanish notebook instead. "I think we drifted a long time ago but were both sort of afraid to see what else was out there." I take a deep breath, then admit to Sabrina what

I haven't said to anyone else. (And who else would I say it to, anyway?) "I looked at her pictures the other day, and she looked so freaking happy. She's a different person, doing different things, and the only thing that really changed in her life between then and now is that I left. So maybe I was holding her back. Maybe I was the boring loser."

The words somehow sound even worse coming out of my mouth now than they did then.

"Or maybe you gave her the push she needed," Sabrina suggests with a shrug. "I mean, yeah, maybe you were a dick about it—"

"I was definitely a dick about it."

"Okay, but I'm your friend, not hers, so whatever. Point is, maybe this was the best thing for both of you and that's all there is to it. You're here for a fresh start, right? So you're getting yours, and she's getting hers."

I'm still stuck on "I'm your friend, not hers," and how I needed to hear it so badly that I can feel tears pricking my eyes and I have to excuse myself to go to the bathroom so I can breathe my way out of crying in front of Sabrina. But then I think of not just Claire and Craig and Sierra but how I'll probably lose Salem to his girlfriend, and Heather will eventually turn on me, and I turn on the sink to allow myself one little self-pitying round of sniffles.

And then I stop. Because I've made friends. And I have to hold on to them, no matter what it takes.

But maybe that also means letting go a little, too. And so even though I know it's only symbolic, that I won't be reaching out and neither will she, as soon as I exit the bathroom,

I make a beeline for my phone and unblock Claire while Sabrina watches approvingly over my shoulder.

I don't know that I feel any lighter. I don't know if she'll even notice, considering I haven't posted anything since emptying out my account to purge my entire Greentree life. But it feels like acknowledging that I'm a little less afraid of something than I was when I got here, and I'll take any little hint of badass I can get.

Friday afternoon it's time to put the focus back on Salem and his self-improvement, so I drag him along with me to community service, and Matt finds the idea so amusing he tags along for the ride. In fact, the van taking us to Pinebrook Forest to do cleanup is completely full—so full that Matt just *has* to squeeze in with Priya, and Ashleigh just *has* to sit on Landon's lap.

I take my time picking my seat in the van, waiting to see if Salem and Jenna will find some clever way to end up together, but when she slides in next to Izzy and Salem loudly informs me that you can't get pregnant just from sharing a seat with a boy, I bump my ass in next to his. Hard.

Despite the fact that they don't interact once the entire ride, I can't stop looking for signs of the thing between Salem and Jenna. How are they playing it this cool in each other's presences? How in control of your own emotions must you have to be in order to sit in a van with someone you're regularly seeing naked and not even acknowledge their existence?

This is the attitude I dream about having. I should be taking notes.

"We're gonna be in the van for another twenty minutes," Jenna observes. "Maybe we should play something fun to pass the time." Her gaze flickers over to me, but before I can decipher it, she's moved on. "I haven't played a good game of Truth or Dare in *forever.*"

My immediate reaction is to roll my eyes—these games are always really boring when you don't actually have secrets. But then I remember that not only do I have a secret, but it's one I have an extremely vested interest in keeping from someone in this van.

And I may be a great bluffer, but I am a horrific liar.

I dig my nails into the underside of Salem's thigh, and when he turns to me to snap, I widen my eyes in pleading. He furrows his brow, as if he doesn't understand what I'm asking, but then gives a dramatic shudder and says, "If I'm so much as in the same room as Truth or Dare, I start to taste truly bad tequila and smell burnt cotton. And before you ask, Never Have I Ever both tastes and smells like the worst weed I have ever had."

As everyone laughs and changes the subject to talking about bad party memories and substance experiences, I could kiss Salem in gratitude. Well, give him a hearty handshake is more like it. But as soon as I catch his attention, I mouth a *Thank you*, and receive a brief smile in return.

The ride is over before we know it, and we pile out and receive our instructions, complete with reflector vests that make us look like convicts doing trash pickup on the side of the road. Which is to say, I feel a little badass and I don't hate it.

What I *do* hate is how much garbage people leave among the trees. I pick up water bottles, soda cans, single socks, empty bags of chips, gum wrappers, and deflated beach balls, but I am absolutely not prepared for the next piece of trash I see. I glance at the volunteer next to me, who happens to be Matt. "Matthew, please tell me that's not what I think it is."

He follows my eyeline and bursts into laughter. "I swear, dormie, that's not mine. I'm, like, ninety-five percent sure."

"Why does Skeevy look like she's about to puke?" Salem asks, walking over from where I can only assume he's been hiding out with Jenna; I haven't seen him in at least fifteen minutes. "What'd you do, Matt?"

"*I* did not do anything," he says, pointing at the used condom. "Perhaps that's from one of *your* woodsy adventures?"

Okay, I know we're all kidding here, but the idea of that being Salem's is about a thousand times worse than the thought of it being Matt's. Salem just laughs and tells Matt to shut up, and while it's nice to finally see some camaraderie between them, I also feel the need to edge over to some more . . . feminine energy.

I glance around until I spot Isabel's gleaming hair and trudge over to where she, Jenna, and Priya have discarded their trash pickers and are standing around talking, laughing, and hollering after Ashleigh to pull her pants on and come back. Okay, so, maybe this isn't the ideal spot either. But before I can track down Kayla and Heather as my plan C, I hear Jenna call out, "Hey! Evie! C'mere!"

Reluctantly, I do.

"I was sad we didn't get to play earlier," she says with a smirk. "I was really hoping to get to know you better."

Oh, this doesn't seem good. "I'm really not very interesting," I assure her.

"I don't believe that for a second, Rumson Girl." Her ice-blue eyes narrow, and I catch a flash of silver in her hand that I'm pretty sure is a flask. This is the weirdest community service ever. "Truth or dare?"

"Jen." Izzy puts a hand on her arm, but Jenna shakes it off, and I know I have no choice but to answer. I just . . . have no idea what the right answer is. But at least, unlike in the van, Heather isn't in my immediate vicinity, so that's something.

The other thing is that we all know exactly what she's going to ask, and I have a perfectly safe answer. "Truth."

"Have you hooked up with any Rumson boys?"

"Nope," I reply, popping the *p*, because I don't actually know where Lucas lives, but it isn't my dorm. And then, because I can't leave well enough alone, I add, "How about you?"

Her smirk is razor sharp. "It's not your turn, Rumson Girl. But you already know that."

I meet her gaze evenly. "I already know a lot of things."

Isabel sucks in a breath, and I silently curse my inability to keep my mouth shut.

But then again, isn't the whole point of this pact with

Salem to learn to stand up for myself, to trust my instincts and not to back down? Maybe this is growth, rather than my just being stupid.

Yeah, I'll go ahead and look at it that way.

Jenna's smile takes on a cruel slant, and I wait for the next bullet to shoot from her mouth, but she's already moved on, wrapping an arm around Priya's shoulders. "How about you, Pri? Truth or dare?"

It's tempting to speak up and remind her that it's my turn, but I don't think there are any answers here that I actually want. So I wait to see how Priya responds instead, but she just laughs. "As if I have any secrets you don't know."

"I swear," Jenna says with a quick, cutting look at me, "none of you are any fun anymore. Take the dare, then."

Priya grabs the flask from her hand and takes a swig. "Fine. Dare."

Jenna grins. "Go to every guy here and ask him how big his dick is."

"But you already know so many of the answers," Priya says sweetly, and I can't help snorting a laugh. Thankfully, Isabel barks one even louder, and Jenna misses mine entirely. "Are you having me do your research so you can figure out your next victim? Is the current one not satisfying?"

I expect a scathing response from Jenna, but instead, Priya receives a languid smile I'd love to twist off Jenna's face. "The current one is deeply, *deeply* satisfying. Some might say enormously so."

Isabel rolls her eyes. "Jenna would say enormously so. I have, in fact, heard her do so on way too many occasions."

Okay, cool, I am definitely out. Even picking up a used condom beats listening to a discussion of Salem's anatomical gifts. I scan the ground for another piece of trash, and promptly find a gum wrapper I'm 90 percent sure is Jenna's.

I stab it with the point of my picker and move on, the girls' laughter ringing in my ears.

I take the same van seat on the way back, but when a body slides in next to mine, it's Isabel's, not Salem's. "You can go take my seat," she tells him dismissively, as if she's calling the shots here and not literally sending him to fool around with his girlfriend in the back.

So much for community service helping him learn how to do "good."

"You okay?" she asks me in a low voice once the ride starts. "Jenna can be a little . . . Jenna."

"She really can," I confirm. "But it's fine." *It's not fine.* "Anyway, we got the forest clean, and that's the point, right?"

Her lips twitch in a smile. "Right."

She pivots to chat with Priya for the rest of the ride while I pull out my earbuds and settle in with Blackpink. After a few minutes, Isabel nudges me to ask what I'm listening to, and I hand her one of the buds. We listen in silence the rest of the way home.

As soon as we get off the van, though, I leave Isabel and the others in my dust, not caring how glaringly obvious it is that I don't want to be near Jenna another minute. I'm most of the way back to Rumson when I feel a hand at my elbow.

"Where are you running?" Salem asks. "We're literally walking to the same building."

"Are we? I thought you might have plans at Hillman House." Okay, my tone sounds way colder than he deserves, but in fairness, his girlfriend is way colder than I deserve.

Doesn't matter; he's barely listening anyway, engrossed in his phone. I can only assume he's exchanging filthy texts with Jenna, which makes me want to pry it from his hands and toss it back into the woods we just came from.

"Brent and Jason are up for a quick game if you are," he says, slipping it back in his pocket. "Pretty sure they think you were having beginner's luck that first time."

"How do you know I wasn't?"

He shoots me a knowing look. "Come up in ten. And bring snacks."

"Who says I have snacks?" I mutter as I head toward my room while he dashes up the stairs.

"You have snacks," he calls back down.

He's right, I do, but I don't want the human trash receptacle that is Jason Hammond devouring my precious Skittles stash, so when I take a quick shower and throw on a pair of sweats and a T-shirt, I grab a couple of bags of chips I lifted from the Beast instead.

The other guys aren't there when I arrive, but Salem and Matt are, and Matt gives me a big bear hug when I enter, nearly smushing the chip bags. "What was that for?" I ask when I can finally breathe again.

He cracks a grin. "Izzy said you might need it after the woods."

"What happened in the woods?" Salem asks.

I take a seat next to him at the table and pick up the deck of cards in front of him, shuffling idly. "Well, I learned you have a big dick, so congrats on that."

Matt throws back his head and laughs as Salem mutters, "Jesus Christ, Evie."

"What?" I ask innocently. "You should be proud. Jenna was definitely proud."

"Please can we not talk about my dick?"

"If I had to hear about your dick, I think you should have to hear about your dick."

"Do you *want* to talk about my dick?"

Fair question. "No, I really do not."

"That's what I thought. Now pass the chips."

I rip open the bag, help myself to a nice, greasy handful, and hand it over.

"You know," he says as he digs through it until he finds a perfect whole chip, "it's kind of like I called your bluff right there. I feel like this can only mean good things for the game ahead."

"Sure, that plus my beginner's luck being over," I say with a flutter of my lashes.

"Oh, you know what?" he says with a grin that definitely means trouble. "I forgot—Matt and I came up with the perfect next task for your Bad Girl list. Community service got me inspired."

"Let me guess." I grab back the bag and take another chip. "You want me to burn down the forest?"

"Of course not," Salem says with a snort. He glances up at Matt, who comes over and drops a box on the table in front of me. "We want *you* to refill the condom stash."

Chapter Thirteen

I MAY NOT HAVE BEEN UP for Truth or Dare in the woods, but I am absolutely kicking ass at the Badass Treasure Hunt list devised and financed by Matt and Salem. It helps that I've brought a backpack, so no one else on Camden's Target shuttle will have to see what I'm carrying back. Oh, and that I'm wearing dark sunglasses, so I don't have to make eye contact with anyone. But still! I'm doing it!

Condoms? Check.

Lube? Flavored *and* unflavored.

Tampons? Okay, not exactly a "badass" thing, but Salem did point out that he would not be playing midnight messenger boy again, and those Lockwood tampons are the awful cardboard kind.

And finally, the most badass item of them all (but only because I flat-out refused to attempt to buy a vibrator at Target): snacks.

When I've finished filling my basket, I rest it on the floor and take a picture for Matt and Salem, making sure the copious amounts of condoms and lube are highly visible. "Who's a good girl now?" I mutter as I shift to get it from different angles.

"Am I interrupting something?"

The surprise of Heather Cherette's voice in my ear has me dropping my phone into the basket, and I carefully retrieve it from the condom-box nest. "Sorry, didn't mean to scare you," she says, glancing down at the basket, her eyes widening.

"I didn't see you on the shuttle." I debate covering up the contents of my basket, but I suspect that ship has sailed. I settle for taking off my sunglasses instead, so I look like slightly less of a weirdo.

"Yeah, I made it at the last second. Realized I could use a few things."

Reflexively, I glance at her basket. It's completely empty.

"Right," she says, her cheeks flushing pink. "So, I'm having some trouble picking *out* those things, and you seem . . ." Her eyes flicker to my basket, then back up. "Um. Could you help me, maybe?"

It takes me a full minute to figure out what she's asking, and when I do, I think I might throw up right there at the corner of aisle 9.

"Condoms," I choke out. "You want *my* help buying condoms?"

Her cheeks get even redder as she nods. "And Plan B, maybe? Not that I need it," she says quickly. "I just think it'd be good to have."

"Certainly can't argue with that," I mutter, the very idea of Lucas Burke procreating utterly vomitous. "But I . . . I mean, these aren't for me. I'm just shopping for Matt." Then I hear how that sounds. "*Not* that I'm screwing Matt. He just asked for help so he can be prepared, because, well, isn't it the person *wearing* the condoms who generally buys the condoms?" I take a beat. "Maybe that's unenlightened of me. It feels like it is. But if you're not comfortable doing it, why don't you have Lucas do it?"

"Oh, he's just as uncomfortable as I am," she says shyly, but also a little . . . proudly? "We're both new to this and have no idea what we're doing. God, please don't repeat that. This is all mortifying. He doesn't even know I'm getting them. I just thought he'd probably be too shy, and so I figured, well. Taking a leap, I guess."

Lucas may be a virgin, but judging by his confidence—and pushiness—that first night, I have a feeling he's nowhere near as "new to this" as he's told Heather he is.

What a stupid fuck-faced liar.

But of course, I can't say that, so I go ahead and help Heather pick out protection so that she can have sex with the worst guy on the planet, feeling decidedly the opposite of badass.

As soon as I get back, I trudge upstairs, eager to get rid of my new purchases. Matt and Salem's door is open, a rare occurrence, and it's immediately clear that Salem's not inside. Matt, however, gives me a huge smile and throws out his arms. "Dormie! Did you make Big Papa proud?"

"Matthew, I really need you to know that if you ever

call yourself that again, I'm going to throw up on every pair of shoes you own. That said . . ." I reach into my bag and toss item after item onto his bed, shoving aside the disappointment that Salem isn't here to witness my triumph. "I sure did."

"Oh, hell yes." He dives in, and immediately makes a face. "Gingerbread-flavored lube? Seriously?"

"It's festive!"

"It sounds disgusting."

"Well, so does eating lube," I point out.

He sighs and shakes his head. "You don't exactly *eat*— You know what? This feels too much like giving my little sister the sex talk, and I'd rather not."

Ouch. "Wow, okay. Even the school player thinks I'm an uncool, immature little girl. Good to know."

"Evie, that's not—"

"I just bought you *condoms*, Matt. Not even just you! Condoms for everybody!" I kick the leg of Salem's bed, wishing it were Lucas's face, and immediately regret it when my toe throbs in response.

"Okay, I'm going to guess that whatever's going on here isn't about me, and since my roommate's not here to translate, I'm just gonna say thank you for these and ask if you wanna talk about whatever bug is up your butt."

It's stupid in the grand scheme of things, I know. Lucas and I didn't exactly do anything earth-shattering, and Heather and I aren't best friends. But still, holding back on her feels like doing exactly what I flipped out at Claire for doing, and the combo of guilt and hypocrisy is a hard pill to swallow.

"You ever . . . wish you could make someone see what you see, and know what you know, but you . . . can't?"

Matt narrows his eyes at me. "You're joking, right?"

"What?"

He sighs. "Yes, Evie. I know this phenomenon very well."

"Yeah, well, there's that, and some drama from home, and I think I'm just gonna go take a nap and ignore the outside world for a while." I head out, but pause to catch my hand on the doorframe. "Enjoy the gingerbread."

For the rest of the week, I throw myself into the talent show, practicing my cardistry, finalizing outfits with Isabel, and watching videos of other people performing so I can practice gestures and facial expressions in the mirror, like the natural I am.

By the time the event actually arrives, I never want to do a card trick again. But I know I'm not the only one who's been practicing to death; I feel like I've already seen and heard everything that'll be happening tonight. Darryl and Jason from upstairs have been rapping in the halls, Kayla's been singing under her breath all week, Henry from a few doors down has been getting us all way too well acquainted with his clarinet, the cheerleaders have been jumping all over the quad, and oh my God why are there so many jugglers?

I text Sabrina on my way out so we can walk together, and she confirms that she and Heather are heading out the door now and will meet me out front. Seeing Heather isn't exactly helping my nerves tonight, and it makes me queasy to see her being extra cheerful and bouncy in her enthusiasm about performing. If I didn't know she was getting some, I would absolutely know she was getting some.

"Hey, lovelies." I overcompensate for my nausea by linking my arms through theirs and leading us across the quad, trying not to get bogged down in my ugly thoughts. "Heather, you nervous at all?"

"Mostly just excited," she says serenely, and I want to hate her so badly that I almost do. "I used to be in all the plays in junior high, and I've been missing performing, so this is really nice."

"Me too." Sabrina widens her eyes to a comic degree and brings her fists to her chest. "I can't wait to get that baton twirling in my hands again."

"Your routine is going to be epic," I agree. "I assume your sequined leotard is underneath that outfit?"

"You know it."

Heather shakes her head, smiling. "You two were definitely meant to become friends."

We find seats inside, and thankfully, Lucas is nowhere to be found. Next to me, Heather is texting him, but there aren't any free seats near us, and hopefully that won't be changing any time soon.

The room quiets down as Hoffman takes the stage. "Welcome, everybody, to the seventh annual Camden Academy

Talent Show!" There's lots of applause, some whistling, and an a cappella outburst that does not portend good things to come. "Can we have everyone named Michael please stand up?"

A few confused looks are exchanged, but finally, a few guys stand up, including one I recognize from Rumson.

"Great, thank you—that concludes the Mike check."

The groans drown out whatever few laughs there might've been, but Hoffman doesn't look remotely fazed. "We have so many great acts to come tonight, so let's get started! Quite literally kicking us off, as always, we have the Camden Academy Dance Team, led by Captain Ashleigh Cartwright!"

The cheering goes wild as the team gets into position, and Ash is front and center, looking absolutely stunning—her warm brown skin glows with glitter, her long dark curls are gathered on her head, and her white crop top shows off abs that belong in a museum. Landon's hollering is the loudest, and I turn to see him sitting at the back with Matt, Salem, Jenna, Isabel, Priya, and Sebastian Giang, the hot basketball player from the club fair. It's weird to see Salem sitting with that crowd, but at least I can pretend for a minute that it's because he wants to hang out with his roommate and not because he's going to abandon me completely for his hot, popular girlfriend.

I exchange a wave with Isabel, letting her know I've arrived, and then the music kicks up and I turn back, not wanting to miss a minute. Ashleigh is phenomenal; I had no idea her body could move like that, but I sense Landon is an extremely lucky man. By the time they finish up, in a pose that shouldn't be physically possible, half the room is on its feet, and I'm pretty sure everyone feels bad for whoever has to follow that.

Turns out, that honor belongs to 10/10, No Notes, the school's premier a cappella group, which absolutely slays a Taylor Swift medley. Then there's a juggler, followed by a gymnast, followed by Henry the Rumson clarinetist, and then Jesse goes up there for his "stand-up" act, which is spot-on but also silly. Priya follows that with an Adele cover that has my jaw on the floor. By the time Hoffman takes the stage again, I'm having such a good time that I forget I'm performing until I hear Isabel's and my names.

Oh God. What have I done? I do not want to perform in front of all these people, actually! This is not even a cool thing to do! What was I thinking?

"Stop freaking out," Isabel mutters in my ear as she wraps an arm around my waist and steers me up to the stage. "You're annoyingly good at this. Just smile and have fun. There is literally nothing riding on success here."

Okay, she has a good point. I adjust the bottom of the blazer I borrowed from Priya, taking care to make sure the lace corset from my mall outing with Salem is being nicely displayed, and then I step up to introduce myself. But before I can, Isabel beats me to the mic, and the mere sight of her in her glittery bodysuit and heels has the room exploding with whistles and applause.

Weirdly, it takes a lot of the edge off to be reminded that as long as Isabel's up there in next to nothing, no one really cares what I do. So when she sweeps her arm in my direction and says, "Ladies and gentlefolk, please allow me to introduce the Magnificent Everett Riley," I'm actually feeling relaxed enough to smile, wave, and curtsy in my little shorts.

From across the room, I catch Salem's eye and see him biting his lip as he tries not to laugh, and I can't help winking.

"As some of you know," I announce into the mic, "though I couldn't possibly say how—so random, right?—I have a particular skill with cards." A couple of the Rumson guys who've lost way too much money to me boo from the back, and the portion of the crowd that knows exactly why laughs. "As such, the cards are only happy to do what I tell them."

I do a riffle shuffle of a new deck I purchased on my condom run as I talk, and then cut the deck with one hand, sweeping it into two individual, impressive fans. There's some polite oohing to start with, but as I run through a series of flourishes and twirls, I see people start to crane their necks for better views.

"I believe you all know my lovely assistant, Isabel McEvoy." I combine the cards into a single deck and sweep them into a thumb fan that I extend in her direction. It took me hours of practice to master that one, and I'm gratified when it works beautifully, even if I'm well aware the applause is for the strawberry blonde next to me and not because of the seamlessness with which I just displayed every card in the deck in my small hand. "Isabel, would you please pick a card?"

She prances over and bends to eye it closely, which has even more necks craning from the audience. Finally, she selects a card, and I dramatically cover my eyes while she shows it to the audience.

"Three of hearts!" yells out a voice from the back I'm pretty sure belongs to my dear friend Archie.

"Seven of spades!" adds another one—Duncan, I'm almost positive.

A few more voices yell out random cards, and it takes everything in me not to let it mess with my concentration. "If the gentlemen in the back could kindly shut their pieholes!" I declare cheerfully, grateful that Isabel waits until they do before slipping the card back in.

I take note of the spot where she returned the card, and cut the deck accordingly. It's a silly trick, one I've practiced with Isabel no fewer than ten times, and it drives her nuts that she can't figure it out. I flash the bottom of the deck to her and show it to the audience. "Is this your card?"

"It is not!" she says triumphantly.

"All right, then! Let's put that card down, and move one to the back of the deck." We go through this for four more cards, and when we hit the last one, I offer a dramatic "Still no?" and Isabel shakes her head slowly and smugly, making the audience laugh.

Thank God I did not attempt to do this myself with a random volunteer, although it would've been fun to pick Salem or Sabrina, just to torture them.

Or Archie. I really would not mind torturing Archie. Would that I were at a level in cardistry where I could kill a man with a two of spades.

As if on cue, someone yells out from the audience, "Rumson Girl fucked up the trick!"

"Language!" calls a disembodied authoritative voice.

I could kill every single one of Archie's friends right now, but thankfully, their cluelessness actually makes this a little more fun. "Oh no, did I?" I gasp dramatically as I take hold of the four face-down cards on the table and flip one over. "Isabel, are you telling me *this* is not your card?"

She holds it up for everyone to see. "It is not!"

"And this one?" I push forward the second card with an exaggerated pout on my face. "This one's not either?"

"She already told you it's not! Can't you hear, Rumson Girl?"

My teeth are going to crack if I clench them any harder, but Isabel plays it cool and just says, "Nope, that's not it either."

"And this third one?" I widen my eyes in panic. "You're sure it's not this one?"

"I'm sure," says Isabel, holding up the third card.

"Then I guess it must be this one," I say, pointing to the fourth. I wait for an annoying outburst from the audience, and so does Isabel, neither of us wanting the punch line to drown in it, but it doesn't come. Finally, Isabel picks up the card, and her face breaks into a huge smile.

"That's it!" she says, holding up the card as if it were a newborn lion. I knew she could act, but the wonder on her face, as if she's never seen this trick before, is perfect. The entire audience cheers, and for the rest of the routine, there's no more shit from the crowd, even when I slip slightly on an aerial and nearly drop the deck.

By the time they announce the end of our performance, I could not be readier to get off that stage.

"That went great!" Isabel whispers excitedly, squeezing my arm. "You really do have to show me how you do that stuff."

"I will," I promise. I go to take my seat with Heather and Sabrina, and watch as Isabel takes hers. Salem catches my eye and gives me a little golf clap, which I respond to with a dramatic bow.

"That was so great!" Heather gushes. "You— Oh! Lucas is up!"

Well, that was some short-lived joy. I take my seat quietly and dig my nails into my thighs as I watch Lucas perform an entire comedy routine by John Mulaney, though he does admittedly nail the voice and intonations. The audience eats it up, despite the fact that they watched Jesse do something similar a few acts ago, breaking into laughter at all the right points, and I want to remind them that it isn't because *Lucas* is funny.

Mercifully, it's a short set, after which Heather immediately goes to find him, tell him he's brilliant, and abandon me and Sabrina to go sit with him. Sabs and I sit through an impressive quick-change routine, an even more impressive singing performance by Heather and Kayla, a tap dance by a girl in my chem class, Darryl and Jason's rap battle, a ventriloquist, and a Shakespearean monologue by the Lockwood prefect. The night seems to be winding down when Hoffman declares, "And next up, we have a late addition to the roster . . . from the illustrious Rumson Hall, please welcome Salem Grayson and his guitar, playing Guns N' Roses' 'Patience'!"

"I'm sorry, it's who doing what now?" But even as the

words leave my lips my eyes track Salem's long, lean body shuffling up to the stage, a guitar I've never even seen before slung over his shoulder.

Sabrina rolls her eyes. "I knew he couldn't resist."

"He *what*?" I'm still stunned by the sight of Salem up there on the stage, hopping onto a stool, admittedly looking every inch the rock star.

Jenna must be so proud. I've never seen her play anything but cool, but the way her eyes are fixed on the stage, a tiny smile playing at her lips, her eyes glittering in the dim light of the room . . . against all odds, she really does like Salem. It's fascinating.

Salem coughs into the mic and says, "It's actually Chris Cornell's cover of 'Patience,' but uh, yeah."

He starts strumming, and from the very first melancholy notes, my breath catches in my throat. The melody is beautiful, yeah, but there's something about the way his fingers look curved around the wood of the guitar's neck, the effortlessness with which they pluck at the chords, and the contemplative look on his face, peaceful but focused, as if whatever—or whoever—is inspiring him right now is right there behind his eyelids.

And when he opens his mouth, his playing is nothing compared to his voice. His *voice*. It's a low rasp coated in honey, achingly romantic, and even though I know those grungy jeans and that Black Flag T-shirt and corded leather bracelet as well as I know my own wardrobe, I cannot believe that voice is coming out of Salem *Grayson*, of all people. The voice and the *words*. He made it sound like he and Jenna are a casual thing, like they're just hooking up, but . . . this isn't a song you sing about a girl you're just having fun with. A song about waiting? Having patience? Believing that you'll make it?

Salem's singing like he's in love.

If I were Jenna—or, hell, if this were anyone other than Salem—I'd be fully weak in the knees by now.

As it is, I'm not feeling too hot. I know he's not trying to rub salt in the wounds Lucas and Craig left behind—he *couldn't* be—but it's so brutal to hear him singing about taking it slow and having a future when I'm still so full of regrets. It almost feels like he knows, like he's somehow reached into my brain and my heart and decided to claw me open and drag me in front of the entire school.

And when he looks up and locks eyes with me for a second, the faintest of smiles on his lips, intellectually I know it's a nod to my saying I knew he'd play guitar at the talent show, but still, it hurts like hell.

When he comes down off the final notes, the room absolutely explodes in applause and whistles, including from Sabrina. It's total chaos, and if I were to look in Jenna's direction, I might see her sailing down toward the stage, claiming her man with a big, proud kiss.

But I don't have time to look in Jenna's direction; I have to take this opportunity to get the hell out of there ASAP. And so without another glance at Salem, without a word to Sabrina, without so much as another breath, I bolt.

* * *

No one follows me out. As far as I know, no one even notices I'm gone. And who would? As far as everyone *else* knows, I'm fine, absolutely fine, everything is *fine*. I have no one to call, nothing to do in my room except solitaire, which seems way too on point at the moment.

So I go to bed, hoping sleep will take me and I won't have to think about any of these things, any of these people. But hours later I've tried everything from counting sheep to recounting all my Spanish vocabulary words, and still nothing. I hear the boys file back into the dorm, loud voices carrying as they talk about the talent show, and there's little I can make out in the individual conversations that twist and tangle together. Eventually, that too dies down, giving way to the sounds of showers turning on and doors closing.

And then, a knock, so quiet I think I'm imagining it until I hear it again, a little louder this time.

"I'm asleep," I call.

The door cracks open, and Salem steps inside. After the reception to his performance, I half expect him to have his clothing clawed to shreds and his face covered in lipstick prints, but it's just my dormmate and study buddy, my pact partner, a hesitant look on his face I can barely make out in the moonlight streaming through my window. "You almost had me."

"Shouldn't you be off somewhere, rolling around in your fandom?"

"Am I— Is this not my fan club meeting?" He scratches his head. "Dammit, I always get lost on the way to my shrine."

"So I was right about you being an emo-boy cliché."

"I guess you were." He steps closer, takes a tentative seat on the edge of my bed. "Are you okay?"

"Of course I'm okay," I lie. "Why wouldn't I be?"

He sighs. "Can we skip that part where you keep lying and I keep asking and just get to it?"

I don't know what's worse—that Salem noticed I'm not okay or that *Salem* noticed I'm not okay. We were supposed to be on equal footing, each of us wanting a life we couldn't quite achieve on our own. But now he's so far overshot while I've failed at attempt after attempt to grow at all, and it hurts just to be in the same room.

Even more painful? How badly I just want a *hug*. I need someone to hold me and tell me things are gonna be okay like I need air. We may not be in the best place right now, but I would give *anything* for my mom to sit where Salem is sitting and give me one of the lazy back scratches she used to when I wormed into her bed for safety during thunderstorms. And looking at Salem, at the concern on his face, I know that if I asked him, he would give me at least a brief squeeze. And it would feel amazing.

But I am not about to ask that of another girl's boyfriend, after everything. And I need him to leave so I can stop thinking about doing it anyway.

"I'm fine, Salem. You should go to bed."

"You're fine? That's why you bolted out of the talent show?" He sighs. "Look, I get that you don't want to talk to me, but you should talk to *someone*. Sometimes, like right now, you just get this vibe about you, like . . ."

"Like?"

His eyes glitter in the darkness of my room. "Like you should talk to someone."

I don't know if he means a friend or a therapist, but I don't have either one—at least not a friend I can tell about everything—so I stay silent, staring up at my dark ceiling and wishing I at least had those glow-in-the-dark stars or something. Way too much of my life right now is staring out into nothingness.

Where do I even go from here?

"It's just . . . you remind me of her when you drift off like this. Of Sabrina. After she and Molly broke up and she couldn't get out of bed. Couldn't eat. Couldn't anything. It was so bad," he says, his voice barely above a whisper, and I'm not even sure he's still talking to me. "I wouldn't have done what I did if I didn't think I absolutely had to, if I didn't think she literally needed to move somewhere else to survive."

"And now you want to be the hero again?" It comes out meaner than I intend, but I'm not sure I even care. It's physically painful, having him so close and having to keep him so far away. Having to keep my secret, to keep my distance, to keep from telling him how badly I just need a fucking *hug*.

To keep from telling him how much his stupid fucking song broke my heart all over again for reasons I can't even begin to understand.

"I know you don't think it's about that," he says flatly. "We both know I'm not a hero. Hell, you had to teach me how to be a decent guy."

"No, I didn't." As I say it, I realize how true it is. "You were always a decent guy. You were always the guy who risked his own reputation and future for his sister, and who helped me when I asked for it, and who brought me tampons under cover of darkness. And now you're the guy checking on me in the middle of the night. It was stupid to think you were anything else just because you dressed like you rolled out of a dumpster and smelled like a bong."

"I'm flattered, I think?"

"I'm not flattering you. I'm telling you that you don't need me and you never did. And I don't need you either. So can you please. Just. Go?"

There's an endless silence where he doesn't respond but he doesn't get up, either, and I pretend my eyes are closed but I'm actually looking at where his hand rests on his thigh and willing it to stroke my hair. It's the stupidest thing, but my entire heart feels like it's seizing in the hopes of receiving exactly that one small touch. *Ignore what I'm saying,* I want to scream, but I don't, of course I don't, and I don't take his hand and I don't move closer and I don't take a breath.

And then he says, "You know where to find me," and leaves me alone to cry in the dark.

Chapter Fourteen

AT SOME POINT, I MANAGE to cry myself to sleep, which I only know because the ringing of my phone invades my dreams until my searching hand finally locates it and shoves it to my ear. "Hello?" I ask without even bothering to check who's calling, because that would involve opening my eyes, and that is simply not a thing I can do yet.

"Are you still sleeping?" My mother. "Aren't you late for breakfast?"

"Breakfast is optional," I murmur, which turns into a huge yawn, which I know my mother will not appreciate. I check the time. "My alarm will go off in three minutes."

"Well, sorry to wake you," she lies, "but I wanted to make sure to tell you before I headed out to work." She takes a breath, and somehow, I know what she's going to say before she even says it. "Unfortunately—"

"You can't make it to Parents' Weekend."

"Did your father tell you?"

"No." I move the phone a few inches so I can sigh in peace. "Just guessed." *Because I tried to think of the worst news you could be delivering, and expected it.*

Another pause, and I know she wants to be offended, but also, I was right, so what is there to say? "It's complicated, and I'm very sorry." She's not sorry. "But I'm sure there'll be plenty of other students there whose parents couldn't make it, right? You'll all keep one another company."

Truthfully, I don't know anyone else whose parents aren't coming, but telling my mom that wouldn't change anything. I don't know if anything would. Her job as a paralegal doesn't come with a lot of time off, and any complaints would be met with a speech I've heard way too many times about why work has to come first to pay for all these things. Considering my tuition is an added expense they'd never counted on, I'm in no position to bargain.

Then again, she hasn't mentioned work, and when work *is* her excuse, she usually wields it with the same excessiveness my sister does mascara. Which makes me suspect this isn't about work at all. But is it something else real? Or is it entirely made up to get out of seeing me?

Do I even wanna know?

My alarm goes off just then, and it makes the perfect excuse to get off the phone, which I desperately need because I don't even know how to react to all of these disappointments anymore. Truthfully, Parents' Weekend hadn't even been on my radar alongside everything else, but now, all the little things I'll be missing out on—the way my mom always tries to fix up my hair and tells me I look beautiful whether she succeeded or not, my dad's Rice Krispies treats and warm hugs—are bringing me right back to the brink of tears.

God, I hate this week.

I also hate showering first thing in the morning, but I feel so disgusting and headachy and in need of a good cry, and the shower is the perfect place to deal with all three. Afterward, I throw my hair in a wet knot—I'll deal with the aftermath later—pull on my most boring clothes, and lumber out the door in search of coffee and a pastry big enough to stand in for all my feelings.

Sabrina's already at the Beast when I arrive, and I'm relieved to see she isn't sitting with Heather. Or Salem, for that matter; I definitely need some caffeine and sugar before I can deal with last night's whole weird visit. I use the tiny bit of energy I have to give her a little wave and then go retrieve my breakfast before collapsing in the seat next to her and taking a long sip of way-too-hot liquid.

"So, you do exist," Sabrina says in a casual tone that isn't casual at all. "I'd been wondering, considering I've barely seen you all week and then you bolted out of the talent show. You know I called you three times last night. And I do *not* make phone calls."

She did. I saw them. But I couldn't answer. I didn't even know if I could get words out last night. I'm still not sure I can get them out now. Because of *course* the last person at this school I'm actually happy to see is mad at me. Of *course* I did something to piss her off. Of *course* her anger is valid. But I don't have the energy to explain or apologize or defend myself or even formulate words. If I open my mouth, I *will* cry.

"I'm sorry," I offer quietly, as soon as I think I can do it without breaking down. "I'm having a bad week, and I needed some air."

"You know, most people talk to their friends about their bad weeks."

Would've been nice if I could, I think with no small amount of annoyance. *I* certainly didn't ask for my boy troubles to involve my best friend at Camden's roommate. "It wasn't something I could talk to you about. Can you just trust me on this, please?"

"Sure," she says flatly, pushing at her limp pancake with her fork.

I know I should continue the conversation, change the subject, ask how the rest of the talent show was, but I don't have the energy. Instead, we sit in silence, her shredding her breakfast into a thousand pieces she doesn't eat and me grimacing at every sip of bitter coffee, until finally another tray clatters down across from us and Salem slides in. "Well, looks like everyone's having a stellar morning."

God, he's annoying. "Guessing yours didn't start with your parents calling to let you know they're bailing on Parents' Weekend."

At that, even Sabrina frowns sympathetically. "That sucks."

"Yeah, I was looking forward to seeing that hair in triplicate," Salem says with a grin, taking a huge bite out of his omnipresent green apple.

"You would've been disappointed anyway. It's from my dad's side, and he's been rocking a shiny head for years now.

My mom's hair's straight and brown, and my sister got hers—I'm the only freak," I say sourly.

"So you'll hang out with our family," Salem says with a shrug. "We're all freaks. You'll fit right in."

I cut a glance at Sabrina, who might still be mad, but she nods. "Our parents will be thrilled that we managed to make a single friend between the two of us."

It's a nice offer, especially since I'm not exactly her favorite person right now, but the only place I want to spend Parents' Weekend now is locked in my own room. "As much as *I'd* love to meet the mythical creatures who somehow spawned both of you, I think I'm just gonna sleep through the whole weekend."

"Okay, that actually sounds much better than hanging out with parents," says Salem, his teeth piercing the shiny green skin again. "I wanna do that instead."

"Not a chance." Sabrina whacks him on the shoulder, and it's such a sibling move that my heart aches at the sight of what it must look like to have a real one. "But anyway, if you change your mind, just text me."

"Thanks," I mutter into my coffee, knowing that there's no way in hell I'll be doing that.

As it turns out, when Parents' Weekend arrives, they text me before I even get to attempt my grand sleep marathon. SOS, Sabrina sends me in a group text with them both. Need you here ASAP.

I glance at the time—6:03 P.M. Which means they're only three minutes into the special show-offy parents' dinner. How could they possibly need me there? I'm sleeping, I write back.

Salem
I keep telling you, Skeevy, that trick does not work.

Sabrina
Plz. Begging.

Evie
If this is an elaborate plan to save me from my own loneliness, I really do not need it.

Which is mostly true, but I'm intrigued; I've read like five pages of my book in the last two hours, and I am b-o-r-e-d. And yeah, okay, maybe my brain keeps drifting over to what everyone else is doing, and what it's like to be sitting in the auditorium-turned-dining-room in the Student Center, poking at pale chicken breast and limp salad along with everybody else.

Sabrina
Uh, no.

Mom is already getting mad about texting. gg see you soon

If my boredom weren't already getting the better of me, my curiosity would be, so even though I feel I am going to deeply regret this, I pull myself out of bed and throw on jeans and the most decent shirt I can find. Then I dab on a little makeup, try to coax my curls into something a little less bedhead-y, and thread in a pair of earrings. Greentree is a small town, and it's been a long time since I've met a friend's parents for the first time. I feel like I should look nice, even if I don't quite know why.

Evie

Where are you sitting?

No answer. Guess their mom *really* didn't like them texting at the table. Oh well. I make my way into the auditorium and start picking my way around the tables, searching for a crew that looks like the Addams Family, when suddenly there's a gasp, a flash of blond hair in my face, a wave of floral perfume, and the squeeze of someone clearly trying to kill me.

Before I can figure out what the hell is going on, the woman holds me at arm's length, a huge smile spreading across her face as she looks me over from head to toe. "It's so nice to finally meet Sammy's girlfriend!"

What the hell, I mouth at Sabrina as her mother leads me to their table a few feet away; the fact that she couldn't even stay seated to keep watch is only one of many, many things blowing my mind right now.

I'm sorry. Please go with it, she mouths back. I glance at Salem, who has a fake smile on his face that doesn't quite go with the look in his eyes that says he knows dinner will be followed by his execution. There's an empty seat next to him, presumably for me, and I slide into it, immediately digging my fingernails into his thigh. He must've expected it, because he grits his teeth but doesn't make a sound.

"Sammy, aren't you even going to say hi?" Mrs. Grayson asks, retaking her own seat. "Evie, I'm so glad you could come to dinner. Sammy said you were studying, but I knew you'd make it here so we could get to meet you." She covers my hand with her freckled one, and I'm struck by the fact that she bears absolutely no resemblance to the twins. "Sammy tells me you work *very* hard."

I'm working *very* hard on not choking every time she says "Sammy," that's for sure. But as long as I'm here, I may as well have some fun with this. "I do," I say, nodding. "Sammy and I study together all the time. He's such a good listener when he needs things explained to him."

"Which isn't often," Salem says through gritted teeth. "But yeah, we make a good team."

God, it feels like he practiced this. *Did* he practice this? Was the whole invite at breakfast the day I told them my parents weren't coming part of this plan? I have so many questions. But now is clearly not the time, because their mom has even more, and I am getting *all* of them.

Yes, I'm from New Hampshire originally.

No, I don't know where I want to go to college yet. Of course Dartmouth would be great, but yes, it is very competitive.

No, my parents couldn't make it—they had to work. Bank branch manager and paralegal. Yes, I also have a sister. A year older. Not sure about college yet either. Maybe UNH, or Radleigh University.

By the time the third degree is over—or at least takes a break for the welcome speech—the Grayson parents probably know more about me than my own do. I kept waiting for Salem to break in, but he just sat there, nodding along as if I were fascinating, because apparently acting is on his list of talents as well. I wasn't, in fact, particularly interesting, and yet the Graysons are looking at me like I'm the second coming. It's both weird and such a nice change from the looks I got from my parents in the few months before I came here that I haven't even stuck a fork in Salem's leg yet for making me do this without warning or explanation.

Then again, I have a much better idea.

"Gosh, I've been talking so much about myself that I haven't even gotten to ask *you* any questions," I say to Mrs. Grayson, clasping my hands on the table. "I am *dying* to know what Sammy was like as a little boy. He *did* mention being very late to potty training."

"I did no such—"

"He told you that?" Mr. and Mrs. Grayson exchange a deep laugh, and now it's my turn to feel claws digging into my thigh. "He must really like you," Mr. Grayson adds.

"I know it's still early," I say with a happy sigh, retrieving Salem's grasping hand and twining it with mine on the table in their full view, "but we really are serious about each other. As I'm sure he's told you."

The beginning of a snort sounds from Sabrina's direction, and she quickly covers her nose and mouth in a bad imitation of a sneeze. "Bless you." I nod serenely in my future sister-in-law's direction.

"Oh, Sammy hasn't told us nearly enough," says Mrs. Grayson, and I'm pretty sure she's looking at my ring finger, trying to figure out my size. "Just that—"

"—we met in English on the first day," Salem fills in, squeezing my hand hard enough to break bones, and I realize I'm not to let on to his parents that I live in Rumson. "And that we started studying together every night—"

"We *do* study together every night," I confirm with a bob of my head. "He takes studying *so* seriously. But you of course already know that."

"We, er, didn't until now," says Mr. Grayson, rubbing a hand over his dark, close-cropped hair, "but it sounds like Camden's been really wonderful for him. I don't know if he told you, but he was a bit of a troublemaker back home."

"Oh, yes, he did tell me." I rest a head on his shoulder, knowing full well he's getting a mouthful of curls. "So hard to imagine, when he's such a good boy here."

"Stop making me sound like a puppy," he growls into my ear.

"Oh, you are in no position to make demands," I remind him through gritted teeth.

We all shut up for another speech, and then they bring out the main course, which is a buffet that actually smells pretty good. But when Salem's parents get up to take food, I tell them we'll be there in a minute, finally seeing an opportunity to get some answers.

"Okay, you have like *one minute* to explain this to me before your mom definitely comes back here and grabs us to make sure we're eating well enough," I hiss. "And you know I'm serious because I'm not even having us dwell on how hilarious it is that your parents call you Sammy."

"I knew this was a mistake," Salem tells Sabrina with narrowed eyes.

"I'm *sorry*," she says to him before turning to me. "It was stupid. My parents were on me about dating and how I need to move on et cetera et cetera and I was trying to deflect, so I kind of accidentally mentioned that Salem has a girlfriend so I could get the heat off me."

"And how did *I* become the girlfriend in this scenario instead of, you know, his actual girlfriend?" I demand, posing the question to Sabrina but narrowing my eyes at Salem.

"Jenna's parents took her away for the weekend, but even if she were here, uh, you just met my mom; you think Jenna would've managed so much as a fake smile for her? Besides"—he slides his finger under his knife and pops it up, twirling it seamlessly before carving lines into the tablecloth I don't think he realizes he's even drawing—"Jenna's not my 'girlfriend.' It would've been weird."

"Okay, but I'm even *less* your girlfriend. This is much weirder."

"Except *you* have a vested interested in making me look

good to my parents," Salem reminds me in a low voice, his gray eyes flashing silver. "Remember?"

That stupid pact. God. It feels like a million years ago.

"And why's that?" Sabrina asks.

Crap. I'd forgotten that she was even here, and that she has no idea what we're talking about. "Just a stupid bet," I mutter, and I guess we're just weird enough for that to be sufficient. "Anyway, what happens when Jenna finds out?"

Salem shrugs. "She'll probably think it's funny. Or stupid. Or both. You really do not have to worry about Jenna London."

Every girl on campus has to worry about Jenna London, I think, and then Mrs. Grayson is calling to us, gesturing for us to get in line. We stand to meet them, but as Sabrina moves forward, I grab Salem's elbow and hold him back. "I'll play along this weekend," I tell him, "but that's the end of this pact. All right?"

He opens his mouth, and I brace myself for mockery, but instead, he lapses into a flash of a smile. "Deal. But you better fill up your plate. Mama Grayson likes a girl with an appetite."

It's a weirdly good weekend, all things considered. My parents do text to say they're sorry they couldn't make it, and I send them pictures and videos of random stuff they're missing. Meanwhile, the Graysons take me in like a triplet, insisting I join them for breakfast, at which Mrs. Grayson—"Please!

Call me Naomi!"—urges Salem to heap a thousand things on his plate I know he'll never eat, and suddenly that first breakfast together makes sense. I beg off for the orientation and accompanying seminar, and I'm still trying to decide how to spend the rest of my day when Sabrina swings by and tells me we're going to lunch.

"Okay, I think there's a limit to just how much Grayson family time I'm gonna horn in on," I tell her as she stands tapping her foot in my doorway. "Seriously, you do not need a fifth wheel. Just go."

"Ew. Did you just imply Salem and I are a couple?"

I roll my eyes. "I feel pretty confident you know what I mean, and you two have been more than implying that Salem and *I* are a couple all day."

"Yeah, that part's pretty damn funny. I keep waiting for Jenna and her parents to show up; Salem doesn't even know how long they're gone for."

"And what exactly is the plan if we bump into them?" I press.

"That's Salem's problem," she says with a shrug, flicking a piece of dust off her ISN'T IT NECROMANTIC? sweater. "Now, come on—you don't want to offend Ted and Naomi, do you? Their children do that enough already."

"Don't you think the more time I spend with you guys, the likelier they are to figure out that Salem and I aren't a couple?"

Sabrina arches one of her thin brows. "Uh, no. Have you seen the way you two are constantly touching and whispering and finishing each other's sentences? Half the time *I* don't remember you're not a couple. Now grab your jacket—it's a wee bit nippy out."

"*You're* a wee bit nippy," I snap, busying myself with hunting down my jacket so she won't see the flush in my cheeks at her comment about me and Salem. We do *not* act like a couple.

"Well, we can't all have your assets," she says with a pointed look at my chest, and as I stomp out after her, slipping my arms into my sleeves, I vow to start making new friends as soon as this weekend is over.

But lunch is surprisingly fun too, and revelatory—I learn about Sabrina's first pet, a guinea pig who lived up to his job title for way too many of her practice spells, and that Salem was afraid of lightning until junior high and Sabrina's not convinced he's over it. ("I'll protect you," I assure him in a serious whisper, patting his hand on the table while Naomi Grayson watches us like she's about to advise on our china pattern.)

Of course, Salem and I are forced to recount our "first date," and while we definitely do *not* finish each other's sentences, it's pretty easy without even discussing it to simultaneously come up with that first movie night as the setting. Naomi is riveted at the detail that Salem loaned me his jacket (naturally, we give it a very different context), and glows as we one-up each other with stupid additions that make it sound more like Salem took me to Cannes than that we walked together across campus to watch a cheesy movie in an auditorium.

"Sammy." I swear she's holding back tears as she squeezes his hand over the table, and okay, maybe I feel a little bit bad for having so much fun with this. "I'm so proud of you. You promised that you'd turn into a real stand-up citizen if you got a fresh start, and you really have."

The guilt at our deception gives way to a little pride, because this means I have *definitely* delivered on my half of the bargain. Judging by the way Salem's cheeks flush as he stares at the tabletop, but without letting go of his mom's hand, this is exactly what he's been waiting to hear. And I'm genuinely happy for him that he's getting to hear it.

This time, when I put a hand on his knee and squeeze, I'm not trying to draw blood.

Still, I find I need a break from the charade; it's all starting to feel a little too real for comfort, and I don't like the way Sabrina keeps eyeing us and smirking. I *really* don't like thinking about whether this is a shitty thing to do to Jenna—much as she sucks—and how, if it is, I of all people should know better. So after lunch, I'm considerably firmer about not accompanying them on the next portion of their weekend, and I spend the rest of the afternoon playing online poker and reading Sabrina's and my next GSA read—this time, it's the football player / cheerleader romance, which Sabs has already grudgingly admitted is better than she expected.

I don't even realize it's growing dark around me until a knock sounds at my door, forcing me to look up from the page. "Come in!"

The knob turns and Salem lets himself inside, holding one of the beige clamshells they keep at the Beast for takeout. My stomach rumbles at the sight; missing dinner may have been a necessary sacrifice for privacy, but it wasn't a welcome one. "Any chance that's for me?"

"You know it is," he says, perching on the edge of my desk. "Complete with extra garlic bread, in thanks for your service this weekend."

"Good thing I won't *actually* be kissing anyone tonight," I say, motioning for him to hand over the food. *Mmm, garlic bread.* "So, your parents seemed pretty eager to buy that."

"Right?" He shakes his head. "It's so bizarre. I think it's a weird PTSD reaction to Sabrina's breakup with Molly, or something. It was rough."

I pluck a piece of garlic bread from the clamshell and take a careful bite; I'm definitely not trying to sleep in crumbs tonight. "Looks to me like they actually care about seeing you happy and well adjusted. Novel concept, I know."

He snorts. "This may be hard for you to believe, but I *was* fine and even relatively well adjusted at my old school. I mean, yeah, I smoked a lot of weed, skipped some classes, and got in trouble occasionally—"

"Salem. You got caught spray-painting unspeakably raunchy pictures of Daniel Tiger on a public wall."

"First of all, that's disgusting. Daniel Tiger is a child. The pictures were of his parents, and it's not my fault they're so foxy."

"Do you ever actually listen to yourself speak?"

"Nah, who wants to hear that noise?" He rakes a hand through his hair, and it falls back in his eyes immediately. "Anyway, thank you. I know we didn't give you a whole lot of choice in signing on for that this weekend, but you made my parents happy, and they really needed a win."

Don't I know that feeling . . . "So, you think they liked me?"

He rolls his eyes. "They fucking loved you."

That shouldn't make me nearly as happy as it does. "What'd they say?"

His mouth quirks up in a grin. "That it was nice to finally meet someone in our circle with an ounce of social grace."

Social grace. I don't think anyone in the world has ever said anything like that about me before, and I like the sound of it.

Frankly, it makes me a little disappointed that it was fake, too. Not because of Salem, of course, but I'll miss his parents and their warm seal of approval.

"Yeah, well, I'm sorry I didn't get to say goodbye," I say, and I mean it.

"Don't worry—I told them you had cramps. They got it."

"Oh my God, I despise you."

He smirks. "No, you don't. I'm the bringer of emergency tampons. And garlic bread."

"And trouble. Always trouble."

"That too. But listen—"

The ringing of my cell phone cuts him off, and we both instinctively glance over and see the call is coming from my mom. "I haven't been able to connect with my parents for more than a text all weekend, so I should probably take this," I say apologetically, grabbing it from my nightstand. "But we'll talk tomorrow?"

He nods. “Yeah, okay. G’night, Skeevy.”

I answer the phone as I watch him go, but wait to speak until the door closes behind him. “Hey, Mom.”

“Evie.” She sighs, and I want to remind her that she called me, and I haven’t said nearly enough to exhaust her yet. “I’m sorry, again, that we couldn’t make it this weekend. We’re . . . we’re with your sister.”

“Of course you are,” I say before I can stop myself. “Of course Sierra’s the reason you’re not here. What is it now? Meeting with Principal Myers? Angry parent? Did she get another bootleg tattoo?”

There’s a long silence, and I worry that maybe I’ve gone too far, until she speaks again. “We’re in a rehab facility in Vermont, Everett. Your sister’s checking in.”

Chapter Fifteen

TURNS OUT, SLEEPING IS REALLY challenging when you find out your sister's popularity has been partially due to her being the school's go-to for pills. There's a whole legal mess my mom clearly doesn't want to dig into and "thank God she's a minor" comes up about a hundred times, but the tl;dr is there was a deal on the table for Sierra to attend rehab and it was now or never. Which I guess does kind of put them not attending Parents' Weekend in perspective.

But it still feels like ass.

The worst part is that I actually want to *talk* to Sierra now, to find out what the hell was going through her mind, and how exactly this fit into everything she did to me. Did Craig know? Did Claire? Were either of them using with her? I would be 0 percent shocked to find out Craig's loser gamer friends were customers.

My brain is bursting with questions and expletives and

more questions, and I break my rule again and look through Sierra's posts, and Claire's, and Sierra's friends', and I see nothing, except then I realize I do see one change, which is that I don't see pictures of Sierra at all. Pictures I know existed on her friends' pages are gone. *Plausible deniability,* I think, and I almost feel bad for her.

I don't know what her life is going to look like when she comes back. I don't know how she got caught in the first place—my mom didn't offer, and I didn't ask. There's definitely some irony in that I took the ticket out she's probably going to wish she had, but she has no one else to blame for that. Saving your sister from herself is strictly a Salem Grayson move, I guess.

Then again, Sabrina doesn't know what really happened, and neither do I; maybe Sierra *was* saving me from a life I shouldn't have been living. I mean, it *is* because of her that I'm here, that I got a fresh start at romance and friendship and making a name for myself. And for once, it's not her fault that I'm hovering somewhere around a C+ at it all.

I argue with myself for hours about whether it's worth reaching out to someone to get some answers, watching the clock move like molasses when my eyes are on it, then way too quickly when I look away. I'm tired, but I won't be getting any rest at all until I can get some of this off my chest. If only I kept a diary.

Then I hear it, the slight creaking above me that means either Matt or Salem is up and about. I look at the clock, and see that it's a little past three in the morning. Probably just a quick bathroom trip. But the urge to talk to someone is so great, I feel it with the same desperate ache I felt wanting Salem to hug me.

It's sad, and it's pathetic, but I just need a *friend.*

I slide into my slippers—designed to look like aces of spades, naturally—and creep upstairs, not particularly worried about being caught by Hoffman at this hour. But my hopes of catching Matt or Salem in the hallway are dashed when I see their door is closed; apparently, no one left the room after all. I stand there, staring at it, willing it to open, but there's nothing other than silence, and no way I'm knocking.

My entire body deflates as I turn to go back downstairs, and then, miraculously, I hear the knob behind me turn.

"Evie?" Salem says on a yawn.

I whirl around, and see him leaning against the doorway in a pair of black drawstring pants and . . . nothing. It never in a million years would've occurred to me that Salem Grayson sleeps shirtless, and the fact that he does and that I am staring at a wall of lean muscle is very unsettling. "Hi," I say, because I have to say something, and also I have to look up into his eyes. His eyes, which look sleepy and soft and a little concerned, long lashes slightly fluttering, and all of this is very confusing.

It is really not a good time to be noticing any of this.

"Hi?" He scratches his chest, giving me permission to glance again. It's not a broad chest, or a particularly defined one, and yet. The urge to feel it under my palm is obnoxiously strong. "It's like three A.M."

"I know. Sorry. I just . . . I've been having a really weird night, and I was dying to talk to someone, and then I heard you moving, so I figured I'd see if you were up. But it's really late. You probably wanna get back to bed. This was stupid."

"Nah, I've been having a weird night too, and then I heard you skulking outside. You wanna come in?" He holds open the door. "Don't worry—once Matt's out, he can sleep through a zombie apocalypse. I've stuck so many things in his nose to test this theory."

I smother my laughter in my hand and join Salem on his bed, curling my legs up underneath me in the corner while he sets his pillow behind his back and sits up to face me. "Are *you* okay?" I ask. "You know, before I dive into talking about my stupid shit for an hour."

"Yeah, yeah. Also stupid shit, but not the kind worth talking about."

I take him at his word, mostly because I'm about to break. "My sister's in rehab. That's why my parents weren't here this weekend. They were checking her in."

"Oh, shit."

"Yeah. And I don't even know how much she's actually using or anything, but apparently, she was dealing, and this was part of the arrangement they made, along with her license getting suspended." I fix him with a dark look. "Please tell me you were never that stupid."

"No way, that would've been way too much work. My dealer was just one of the guys in my band back home."

"You were in a band? God, I really did call it from the beginning. I can't believe you lied about playing guitar. Who lies about that?"

"I didn't lie about playing guitar; I said I wasn't going to be giving an emo acoustic performance, and that my guitar's name wasn't Betty."

"Okay, so what's her name?"

He sniffs. "Janis."

I burst into laughter, and Salem dives forward to cover my mouth with his hand. "Okay, I hadn't considered that your laugh is *louder* than the zombie apocalypse," he growls.

"Hmph." I press my lips together to stop myself, but now I'm hyperaware that Salem and I are in his bed, touching, so close I can feel his body heat through my thin tank top.

I am not thrilled about noticing this, either.

Or that my next thought is that I could swipe my tongue out and lick his palm.

I don't know if similar thoughts are running through his head—probably not, because unlike me, he is neither single nor deranged—but he releases me and backs away with a quickness, leaving me nothing to do but pretend to be offended by the entire exchange before we finally steer ourselves back to the conversation at hand.

"You *did* give an emo acoustic performance," I point out, though I omit the fact that it was one of the most beautiful things I've ever heard in my life, because I don't know how to begin to process that.

"I did," he concedes with a sheepish smile, "but I honestly didn't plan to at the time." Now it's his turn to furrow his brow at me. "Did any of this stuff with your sister have to do with why you ran out after it?"

God, it would be so easy to say yes, and even easier if it were the truth. Right now there are so many question marks in my brain and I really do not like where it leads when I try to come up with the answers.

Especially with this added shirtlessness component that's making it a lot harder to ignore the creeping, inconvenient truth of my feelings.

But when school was just beginning, I talked myself into a stupid mistake with the wrong boy, and now Salem's with the wrong girl, and *this* is why I cannot be trusted with my own heart, my own body, and God, are those tears, *again*? How am I not completely dehydrated already?

"Evie?" Salem reaches out to place a hand on my knee, and while words and my brain can lie to me, the lightning that travels through my entire body at that contact can't. "Hold on, let me get you some water." I watch him grab a bottle from their little dorm fridge, and when he heads back toward me, my savior with drink in hand, it hits me like a cannonball to the gut.

The Knight of fucking Cups.

I am so stupid.

I am so, so stupid.

I have to get out of here.

"Thanks for the talk," I babble, leaping off the bed, "but I'm good now. I'm gonna go to sleep. I'm sure I'll be just fine. I—"

"Evie." Salem looks down at the hand that was just on my knee, and back up at me in horror. "I wasn't trying to—"

"No!" I blurt. "I mean, I know. Of course I know. You're . . . I mean. I did *not* think that. Jenna! I mean, hi, I know about

Jenna. You guys are great. So cute. Well, not cute, because she's kind of a she-devil, but—"

"Evie." Salem stands and slowly approaches like he's trying to soothe a wild animal, and that's how I feel, caged by this room and the sight of that bed and the fact that I want to pull him down into it and kiss his stupid emo face. He's standing between me and the door, and I can't bring myself to go any nearer, to get a closer glimpse of that concern, of those shoulders, of the way his pants are hanging way too low . . .

The rope ladder! How could I forget? This is the one room at Rumson that comes with its own alternate exit. I run to the window and grab it, trying to toss it over, but it's heavier than it looks and not nearly as seamless a motion as when I've seen Matt do it. Stupid basketball biceps.

"Evie!" he whispers fiercely. "What are you doing? This is crazy."

This is crazy. Where have I heard that before? Oh, yeah, when I went down to Craig's basement to find him rolling around with my sister. Apparently, it was "crazy" to lose my temper at that, and "crazy" to throw his stupid video game controller at him. Crazy Evie, always overreacting.

And maybe this time I am, but I am just so *tired* of screwing things up. The way I hated Craig and Sierra in that moment is the way I hate myself now, for trying so hard to become someone else, and for what? To prove I could be as fun and spontaneous as my sister? To make myself desirable so I can keep falling for the wrong guys?

There will always be girls who are better people than I

am, like Heather. And there will always be girls who can beat me, who can have everything they want—everything *I* want—like Jenna. And there will always be girls like Sierra, who'll do anything to get their way, and mostly succeed.

But where in there do I fit? The girl who isn't nice enough or fierce enough or compelling enough or just simply *enough*—

"Evie! You have to—"

Or smart enough to secure a fucking rope ladder is my last thought before I hit the ground and everything goes black.

What follows is total chaos that, between pain, drugs, and exhaustion, passes in a blur. By the time I wake up in the infirmary, the sun is high in the sky, my ankle is on ice and elevated, and all at once, the previous night floods back in a humiliating rush.

"Oh, thank fuck you're up," Sabrina says on an exhale, jumping up to peer into my eyes. "Are you okay? Do you know who you are?"

"Jesus, Sabrina, yes, I'm fine, thank you. At least I think I'm fine. How long have I been out?"

"A while, but some of that was the doctors keeping you out to deal with your ankle. Turns out it's only a sprain, but they were worried it was dislocated." She points to the corner of the room, where a pair of silver crutches stand. "You'll have to be on those for a bit. Good thing you already have an accessible room, right?"

"How long have you been here?"

"Not that long—the doctors came in about ten minutes ago, which is the only reason I know anything. Salem had to get to class—he has a quiz—so he asked me to take over. No one gives a crap if I miss art."

"Salem was here?"

"Wow, you really have been out," she says with a tip of her head. "Salem's the one who found you. Said he heard a thump outside that woke him up, and realized you'd fallen out of your window. Which raises the obvious question: What the hell were you doing falling out of your window?"

I register a whole lot of things at once, most importantly that this is the story we're going with in order to keep Salem, me, *and* Matt out of trouble. And that's fine with me—the last thing I need is anyone knowing where I really was last night. But I guess this is an element of the story Salem couldn't make up for me, which means I have to come up with something believable, fast.

And it's Sabrina, who, against whatever odds, has become my best friend at this school other than Salem, so I give her the truth. Well, most of it anyway.

The parts that don't involve her brother and my realizing I've got a heinous crush on him, specifically.

When I'm done, Sabrina gives me a hug, and fills me in on this morning and the news spreading around campus. Apparently, some people think I was trying to off myself, which is just sad. Others think I was meeting someone outside, which is mostly funny, considering my access to tens of guys within my own dorm. To everyone, I'm pretty much that deranged klutz who fell out of her first-story window.

It's all not great.

The nurse comes in and gives me the rundown of my care, tells me I'll be staying there for the next twenty-four to forty-eight hours so I can be monitored for a concussion and stay off my ankle until my parents pick me up to bring me to a specialist. Honestly, hiding away for a day or two sounds so good, I think they might expect a protest from me, but they don't get one.

Then they tell me the dormmate who found me will be coming back later with my clothes, toothbrush, and whatever else I need.

Which means I have just a few hours to figure out how to talk to Salem again.

Sabrina leaves for her next class, telling me Heather plans to visit later, and I plaster a smile on my face as if that doesn't make me want to put all my weight on my ankle right now just to black out again. I don't have my phone or laptop or even a deck of cards, but I'm still plenty exhausted from last night, and woozy from what I assume are pain meds, so I let my eyelids flutter shut and hope I'll just sleep through Heather's visit.

When I wake up, Salem's sitting in Sabrina's seat.

"Hey," he says, so softly I don't even have a second to convince myself my feelings aren't real. "You feeling any better?"

"Depends." At the sound of my dry, raspy voice, Salem pours me a cup of water from the little plastic pitcher on the nightstand, and I take a sip before continuing. "Has 'the Klutzy Slut' caught on as a nickname for me yet?"

"It's still being workshopped."

"Oh, good." I struggle to sit up, and Salem reaches out to help me, then thinks better of it and lets me do it alone. "I guess you guys got the ladder back up in time."

"Yeah." I expect a snarky follow-up, but none comes. He just looks . . . drained. "Fuck, Evie," he mutters. "You fell out my *window*. I don't know what I did, but—"

"Nothing," I say quickly, and this time, I'm the one to grab his arm, even though I know I'll regret it. "You were really, really nice to listen to me last night. This is all me. Crazy Evie," I add through gritted teeth.

"You're not crazy."

"Yeah, well. Maybe I am. It wouldn't be a brand-new nickname, even."

He clicks his stubble-shaded jaw. "Ableism is shitty. And I'm guessing so's your sister. Or your ex. Or both."

"Both is good dot gif."

"Is it weird that I hate everyone in your life?"

I snort. "I hope not, because so do I." *Except you.* The thought spirals until a question occurs to me, and I hate myself for how much I'm about to sound like Lucas Burke, except that I'm going to keep it neutral—Salem's answer is up to Salem. "Did you tell Jenna what really happened?"

He laughs dryly. "I didn't have to. She broke up with me. Literally on my way here."

"*What*? God, Salem, I'm sorry." I mean, selfishly, I'm not remotely sorry, but Salem deserves better than to be unceremoniously dumped because he happens to have befriended a freak. "What happened? Is it real, or is this, like, a silly miscommunication that will resolve over dinner? Because if she thinks anything *untoward* was happening in your room last night—"

"She doesn't," he assures me. "She doesn't even know for sure that you were in my room, and she's mad anyway."

"What's she mad *about*?"

He shrugs. "She thinks I'm into you."

Oh, Jenna, you sweet summer child. "Aaaand did you correct her?"

"What's the point?" he asks, rolling his eyes. "It was gonna end soon anyway. I'm tired of being a secret fuck-buddy to someone I barely even like."

I hadn't realized how tightly wound every muscle and organ of my body was until I feel my chest loosen at that proclamation, and a laugh bursts from my throat. "Oh, thank God you just said that. The world finally makes sense to me again. I still have *so many questions*."

"Yeah, well, I have no great answers. I *do*, however, have your bag"—he pats the familiar backpack sitting on the floor next to him—"which has your phone, deck of cards, a book, and some clothes. Not gonna lie, it was fun choosing your underwear. I went with the heart print. It just said 'healing' to me."

"Have I mentioned how much I hate you?"

"Not in the last ten minutes, which feels like a new record," he says with a grin. "I gotta run again—they told me I can only stay for a couple of minutes, and then you need to eat lunch. I'll come back with some visitors tonight, see if we can't get a poker game going."

"Sounds perfect." We say our goodbyes, and the nurse

wheels in a tray of some kind of pasta and obviously canned vegetables. Somehow, I don't think the infirmary fare is the same stuff they're serving at the Beast, but the convenience of being able to eat in bed is pretty great.

I'm just finishing separating out the lima beans when my brain flashes back to Salem telling me that Jenna broke up with him. I still can't believe he let her dump him over something that isn't even true. Okay, so he wasn't exactly in love with her, but he must've been enjoying himself enough to stay with her until now, to sing that song to her. So why *did* he let her, instead of denying it? Why didn't he just say she was being ridiculous?

Unless . . . she wasn't?

"As if that's how things work out in my life," I mutter as I stab my spork into a noodle. "He told me exactly why he didn't tell her the truth, and it didn't leave a lot of room for interpretation." These pain drugs are good, but clearly, they inspire way too much wishful thinking.

Unless . . .

Oh, shut up, I tell myself, and I pull out the deck of cards and shut my brain off completely.

Chapter Sixteen

EVENING COMES AND GOES. I read Sabrina's and my GSA book, and text her all my thoughts. Heather does show up—we play spit, which keeps conversation to a minimum—and then she leaves for dinner. True to his word, Salem returns with Matt and Jason, and the four of us play poker until a nurse catches wind of what we're doing and kicks them out. Then it's just me and my thoughts again, and I pick up my phone to see if any more info about Sierra has been posted anywhere.

Still no, but Claire has a new set of pictures—displays of her work at the Greentree High Autumn Art Show. It's mixed media, but primarily beading, which is something she'd been working on forever. The art is incredible—vivid and textured and unlike anything I've ever seen. Half of them are landscapes: beaches using actual sand, sea glass, shells, and seaweed; a cityscape of stones and coins for windows, cotton clouds. The other half are portraits, using tiger's-eye and slivers of ebony and mahogany for her parents, her favorite cousin.

And then, at the end, a solitary work that doesn't fit in with the rest—a two of spades crafted of a combination of cards and photographs. Only when I zoom in do I realize each spade is actually two hands, joined in prayer. Or . . . apology, maybe.

My heart leaps into my throat and I don't allow myself a second thought before I leave a comment: *This is incredible, ClaireBear. You should be so proud.*

I look at it for a minute before deleting "Bear," then hit the button to post.

Her reply comes in the form of a text thirty seconds later. I wasn't sure you'd ever see it.

So she knew she was blocked. I wonder if she knew when she was unblocked. I'm glad I did, I write back.

The chat goes silent then, and I'm tempted to leave it. But my eye catches on that two of spades again, and I think about how hard Claire must have worked on it, how difficult it must've been to push herself to finish it without ever knowing if I'd even see it, let alone respond, especially when she had no way to tag me or text or call and tell me to look. It was a leap of faith, which has always been more Claire's specialty than mine—she'd certainly be in chapel every Sunday, same as she always went to church right after our Dunkin' trips—and maybe it's time I take one.

I open up my contact list—Claire no longer resides in Favorites—and make the call.

She answers immediately, and the way she says "Hey, Eves" makes me feel a little like I've just come home.

"Hey, ClaireBear." It just comes out. I've used that name so many times, I can't help it. "Long time."

"Yeah. Good to know you're still alive."

"Well, I'm in the infirmary after falling on my ankle, if that makes you feel better." Okay, this is not the path I wanna go down. *Think of the card. Think of the card.* "But your art really is amazing. And you . . . you look really happy since I left."

"I am," she says simply. "I mean, not *because* you left. I did want to apologize to you, but I couldn't exactly do that when you had me blocked everywhere. Our fight made me think about a lot of things, though, and stuff I wanted to change, and I started hanging out more with art kids and my cousins, and yeah, it's been good."

"So you didn't become BFFs with Sierra in my absence?" I can't help asking. "Because I kinda thought that's what you were going for."

There's a pause, and then, "This is probably a stupid question, but you heard about Sierra, right?"

"I did, from my parents. They didn't tell me much. Did you know anything about it?"

"Of course not," she says, and I believe it. "Craig might've. I don't know. But no, she and I were not friends, and I had no desire to be."

I think of the questions that've plagued me for the last couple of months, about Craig and Sierra and whether they ever became a real couple, how long they lasted. Claire would know the answers to all of it. She could tell me exactly how things went down. She could fill me in on everything I've missed in Greentree.

But now that I'm actually talking to her again, hearing about how she moved on, and knowing how I did, I don't know that I wanna go back there.

"He sucked" is all I say. "I'm sorry I didn't realize that sooner."

"I'm just glad to hear you say it now. I didn't think you'd listen to me if I'd told you, even about Sierra. It probably wasn't the right way to go about it, but I just thought . . . I thought if you found out yourself, then you wouldn't be able to deny it. And you wouldn't associate me with it. I hated keeping it a secret from you, and I'm sorry I did. I should've trusted that you'd listen to me."

"Yeah, I wish you would have," I say honestly, but I think about Heather, how I've been torn between telling her and keeping my mouth shut every single day since orientation. "But you're right—who knows? Maybe I would've continued being stupid and taken it out on you. Maybe I wouldn't have believed you, or maybe I would've even found some way to blame you; Lord knows I made some stupid calls where Craig was concerned. I think I get it, though, why you didn't want to tell me yourself. Some people are just really good at hiding being pieces of crap."

"Too true," Claire says with a snort. "And how's it going over there? You haven't posted anything. Have you found a new BFF? Did you find someone to take your mind off Craig?"

Now it's my turn to snort. "Craig helped me take my mind off Craig. And I've made some friends," I say cautiously. I'm dying to spill about Salem, about Lucas, about what a screwup I've been, but now that she's finally free of my drama—and clearly thriving because of that—I don't want to drag her back in.

But God, I'm gonna burst if I don't say something to someone, and there's no one safer I could tell. "There is a guy, sort of. He's kind of my best friend here, and I really did not look at him like that . . . until I did, and now I can't stop. Which is really bad, because he does not feel the same way."

"How do you know?"

"Well, he was hooking up with one of the hottest girls in school until like five minutes ago." I decide to leave out the part about why they broke up, because I don't need her reading into that. If it'd been true—if Jenna were right, and Salem wanted me—wouldn't he have told me on the spot? Wasn't that his opening?

"And? Sounds like he's single now. So did you tell him you like him?"

"What? God no. I mean, I don't even know if I do. He's obnoxious and annoying and he calls me Skeevy. It's just . . ."

"It's just . . ."

It's just . . . I think of how badly I've been wanting him to touch me. How my meals feel incomplete without the scent of his green apple. How he knew exactly what to put in the bag he brought here, because somewhere along the way, Salem Grayson became the person who knows me better than anyone else in the world.

How he looked when he opened the door last night, soft pants slung low on his hips.

How it felt to find that stupid underwear in his bed. How it felt to hear him sing that song to someone else.

How could he have sung like that to her if he feels the way about her that he says he does? A lot still does not compute, but for all I know, he's just covering up hurt he doesn't want to admit. And that is a confession I have no interest in extracting.

"Nothing. We're friends. He's my best friend here. I can't lose him." And I really cannot survive another heartbreak, especially if I don't have him to go to afterward.

"Okay, Evie, now that we've established that Craig sucked, I'd like to emphasize just how much he *sucked.* And I don't mean he sucked for cheating on you with Sierra; he obviously did. But he sucked the entire time. He never did shit for you. He forgot your last *birthday,* even." Oh, God, I'd completely forgotten about that in the wake of everything else. "And yes, I should've told you when I found out about them, but I also couldn't believe you just didn't *see it.*"

I don't know what to say to that, so I don't say anything. I feel stupid for all those wasted tears, all that wasted energy. The whole point of my pact with Salem is to become someone who's stronger than that, who understands the world better than that, who can see guys like Craig coming a mile away because I've seen bad behavior from the other side.

But all I'm seeing is me becoming a sucker for a guy, *again.*

"I wanted to talk to you about it," she continues, "but the

fight we had was . . . a lot. I wasn't ready to talk yet, and you weren't ready to talk yet, and then the days just got away and I spent the summer at my grandma's, and then you were gone. It feels like you disappeared really, really fast."

"Funny," I mutter, staring down at my stubby nails, "because it feels to me like I've been disappearing very, very slowly."

"Does this guy see you? Your hot friend?"

"I didn't say he was hot."

"He is, though, right? I mean, if you've got a thing for him."

I've been trying very, very hard not to think of him that way, not to think about his long fingers strumming the guitar, or the stormy gray eyes that crinkle so surprisingly when I get a rare smile, or the way his biceps ripple when he takes a shot. If I think too much about how badly I want to press my thumb into his slightly pouty lower lip, or curl into his long, lean body every time we're sitting on the same bed, I'm afraid I'll just . . . do it. "Some might say so" is all I'm willing to give.

"Uh-huh. So, does he? See you?"

I think back to the talent show, not the during but the after, when he came knocking on my door to make sure I was all right. To the very fact that he knew I wasn't. "He does."

"Good. You deserve a guy who does. That's all I'm saying."

"Noted. Thank you," I add softly. "And you? Anyone new in your life I should know about?"

There's a pause, and I jump on it immediately. "Oh my God, there *is*. Do I know him? Or her? Or them?"

"Them," she says shyly, and I can't help squealing into the

phone because I have *never* heard Claire express interest in anyone in the entirety of our friendship. "And you are *not* to make a big deal out of this."

"Are you kidding? I have talked your ear off about boys for years, and now *you* have a person, and I must know everything. Do they go to Greentree?"

"Their name is Lowen and they go to my art camp. We've been hanging out the last few weeks. They're, uh, also ace, which is nice."

"That is nice," I say, smiling into the phone as I settle back into the pillows. Guess Claire's figured out a lot in my absence, and it's not lost on me that she's actively choosing to share it with me now. "Maybe I'll get to meet them when I come home for Thanksgiving?"

"That'd be cool," she says. "I have to run—my mom's been calling me down to dinner for like five minutes already, but send me a picture of the guy. I'll tell you whether it's worth it."

"Deal. Talk soon?"

"Hell yeah."

We hang up, and I dig through my photos until I find one from my Bad Girl Day, a photo of Salem doing a model pose with his hand on his chin. At the time I thought it was funny in an absurd way, his silly photo shoot following mine, but now that I look at it closely, I . . . can't stop looking at it.

Crap.

I send it to Claire, and I'm not even surprised when the reply comes less than a minute later.

Claire
Oh my god?

My mom says to call him rtfn.

I sigh and bury my face in my pillow. I am so screwed.

After two days of being closely monitored for worsening concussion symptoms, I check out of the infirmary during lunch, painkillered and booted up with Salem at my side to carry my bag. It's so difficult to ignore the boyfriendy feelings I get from having him pick me up, tote my stuff, and give me his arm as necessary, but he's just joking around as always, even as he helps me pack. My brain keeps filling with words, but they won't leave my tongue.

My dad's coming to pick me up in an hour so my parents can bring me to an orthopedist for a second opinion and give me a day at home to get more used to my crutches before I have to start hobbling around campus. I'm praying the time apart will also function as a much-needed mental refresh so I can remind myself that Salem and I are strictly friends.

Now I just need to stop imagining Salem and Jenna getting back together while I'm gone.

Or another girl swooping in.

Or—

"Skeevy?"

I blink. "What?"

"I said, 'Do you need me to help you to the parking lot when your dad gets here?'"

"Oh." God, he's being so nice. I don't know what to do with a nice Salem. I don't even know what to do with the usual Salem. "Thanks, but Hoffman's bringing me. Probably dying to kiss my dad's ass so he won't get sued about this happening on his watch."

"Are your parents *planning* to sue?"

"Absolutely not, but Hoffman doesn't need to know that." I look up at Salem, standing in the doorway with one foot in the hall, and I realize he's probably gotta run to his next class. "You're in the clear," I tell him with all the smile I can muster. "Go on. I'll see you tomorrow."

He nods, and for a second, I swear I see a flash in his eyes of wanting to say something, but then I realize it's just my own reflection. "See you tomorrow." And then he's gone, and an hour later, so am I.

The car ride is chatty, because my dad is chatty, and we end up talking about everything from my uncle getting a root canal to the neighbors starting to put up Christmas decorations in October. He asks, again, about the food, and about the Rumson boys, and what friends I've made, and if I've broken any of my winning records at cards yet, and what classes I'm enjoying, and by the time we pull into the driveway of our small white colonial, he's whistling like things are totally normal and he didn't just pick me up from boarding school because I fell out a window.

Not once has Sierra's name come up.

It's strange how quickly a place you've called home can

feel so alien, but from the minute we enter through the familiar red front door, everything feels wrong. If you don't know that the Riley house is supposed to sound like blaring music and incessant telephone chatter and have the smell of three different perfume samples sprayed onto one little wrist, then maybe it seems normal. And if you haven't spent weeks getting used to being in a dorm with twenty-two boys who are always shouting, smell like BO, and constantly drip on the floors so that every walk down the hallways is an adventure, then maybe this could even seem like a lovely place to live.

But right now, it isn't my home, and it doesn't feel like the place I grew up in, and the silence is thick enough to choke on.

"Your room's just as you left it," Dad says quietly, as if trying to match the tone of the house. "Mom will be home in a couple of hours. You want something to eat?"

"No, thanks. I'm just gonna go lie down."

"Okay. You go do that and I'll bring you an ice pack."

He helps me get set up on the living room couch with a pile of pillows under my ankle and the ice pack bound to it, and then heads out to make a work call while I turn on the TV, hoping to drown out all the noise in my head. I keep glancing at my phone, even though everyone I know is in class right now, and contemplate telling Claire I'm here to see if she'll come over after school, but decide our makeup is still too new and tenuous to rush into that.

Instead, I watch old poker championships until I fall asleep.

When I wake up, it's to the buzzing of my phone under my arm. I wipe the puddle of drool off my face and the inside of my elbow and squint at the screen.

Salem
Have you managed to go the whole afternoon without further injuring yourself?

I can't help it; I can feel my lips tugging into a smile at the sight of his name.

Evie
No :(

I'm in a full body cast now, so be nice to me

Salem
I'm only like 69% sure you're joking

Evie
:) :) :)

Salem
Who types like that

Are you my mom

Evie

Well, actually, this is awkward, but

. . . yes

Yes I am

Salem

I'm done with you

Evie

Cool, send Archie to text me next

I miss him

Salem

brb going to make you regret that joke in 5

4

3

2

Evie

Salem jfc do not

. . .

Salem, what did you do

Salem

We're gonna fight this
together, Skeevy

He says the baby's not his,
but I told him you have
proof

Evie

Oh my god you better not be
doing this in public

Salem

What are you talking about

You specifically said to
make a scene at a school
assembly

God, it feels good to laugh. I take off the now-defrosted ice pack, try moving my ankle, immediately regret it, and rewrap the loosening Ace bandage.

Evie

Lose my number, Grayson

Salem
Too late

Went back to the mall

Chick with the blue hair tattooed
it on my thigh

I do not need to think about Salem Grayson's thighs. Or the way Salem looked at said chick with the blue hair at the Ink Spot.

My dad calls to me from the kitchen before I can think of a clever response, letting me know my mom's pulling into the driveway and he'll be putting dinner on the table in two minutes. Instinctively, I open my mouth to tell him I'll come help, then remember that I can't carry a damn thing. I use the two minutes to maneuver my way to the table on crutches instead.

"You do not make those look very comfortable, kiddo," he says with a sympathetic smile as he puts a pitcher of water on the table, then returns to the cabinets for three glasses. I half expect him to grab four out of habit, the way I probably would, then remember he's had two months now to get used to having only three people at dinner. And lately, it hasn't even been that.

The urge to apologize for leaving is strong, and the words are on the tip of my tongue when the door opens and my mom swoops in, planting a quick kiss on my dad before giving me one of her lukewarm hugs. "It's good to see you, sweetie," she says, holding me at arm's length as she sizes up my whole crutch situation. "I hope it doesn't hurt too bad."

"It's okay." Which is true, because they gave me painkillers at the infirmary just before I left. "Mostly, I'm hoping the doctor will tell me tomorrow that I don't have to stay on these crutches. I suck at using them."

She sets her bag down on the counter and puts her keys in the tray by the door—moves I could choreograph in my sleep, even after months away. "How have you been getting around campus?"

"A friend helped me out." I feel a little warmth rise in my cheeks at the thought of wrapping myself around Salem, or vice versa, and hope it doesn't show on my face.

"I'm so glad you're making friends." My parents are a well-oiled machine, bending around each other at just the right angles for salad, lasagna, grated parmesan from its same-old spot in the fridge. I don't need anything more than the fact that the clear plastic cylinder is still nearly full to remind me that Sierra isn't here; she could eat a leather shoe if you put enough cheese on it. "Did you tell Claire you were coming home? Or are you two still having trouble?"

"We're okay now, Mom," I say as we take our seats and start passing things around. "But no, I didn't mention coming home. I don't really feel like seeing anyone when I'm like this. Maybe over Thanksgiving."

"That'd be nice." She fills three-quarters of her plate with salad, then hands me the bowl. It's kale, which I don't think I've ever seen at the Beast, and haven't been missing. But my mom thinks the dark leafy green is God's gift; she consumes it almost as frequently as Salem eats green apples.

I take a little bit, just to show I'm making an effort.

My mom asks the same questions my dad already did, and I give the same answers. Finally, she broaches the one subject my dad didn't. "Have you spoken to your sister at all?"

She has to know that I haven't. Do they even allow you to keep your phone at rehab? But I just say "Nope" and push the kale around my plate, hoping that'll be the end of it.

"I think she'd really like to hear from you."

"*I* think she has enough on her plate already." I let the tine of my fork scratch the dish, just enough to get a little screech out of the contact.

"Evie—"

Jesus. "No, Mom. Please, just stop." I drop the fork onto the plate and meet her eyes with mine. They look tired, and sad, but even as it hurts my heart to look at her, I know I positively cannot do this. "You said if I left, I'd miss her. Let me tell you something—I don't, okay? I don't miss her, and I don't want to talk to her, and I am *loving* finally having my own life that doesn't have her in it. So stop trying to shove things back where they don't belong."

"Everett, don't talk to your mother that way."

Oh good, now they're both mad. Well, turns out, so am I. And I may have been a sweet, doting daughter the last time I was home, but I'm the Rumson Girl now. "Then how exactly would you like me to get this message across, Dad? Because apparently begging to go to *boarding* school didn't do it. Straight-up telling you both that I don't want to talk to her isn't cutting it. So how about I tell you this: she slept with her own sister's boyfriend." The sharp inhale of my mother's breath is only mildly satisfying. "And, by the way, she's never once said she's sorry. So if you can't understand *me*, I hope you can understand that. Thank you for dinner, but I'm gonna go ice my ankle again."

There's no fight as I stand up and crutch-hop away.

After dropping that, it's a little awkward to then ask my parents for help, and they've locked themselves away in their room for a conversation I'm clearly not meant to hear and don't particularly want to, anyway. It's too hard to handle making my own ice pack while I wait for the one I used before dinner to refreeze, so I settle for elevating my foot on my bed while I finish my GSA reading and glance at my phone every five minutes, willing it to light up.

I really, really hate missing Salem Grayson.

You don't miss *him*, I chastise myself, tossing the book onto my nightstand and collapsing back into my pillow. *You've gotten used to him helping you. And you had an unfortunately timed shirtless run-in that's scrambling your brain a little. That's* it.

Well, and the guitar playing. And singing. And returning your stolen goods for you. And buying you candy cigarettes.

Ugh, where did *those* even come from?

And offering to walk you into class when Duncan was giving you shit. And being such a good brother that he got himself kicked out of school just to buy his sister some space to breathe. And taking incredible care of you when you got injured. And—

"Oh my God, shut *up*!" I yell at my own brain.

"Evie!"

My eyes snap open and I'm horrified to realize that my mom is standing in the doorway, looking completely stricken. "Oh, God, Mom—that was *not* at you, I promise. One hundred percent talking to myself. Didn't even realize you were there."

She nods and walks over, ice pack in hand, and sits on the edge of the bed, wrapping it around my ankle. "Sounds like you might need to be kinder to yourself, then, too."

"Trust me," I mutter, staring up at the ceiling, "my brain deserves it. It's being very, very stupid."

"You, Evie, are a lot of things, but stupid is not one of them." She reaches over to stroke my hair, and my eyes instinctively flutter shut. It's exactly the touch I've been craving, and it isn't something she does often. My hair does not look inherently strokeable, and my mom isn't particularly physically affectionate, at least not with me. "You've been having a hard time, haven't you."

I inhale a deep, shaky breath, willing myself not to cry as I nod.

She presses a kiss to the top of my head. "Do you want to talk about it?"

"Just a hug, please," I mumble into her shoulder, and as she wraps her arms around me, I let myself melt into her until I can finally breathe.

Chapter Seventeen

EVENTUALLY, I FILL HER IN on the basics, ignoring the smile playing on her lips when I tell her that I might like a boy. As if on cue, my phone buzzes with a message from Claire, begging me to send her an update on The Guy, and my mom leaves so I can chat with her. Much as I hadn't wanted anyone to see me like this, as soon as I tell her that I'm home for an appointment and she asks if she can come over, I say yes without any hesitation.

I have really, really missed my best friend.

It seems she missed me too, because twenty minutes later, we're chatting on my bed like nothing has changed. "Wait." I curl my fists in the blanket to stop myself from flailing. "Lowen told you they like you on a *Post-it Note*?"

"It was cuter than it sounds!" she insists, whacking me with a pillow. "It was very sweet and very brave and you do not get to mock *anyone*, considering you have not told Salem in any way at all."

"That's different," I grumble. "And we are not talking about it. So tell me what else I've missed."

"Well, you can probably guess the biggest news around school . . ."

"Tell me what I missed that *doesn't* have anything to do with my sister. Or Craig. I don't need to know a thing about what he's up to."

"Good. Trust me—that boy remains trash." Claire takes a drink of water from the purple Nalgene she carries everywhere. "But Oscar and Vivien broke up, and then got back together, and then broke up again when she found out he hooked up with Kaya while they were broken up. Oh, and Mrs. Taber got knocked up again. She's leaving at the end of the semester."

"Remember last time, when she said she wasn't coming back?"

"Pretty sure she means it this time," she says with a grin. "Oh, and my cousin Angi got engaged."

"Angi of the sublime mac 'n' cheese?"

Claire throws back her head and laughs, and I wish I could bottle up the sound and take it to Camden with me. "She will *love* that that's how you know her, oh my Lord. Anyway, that's about it. You already saw all the art from my show, and I have another one coming up in the spring. Otherwise, you haven't missed much. Frankly, your life at boarding school sounds way more interesting. Or it *would* if you'd tell the boy how you feel."

"How I *maybe* feel," I amend stiffly, because part of me is clinging to the idea that this is some sort of temporary brain blip, confusion born of a combo of his surprising talent and even more surprising caretaking.

Judging by the roll of her big brown eyes, Claire's not buying it. "Do you miss him?"

Shockingly badly. "People miss their friends," I say defensively. "Hell, I missed *you.* A lot."

She takes one of my hands, squeezes it. "I missed you too, Eves. Let's not do this again."

"My doctor's appointment isn't until one, so I'll still be here tomorrow afternoon. Dunkin' run after school?"

"It's a date." She leans over to give me a hug, every bit as warm as I remember. "I should get home, but just FYI, I'm *going* to need an update when you talk to that boy, and I'll point out that if you're nervous about talking to him face-to-face, I'm pretty sure you've got his number in your phone."

"Or I could just leave him a message on a Post-it."

"Shut *up.*" She whacks me with a pillow again as I crack up, and I don't mind it at all.

Claire's comment about calling Salem is still ringing in my head an hour and two episodes of cheesy TV later. Avoiding having to look at him when I say something *is* tempting, but avoiding the issue entirely sounds even better.

Then again, what if I avoid it so hard that Salem sails right into someone new? I hadn't seen him and Jenna coming;

what if someone else slips in? The thought is enough to make me grab my phone without even realizing I'm doing it until my fingers curl around the rubber case.

Am I really gonna do this? What do I even say? I'm tempted to put my phone back down, but then I think about how Claire will be asking for updates, how Lowen found a way to ask her out even though they were clearly nervous about it, and how I want to be able to tell her I got brave too. Without giving it another thought, I dial his number.

He answers way more quickly than I'm ready for. "Skeevy? Is everything okay? Did you die?"

Ugh, I really did miss his stupid voice. "I hope not. It'd be such a waste of a good hair day."

"Skeevy. Are you *really* having a good hair day?"

I yank out a curl and let it bounce back. "Can you not just let me have this, please?"

"Never."

Never. That one word seems to inflate like a balloon until it's taking up all the space in my brain. Is it playful? Cruel? A harbinger of romantic doom? A hint that he knows why I'm calling and he wants to cut me off at the pass before I embarrass myself?

Or, you know, is it just the logical next word in our conversation? Who can say, really??

"Skeeves? You there?"

"Whoops, sorry! Yes, I'm here."

"So what's up?"

Oh, right, I called him. I have to actually say something.

This is so much worse than talking face-to-face somehow. There is no chance on earth I am doing this right now. Is it too late to pass this off as a butt dial?

"Um, nothing. I just . . ." Just *what*? How do I possibly finish that sentence? "Wanted to make sure you hadn't burned Rumson down in my absence." God, that was pathetic.

"Can promise I have not burned the dorm down. Can *not* promise I haven't been using your private bathroom."

"Salem!"

"Your shower is so much bigger than ours!"

Cool, cool, Salem's been naked in my room. That's fine. I am definitely not picturing it. *Definitely* not thinking about how he looks without a shirt on, now that I possess that information. "Don't get used to it," I manage to choke out. "I'll be back tomorrow night."

"Got it. Morning shower it is."

I am simply going to die on the spot. "I better return to a *spotless* bathroom, Grayson."

"You know you didn't leave a spotless bathroom behind, right? Your hair shit is everywhere."

"Because it's *my* bathroom! But feel free to make yourself useful and neaten it up."

He snorts. "You haven't made me *that* good, Peach."

My teeth find my lip and bite so hard I nearly draw blood. I have to get off this phone call. Now. "I gotta go ice my ankle. I'll see you tomorrow, okay?"

"Try not break anything else before you get here. But if you do, I totally claim your room."

"Oh, screw you." I hang up over the sound of his laughter and fall back onto my pillow.

Yeah, I don't think romance is in the cards for us.

The visit to the orthopedist the next day thankfully goes well, with the X-ray confirming there's no break and the doctor graduating me from crutches to a boot. It's still clunky and makes for uneven walking, but at least my armpits aren't sore anymore. I celebrate with a Dunkin' run with Claire after school, and then my parents drive me back up that night when they get home from work, the sun having long faded behind the fiery golden leaves lining the highway.

We're already past dinnertime at the Beast, so we make a stop at a roadside diner about halfway to school and I get a BLT with a mountain of delicious greasy fries. Then we get back on the road, and as we pull into campus, I realize that my parents have never actually seen the school. "I wish I could give you a tour," I say as they park in the lot nearest Rumson. "But between the boot and the dark—"

"We'll find another time to come see everything, honey," my mom assures me, reaching back to squeeze my hand. "I'm sorry we had to miss Parents' Weekend. We really wanted to be here."

Talking about Parents' Weekend feels like a minefield, so I just give a brief smile and then together, we get me and my things into my room. I point out as many buildings as I can along the way, but I can see they're eager to get back home, so I let them go with hugs goodbye and collapse onto my bed, pulling out my phone.

There are about fifty messages from Claire, begging for updates. In the middle of them is a photo of her and Lowen, both of them cheesing for the camera with their cheeks pressed together. Lowen is extremely cute—their curly brown hair frames a face with dimples big enough for their own zip code—and beneath them, Claire has texted You can have this too!

With your own person, she added underneath, making me snort.

Even in the best-case scenario, I don't think I'll be getting Salem to smile hugely for any cameras, but it does look nice. Stop bullying me, I text Claire back. I just got back.

She replies with laugh-cry emojis, followed by some big eyes, and I groan and tuck my phone under my pillows, then rest my head atop them and close my eyes.

A minute later, I hear footsteps through the ceiling.

He's there. One floor above me. All I have to do is drag this stupid boot up one flight of stairs.

I can't.

I try to go to my happy place, reflecting on some of my best poker hands, but once again, Claire gets in my head. *Why are you so good at gambling when it comes to everything but your own happiness?*

Fuck it. I've worked too hard at becoming a badass to stop going for what I want now.

Embracing my newfound courage for as long as it lasts, I retrieve my phone and tap out a new message.

Evie

In the interest of honesty, I need to admit something.

I am kind of head-over-ass for your brother.

And I'm going to tell him.

I'm sorry.

Please don't hate me.

Then I toss my phone to the side, take a deep breath, and hobble upstairs.

My heart is pounding so heavily that I can't even hear the sound of my fist knocking on Salem's door. For all I know, it's silent. Except then, the door opens, and Salem is standing there, and my first thought on seeing him and the flannel pants hanging off his hips and his mess of midnight hair is *I cannot believe I ever thought there was anything about this boy that needed fixing.*

"Evie, hey, you're back. And booted! That seems promising." When I don't respond, don't—can't—even smile, his face grows serious. "Everything okay?"

I shake my head, and he steps aside to let me in, then closes the door behind me. My eyes sweep the room, not just looking to confirm Matt's out (he is) but to drink it all in. So many of my memories of this first semester at Camden are wrapped up in this room, and if this all goes to hell and I'm not welcome back here, I want to at least know that my last time is my last time.

"You're kinda freaking me out," he says as he sits in his desk chair, rolling back and forth across the linoleum. "Are you leaving? Don't tell me you're leaving."

It's something to cling to, so I do, wrapping myself in it as I take a seat on his bed so I can elevate my ankle. In an ideal world, I'd have a quicker escape route if I need it, but nothing about this is ideal. "Would you be upset if I was?"

He furrows those dark brows. "Is that a trick question? We've been over this. I know I'm an asshole, but yes, Evie, if you need to hear me say it, we *are* friends. Happy now?"

"Even though I ruined your relationship with Jenna?"

"*You* didn't ruin my relationship with Jenna, if you can even call it that," he says with a roll of his eyes. "Nothing about that was your fault."

"Well, it's my fault if she was picking up . . . feelings." I take a deep breath, steeling all my nerves. "Because I think I have them. For you, I mean. And I don't just think; I don't know why I said that." I shake my head, trying to get out a little of the panic. "I'm a mess, I know, and this is probably not the kind of thing you want to hear from me, but I feel like I *miss* you and maybe I've been missing you a little bit ever since you took your arm off my shoulders at the movie that first Friday, like I've just been waiting for you to put it back. And instead you went to Jenna, and I get it—*obviously* I get it, she's *Jenna*, and I'm me, and clearly she realized this before I did, but—"

"Evie." He braces his hands on his thighs, those long fingers fidgeting against the soft fabric. "Stop. Breathe. And hear me when I tell you that Jenna picking up vibes isn't your fault either."

"What do you mean?"

I've been avoiding direct eye contact, but his gaze locks on mine, as stormy and serious as I've ever seen it, and I can't look away. "I know how to do my own damn laundry."

I snort at the weird turn this conversation is taking. "I should hope so, after I spent an entire evening—"

"No." The slightest of smiles creeps onto his lips, twisting something inside of me. "I *know* how to do my own damn laundry. You really *should* do whites separately, by the way. And unlike you, I even know how to use fabric softener."

"Now you're just bragging," I say, trying to keep my voice light so it doesn't shake like the rest of my body is trying to.

"No, I'm bragging and I'm telling you that the reason I didn't 'correct' Jenna is because she was right," he says as he rolls up to the bed, "and it would've been a dick move to pretend she wasn't when everyone knows it except you."

"Everyone knows . . ." My face flushes with warmth as my brain finally catches up and registers what I think he's saying. What I hope he's saying. What I really, really need to make sure he's saying. "Words, Grayson. I need words."

"Do you, though?" And then the warmth is everywhere as he slides onto the bed and slips one of those rough, callused hands into my hair, pulling my mouth to his. The kiss is soft, tentative enough to let me pull away, but I kiss him back without hesitation and it quickly turns hungry. Fevered.

Electric.

And I know that this time, I finally got the person right.

At that thought, I yank myself away, because I can't start something here without putting everything else behind me.

"I'm sorry," I tell him as I catch my breath. "I . . . really, really want to keep doing that—like, wow, a *lot*—but I need to tell you something. I said honesty was important to me, and you deserve it too, even if it's going to make you think a little less of me."

He rubs his bottom lip with his thumb, as if he's still feeling a little tingle there. Lord knows I am. "If you're the one who drew that picture of Hoffman on the bathroom wall, for the record, I support that a thousand percent. It was hilarious."

"I thought *you* did that."

"Oh, yeah, I did do that."

"Salem."

He flutters his eyelashes innocently, and God, I am so mad at how attractive I find him. People should *not* be able to creep up on you like that. But there's no question—Salem and his rock-star hair and angular jaw and stormy eyes are stupid hot. Which, considering he landed Jenna London, seems like another thing everyone knew before I did. "Peach, whatever it is, it's going to be fine."

"Maybe, maybe not." Another deep breath. Another silent prayer for courage. Maybe I should be going to chapel on the weekends after all. "I made out with Lucas."

"Oh." He scratches the back of his neck and looks up at me. "Wait, Lucas Burke? I thought Sabrina told me he's been with Heather since the school year began."

I look away, and get another, quieter, more heartbreaking "Oh." He takes a deep breath and shifts a few inches away from me on the bed; it feels like miles. "That . . . doesn't really seem like you."

"It isn't," I say quickly. "I mean, I didn't know he was with Heather—it was literally my first *day*. But he'd seemed sweet, and interested, and after everything with my ex and my sister, I just . . . wanted to be with someone who chose me, I guess? And of course, even he'd chosen someone else first. So much for being a nice guy."

"You know he's the kind of guy who tells everyone what a nice guy he is and is an actual, certifiable douchebag, right? Everyone on the team hates him."

"Well obviously I know he's a dick *now*." I swipe a tear off my face, and another one quickly appears in its place. "Anyway, there you have it—I'm a bad girl after all. Sooo proud."

"Hey." He lifts my chin, wipes the new tear gently with his thumb before tugging on a curl. "You are like goodness incarnate, Evie Riley. You are a fucking literal ball of sunshine. I was dreading everything about this year, thinking how incredibly fucking stupid I was getting myself sent to *boarding* school, and then you rolled into that orientation you shouldn't have been at and made me *laugh*. Do you know how many people here make me laugh?"

I open my mouth to answer, and he adds, "Intentionally?"

"Oh. Probably not a lot."

"No," he says, sweeping my hair behind my ear, "not a lot. And then you just kept on finding new ways to be such a cute fucking weirdo, and I fell so damn hard for it. Hell, I'm still falling. You are magic to me, Peach, and the best person I know."

"Most of the people you know are terrible," I say with a sniffle.

"I didn't say it was a high bar." His hand lingers on my skin, so warm and gentle as he swipes away another tear. "But even if you'd known about Heather, there's a difference between doing something shitty and being someone shitty." He cracks a grin. "Kind of like doing something slutty and being someone slutty. And if I recall correctly, you're the one who ripped me a new one over not getting that."

I know it's supposed to make me laugh, but all I can do is look up at him in wonder and, if I'm being honest, a little confusion. "That's it? You're just . . . cool with it?"

He shrugs. "I mean, unless you're still into him?"

"Oh, hell no," I say with such certainty that Salem laughs, and I take his hands and squeeze them. "No, no, no. I am very firmly in the Salem Grayson cheering section. But if you've had feelings for a while, why didn't you say something?"

"Do you not remember how firmly you said that you had no interest in being with any guys when we established that ridiculous pact? Because you were pretty damn clear. And then Jenna came by and flirted with me, and I guess I just . . . also wanted to be with someone who wanted me back. She clearly wasn't taking it seriously, and I figured it'd help me get over you, but."

"My charm was too much to resist?"

"Something like that." He wraps his arms around me and pulls me onto his lap, and he feels so warm and so good, more solid than you'd think considering his skin-and-bones build. "I wasn't a hundred percent honest about what Jenna said when she ended it."

"She didn't say she thought you were into me?"

"Oh, she did," he says with a wry smile, "but she didn't care about that; she's always figured. It was everyone *else* knowing it that was where she drew the line. Somehow she figured out a song about having patience and being in it for the long haul was . . . not about me and her, and she did not appreciate my singing it publicly."

Now it's my turn to say "Oh."

That song. That gorgeous song. *Our* song. Hot damn.

"Yeah. It didn't exactly make me feel optimistic when you ran out after hearing it," he says with a low laugh. "And I knew I was an asshole for singing it. I hadn't planned to. But then you did that ridiculous card-trick show and you were just so . . . I had to."

"Of all things to trigger it." I bury my face in his shoulder, smothering my laugh in the flannel. "That stupid talent show. God. I heard you singing that song, and I thought it was for Jenna, and it also reminded me of Craig and Sierra, and Lucas, and I couldn't stand it. That's why I ran out. But for what it's worth"—I look up, meeting his affectionate gaze with mine—"it was extremely hot."

"Was it now?"

"It really, really was. Like, irritatingly hot. Taking the rock-star cliché just a little too far. Ten out of ten would throw my bra onstage."

That low laugh again, warm against my ear, tingling down

to my toes. "Would also accept that lace thing you bought at the mall. I am a big fan of that lace thing. That lace thing is at least sixty-nine percent responsible for my poor decision-making at the talent show."

"Noted," I say with a wicked little grin that has him biting the corner of his mouth. "So now you know everything." I rest my chin on his shoulder. "You still wanna be with me? This is your last call to bail. After this, you're required by law to be on my side for everything."

"That's the dating law, huh?"

"I mean, I only have an incredibly awful dating history, but I'm pretty sure that's how it works."

"Okay then."

"Okay?" I look up at him, imagining hope shining in my eyes making me look like a Disney character.

His lips curve into a smile. "Okay. I'm on your side for everything, Peach."

"You're really sticking with 'Peach'?"

"Feels like one should probably not call the girl he's kissing 'Skeevy,' but I can go back to that if—"

"Don't you fucking dare." Truthfully, "Peach" has kinda grown on me.

And then another thought hits, and I drop my gaze down to my hands. "I really, really hate that you're not my first kiss here."

He lifts one of those hands and gently bites my thumb. "You weren't mine either—who cares? I'm pretty sure the point of being in a relationship is for someone to be your last, not your first."

Just like that, I feel the last of the bricks weighing my shoulders down fall away, and I settle into the warm flannel feel of him, curling into his arms exactly as I've been dying to do for days. "You know, for someone who floated into Camden on a cloud of pot smoke, you are oddly profound, Sammy."

He snakes an arm around my waist and turns me, quick as lightning, so that our lips are mere inches apart. "For fuck's sake, please just call me Salem," he mutters before kissing me into oblivion.

Chapter Eighteen

I WAKE UP THE NEXT MORNING with my lips feeling bruised and my brain feeling dangerously full of happiness and excitement in a way I haven't felt in . . . ever, maybe? Which of course means I immediately assume it was all either a dream or a mistake, and any minute now Salem's going to wake up and tell me the latter.

But when my phone does light up with a text from him, all it says is Beast in 5?

Despite the fact that Salem and I do eat many of our meals together, we've never, ever planned it, which does seem to confirm the possibility that last night was real and there will be more kissing in our future. I text back a quick confirmation, and then look at the other text that'd been waiting for me this morning.

Sabrina

fucking finally

My smile at that is so huge, it's somehow embarrassing me even with no one in the room to see it. But I don't have time to dwell on my relief at getting Sabrina's blessing, so I run to brush my teeth and throw on clothes.

And in five—okay, seven, because punctuality still isn't Salem's strong suit—minutes, when a knock sounds at the door and I swing it open, the smile that spreads slowly over Salem's extremely kissable mouth when he says "Hi" would suggest that last night was very, very real indeed.

"Hi," I say back, feeling inexplicably shy. This is *Salem*, and yet I suddenly have no idea what to do in his presence. Can I kiss him? Can I take his hand? Do we have to keep us a secret because of Jenna or just my generally being an embarrassing human?

He leans against the doorway, his long, lean body filling the frame and making it even harder to think. "Having second thoughts?" he asks, his lips still twitching with a smile that suggests he does not actually think that's what's going through my brain.

"Just . . . trying to figure out what to do here."

His smile widens with a mocking lilt, and apparently, having feelings for somebody doesn't mean you give them a break, ever. "What is it you want to do here?"

"Salem, stop being annoying. You know what I mean."

"Are we having a 'how do we label this' conversation already?"

Great, another concern to add to the pile. "Well, we *weren't*, but—"

"Evie." Finally, Salem cuts me some slack, grabbing my bag from where it sits at my feet and slinging it over his shoulder, then pulling me out of the room with his other hand. "Shut your brain off for five seconds and let's go get breakfast."

I nod and close the door behind me, waiting for him to give me my bag or let go of my hand.

He does neither.

"You're my boyfriend, aren't you," I say with wonder as he pushes through the exit onto campus.

"That's kinda the position I've been angling for, yeah," he says without missing a beat. His thumb softly strokes the inside of my palm, sending jolts of lightning throughout my entire body, and it's so unfathomable to me that it can be like this, feel like this.

Why did I ever give a shit about Craig or Lucas when they were never, ever capable of making me feel anything like this?

"You okay?" Salem asks, and I realize I've stopped walking, and now, so has he.

I rise up on my uninjured toes—he is really damn tall—and throw my arms around his neck, kissing him with every ounce of strength in my body, despite the fact that we are very much in public. I don't care. I can't wait. And judging by the way an arm circles my waist, holding me close as he kisses me back, his corded leather bracelets pressing into my skin as if to leave no doubt as to whose arm it is, he doesn't mind one bit. Not even when people start whistling and catcalling.

"Wow, okay," he says, a little dazed, when we finally part and I retake his hand, swinging it as we walk toward the Beast. "So that's a yes on the whole boyfriend thing, then?"

"Were *you* looking for a 'how do we label this' conversation?" I ask in disbelief.

"In my defense," he starts, and I love that his vampiric skin can't hide the hint of heat creeping into it, "my parents have been bugging me about you every single day. I just wanted to know what I was supposed to tell them."

"Tell them the wedding's still on, and I'm ready to call them Mom and Dad as soon as they are. Which I guess was probably last week."

"Now *I'm* having second thoughts."

"No, you're not," I say, and it feels so good to trust it. Well, mostly trust it—it's not like I've shed *all* my baggage.

"No, I'm not." He pulls me close and kisses the top of my head, and I float the rest of the way to breakfast.

Of course, the bliss lasts only a few minutes, and then, as I'm standing in line for waffles while Salem heads to the fruit table for his apple, I bump into the most smug, annoying smile on the entire campus. "All those guys in Rumson and you choose to fuck Grayson?"

Ugh, Duncan. Of course he would find a way into my space when I'm just trying to enjoy my waffles. I whirl around and meet his mocking gaze with my own. "All those guys in Rumson and you choose the role of Archie's bootlicker? It doesn't seem like you're in any position to dole out relationship advice."

His face turns a satisfying shade of red at that, but whatever nasty reply was hovering on his lips dies the very instant a solid arm wraps around my shoulders. "Hey, Peach." Salem takes a big bite of green apple and chews loudly. "Did you know that Duncan here's nickname at his old school was Crustysox? I guess *he* didn't know how to do his own laundry. Still, such a strange choice of moniker . . ."

I barely smother a laugh behind my hand as Duncan's flush gets even more fierce. "You two are so fucking annoying," he mutters as he moves on.

"Key word: fucking!" I call after him, relishing the look of disgust I get in response.

Salem looks down at me, a smile playing on his lips. "Did you just lie about us having sex in order to look cool? You *are* a Rumson guy."

"Oh, shut up." I dig an elbow into his side, and he laughs. "He started it."

"Hey, I'm not complaining. I like where your mind's at."

I roll my eyes, but kiss him anyway. I've already told him I'm not ready to move at the speed he did with Jenna—and unlike Lucas, he was perfectly cool with it—but that doesn't mean I'm not thinking about it. Constantly. Which he does not need to know. Yet.

"I'm gonna get us seats," he says as my turn comes up on the waffle line, giving my fingers a quick brush with his. I allow myself a few seconds to watch his butt as he goes, then treat myself to a perfect golden waffle I fully intend to bury in whipped cream and berries. I get my bliss back for all of one minute before yet another boy swoops in to ruin it with the worst four-word sentence in the English language.

"We need to talk."

Salem's been gone for two seconds, and already I'm regretting letting him leave my side. "What could I possibly have to say to you, Lucas?" God, there really *are* trash boys everywhere you look, but I guess I'm evolving because I sure can pick 'em out now.

"Can we please talk somewhere else?" He touches my arm as he asks, and I instinctively pull it away. It's amazing how quickly you can go from dying for someone to kiss you to finding their touch utterly repulsive.

"No, right here's good, if you *must* say something." The line moves down, and I grab the whipped cream and spray on thick spirals. "Though if this is about Heather, no, I haven't said a word."

"It's not about Heather," he says through gritted teeth, even though I haven't seen her in the room. "It's—did you do it because of me?"

I move on down the table toward the berries and pour on a pile. "Do *what* because of you?"

"The window." He gestures down at my ankle, still wrapped in an Ace bandage and surrounded by a boot. "Did you throw yourself out of a window because of me?"

I blink. "Are you for real?"

"Can you just answer the question?"

I glance past him at my table, where Salem's doing something on his phone, paying no attention to me and Lucas. He's got a green apple in hand, and his hair hanging in his eyes, and all I want to do is brush it back into place. Truly, I do not have time for a minute more of Lucas Burke's bullshit.

"I didn't throw myself out of a window, period," I snap, keeping my voice low, "but even if I had, rest assured that your being a lying, cheating asshole would not be the reason. You're someone else's problem now, much as I think she deserves way, way better than you."

If my venomous response has fazed him at all, it doesn't show. "You better not say a word to her."

I roll my eyes. "I didn't, and I won't, because I'm not interested in hurting her, and you're the person she should find out from. Personally, I think Heather deserves better than being lied to. I *did* tell *my* boyfriend." God, that feels good. "But you do you, as long as you do it far the fuck away from me."

His eyes are burning a hole in my back as I make my way toward Salem, but he doesn't stop me, and I don't turn around. I can't prevent him from being in my English class or dating my friend, and I'll have to see him around far more than I'd like (read: ever), but he's taken all he's going to get from me, and he doesn't get another minute.

Bad Apple Evie is racking up a whole lotta points this morning.

Salem looks up as I put my tray down, and he gestures to where his phone lies on the table. "You didn't get my text, I take it."

"Like, just now? No." I pull out my phone, and sure enough, there's a message from Salem.

Want me to kill him and make it
look like an accident?

I bite my lip to stop an embarrassing smile from spreading over my face as Salem takes another bite of his apple, the juice spraying onto my cheek. He wipes it off gently with his thumb, and I send my own reply text:

Wanna cut English and make out?

He laughs as his phone buzzes with the message, and we text-flirt through the rest of breakfast. When we do head out to English—a far inferior choice to my plan, but whatever—I see Lucas taking stock of us from across the room, registering exactly who my boyfriend is, a.k.a. the only other person on campus who knows his secret.

I should probably warn Salem before they face each other on the court tomorrow night.

Although, who am I kidding—Salem could wipe the floor with him.

And I'll be there to cheer him on when he does it.

Word must travel fast, because Isabel catches up with me on my way back to Rumson from Baking Club, helps herself to one of the raspberry scones in the box I'm transporting, and says, "So, you finally pulled your head out of your ass. Congratulations."

"Excuse me?"

"Oh, don't get me wrong—I'm glad you held out so long; you made me fifty bucks. Matty thought for sure you'd hook up within twenty-four hours of the talent show, but I said, 'No, I know my girl Evie—she is absolutely going to find some way to bungle this.' And look! I was right!"

I stop in my tracks and turn to her, watching her take a delicate bite of a scone I just pulled out of the oven fifteen minutes ago. "He wasn't even single that night! Wouldn't I have been an asshole for kissing your best friend's boyfriend?"

"Please, that was a technicality. The only reason she didn't dump his ass on the spot was because we were in public."

"Okay, well, technicality or not, I don't fool around with other people's boyfriends." At least not on purpose. "Have been on the receiving end. Am not a fan."

"Such a good girl, Everett. Matt's not right about a lot, but he was right about that."

"I don't know about that," I say as we resume walking, although I have no intention of elaborating. "But why were you and Matt even talking about me?"

"Well, he had to convince me that we should tell you about Salem and Jenna hooking up. He said you deserved to know, that it would take forever for you to figure out you had feelings for him otherwise. He can be very persuasive when he feels like it."

"Matt said *what*?" I shake my head. "And you *didn't* tell

me about Salem and Jenna," I point out, breaking the edge off another scone.

Isabel rolls her big green eyes. "Does Jenna really strike you as the type to leave her underwear behind, Evie? Or have you considered that maybe, just maybe, someone put them there for you to find."

Someone put them . . . "How could you possibly know I'd find them?"

"First of all, I saw you at the poker night, getting all comfy in his bed; I knew you'd end up back there. But just in case, there were five different pairs hidden around Salem's stuff. You owe me a hundred bucks, by the way."

"Cute. And completely ridiculous."

She swallows the last bite of her scone and grins. "You say that like it didn't work. Tell me it didn't work."

I keep my mouth shut. You don't need to be in AP Psych to know when you're not winning a battle against Isabel McEvoy. "Honestly, I can't believe you're still allowed to talk to me. I'd think Jenna hates me."

"She does," Isabel says coolly, "but she's Jenna; she'll find someone new by next week and forget all about Salem."

"And me?" I ask hopefully.

"Oh, no—you, she's gonna hate forever."

I laugh, assuming Isabel's kidding, then stop when it becomes obvious that she isn't. "Oh."

"Yeah, she's like that."

"And you still wanna take the risk of being friends with me? Is this a 'keep your friends close, enemies closer' type of thing?"

"No, please, I'm not that bored," she says with a snort. "But I think you're interesting. You surprise me. Not a lot of people manage to do that."

"I can't tell if that's more egotistical or patronizing."

"See?" She flashes a broad smile. "Who talks like that to me? Nobody."

"But like, what was even the point? Why did you even *need* a middleman? Jenna could get any guy she wants by just blinking pointedly in his direction. Did she really think he wouldn't fall down at her feet if she just said hi?" I mean, *I* like to think he wouldn't, but I'm a realist.

Isabel fixes me with a Look. "You *do* know he's a sophomore, right? Jenna would never."

"Jenna *did*," I remind her. "And I'm a sophomore too."

"Okay but it's one thing to be friends or hook up with a sophomore when you're a junior; it's an entire other thing to *pursue* one." She nods down between us. "Honestly, this friendship is bad enough."

"I really appreciate your humbling yourself." I'm not even entirely sure I'm kidding.

"Well, there *is* one more thing I want, and before you get mad, I'm telling you. Directly. So this is different, and born of friendship."

"I suppose I can appreciate that. What is it? A voodoo doll of Salem's hair? A lifetime supply of scones? A kidney?"

"Nothing like that, you drama queen."

"What, then?" I ask as we reach the fork on campus where we'll part ways.

At first, I assume from the smirk on her face that she isn't going to tell me after all. But then she wraps an arm around my waist, pulls me close enough to kiss my cheek, and says, "Hook me up with your boyfriend's sister."

Then she winks and heads down the path toward Hillman, leaving my jaw on the ground.

Chapter Nineteen

THE WEEKS UNTIL THANKSGIVING ARE like an entirely different experience at Camden, one that erases every single doubt I've ever had about going to boarding school.

Yes, I'm still in Rumson, but no one dares mess with me about it anymore. Having your boyfriend upstairs is a pretty damn huge perk, especially when the housing office looks the other way because dealing with it is too complicated.

Sabrina and I keep up the GSA, and sometimes, Salem or Heather even joins. Eventually, Sabrina finds out that a Ewing resident is nonbinary, and together, we all agree to re-petition for an official club for the spring.

I find actual study groups for the classes I don't share with Salem and am reasonably certain I kick ass on all my mid-terms.

The biggest surprise of all, though, is what doesn't change: Salem and I decide to continue our pact, in a way. Every week, I get to make him do two things I think are good for him, no questions asked—this usually involves either going to study groups he was gonna blow off, shooting around with Matt and the other guys in the gym, or joining me for the nature options on weekends, which I point out accomplishes both our goals by making me a hiking, climbing badass and him a do-gooder nature lover who takes gorgeous pictures of fall foliage for his mom.

And every week, he gets to suggest two things that he thinks will further my experience in badassery, which usually means either working on my "musical education" or making out. (Often both simultaneously, which I suspect is Salem's master plan of giving me positive associations with his faves. Unfortunately, it's working.)

But the day before we head home for Thanksgiving, he has a different request, and for the first time, I say no.

"You really don't think it'll make you feel better?" he asks, twirling one of my curls around his finger as we lie intertwined in my bed, watching but not watching an episode of *Stranger Things* on my laptop. My room is slightly more decorated now. Salem got Claire to send him a file of the two of spades art and had it printed and framed; Sabrina gave me the cards from my original tarot reading so I could hang them over my bed; and Isabel picked up the world's most hideous LIVE, LAUGH, LOVE sign she could find in a clearance bin and presented it to me with a flourish.

"I don't think talking to my sister has ever made me feel better in my entire life," I say sourly, fiddling with the soft hem of his flannel. "Why would it start now?"

"Because now you have a dreamy boyfriend."

I snort into his side. "Great, so she can try to lure you away. And considering her track record, it'll probably work."

"Interesting. She hot?"

"Don't you *dare*." I whack him right over his belly button, hoping he's cursing having no body fat to protect him right about now, but he just laughs.

"One Riley woman's enough to handle, thanks very much." He tilts my face up for a kiss, and as I melt into him, I can't help but think that maybe he has a point. I have to see her tomorrow when I go home anyway. Maybe it's best to break the ice from here, where I feel good about my friends and boyfriend and the space I've created for myself, rather than waiting until we're both back on what, let's face it, has somehow always been her turf, even while being my home.

I'd kill to have a sister like Sabrina; for all that she and Salem torture each other, I know they'd take a bullet for each other. Hell, that's basically what Salem did, coming here. And I thought she'd kick my ass for getting with him, but the only thing she said about it when she saw me at lunch that first day was "So you're screwing my brother. Gross. But at least that'll keep my parents' heat off me for a while. Welcome to the fam."

"What would I even say?" I ask when we part. "'Hey, how was rehab? Wanna talk about why you banged my ex?'"

"How about you start with 'Hi'? Chatting about banging the ex is more of a 'five minutes in' conversation topic."

"It all sounds terrible. Why exactly are you making me do this?"

"I'm not *making* you," he says gently. "But, selfishly, I'm asking you to because you're right—it's probably going to suck. And if you wait until tomorrow, when you're home, then I won't be there for the aftermath. But if you do it today, then you can use me as a human punching bag for those tiny balls of rage you call fists. Or get a hug. Or both."

Oh. That is . . . nice. And compelling reasoning. And I wish it weren't making me a little teary to have someone like that in my corner. "Doesn't seem like there's a whole lot in it for you," I say, sniffing.

"Well, I'm assuming you'll end up desperately grateful for my presence, which can only translate to extreme horniness and/or letting me choose what movie we watch tonight."

"You are the literal worst," I tell him, but he isn't, not at all, and so I kiss him again.

I stare at my phone for a solid five minutes after Salem goes back upstairs, playing endless games of "What's the worst that could happen?" in my mind. There's such a disconnect between me at a poker table and me trying to function in reality; in the latter, I never seem to see anything coming, can't call anyone's bluff or guess their next move.

There's a reason I love cards.

But what *is* the worst that could happen? I have nothing to do with her going to rehab. I have nothing to do with whatever punishments my parents have meted out. I already know she hasn't successfully brought Claire over to the dark side, and if she *has* taken Craig, well, I can't imagine something I'd care less about at this point.

So I guess there's not a whole lot to worry about.

Maybe.

I make the call.

But the voice that picks up on the other end isn't hers.

"Evie?" Mom sounds puzzled. "You're trying to reach Sierra?"

"I figured maybe we should talk before I see her tomorrow, but that's okay. I can definitely wait." I pause. "Why do you have her phone?"

She sighs. "Sierra's phone privileges have been restricted. But I think we can make an exception in this case. Hold on, I'll get her."

So much for that out. I mutter a "thanks" and wait for a full two minutes before I finally hear the voice I've been avoiding for six months.

"Finally decided to acknowledge my existence, huh?" is a hell of an opening line.

"Are you *fucking* kidding me?"

On the other end of the line, Sierra whistles. "Wow. Somebody got a spine up at fancy boarding school. Maybe Mom and Dad taking out a second mortgage so you could get away from your loser boyfriend was worth it after all."

"Apparently it's more than you learned in rehab," I snap back. "And was that free because it was court-ordered, or . . ."

"Fuck you."

"Right back atcha, sis." I can't believe I bothered calling.

I can't believe I let Salem convince me there was even an ounce of merit to this. I want to hang up on her, run upstairs, and yell at him for even suggesting it, but then I remember that's exactly what he wanted to enable me doing today, and it cools my temper, just a little. "Anyway, thought maybe we should connect before seeing each other tomorrow, but turns out I haven't missed a thing—you're exactly the person I left behind."

"How could I possibly be anything else? Perfect Everett Riley's screwup sister. God, you had *everything* and it still wasn't enough for you."

I had everything. *I* had everything? My jaw drops to the floor.

Last fall, Claire was experimenting with lenticular prints, and I remember her going on about how fascinating it was that one piece of art could have completely different sides never seen at the exact same time.

Clearly, my sister and I are a lenticular print, because I have no idea what the hell she's imagining if she's thinking about the Evie of a few months ago.

"You think *I* had everything? No, I had two things you didn't in the entire world: a boyfriend and a best friend. And you, who had friends and parties and apparently a boatload of drugs, took them both without even really wanting either one. I came here without anything or anyone, because of *you.*"

She snorts. "Yeah, great friends I had. No one's even talking to me anymore."

"That certainly isn't *my* fault."

"Of course not. Everything's my fault. Everything is always my fault. Craig hit on *me*, you know."

"You're aware that just because a guy hits on you doesn't mean you need to reciprocate, right? I feel like 'Hard pass, you're my sister's boyfriend' is a pretty solid rejection."

"Okay, this was like a million years ago. How can you possibly still be hung up on that guy? He's pathetic."

"I'm not hung up on Craig; I'm hung up on how you hurt me, and how I can't trust you, and how shitty that is."

"Yeah, well."

I wait for a follow-up, but nothing comes. "Is that seriously all you have to say about it?"

She lets out an aggravated sigh. "What do you want from me, Evie? It happened. It's over. Neither of us cares about him anymore. And as for Claire, I assure you, no one's trying to steal your boring friends. My life is shit. Your life is great. Tomorrow you can gloat about it in person. We all set?"

God, I knew this conversation was gonna be bad, but I truly didn't know it would be *this* bad.

The thing is, though, at this very moment, my life *is* great. I do have everything. And while I'm sure Camden will continue throwing its curveballs, fighting with Sierra right now is basically just kicking a dog when it's down. What's the point? She isn't sorry. I'm not forgiving. And this isn't worth the mental energy for either of us.

It's time to wrap this up, but I'm *not* going to let her make me the bad guy as we do it.

"I don't want to *gloat*, See. I've never felt worse in my entire life than when I came here, by myself, having begged

Mom and Dad to spend money they didn't have, minus a boyfriend, a best friend, *and* a sister. Whatever you think I had when I started here, I'm telling you now, you were wrong."

I take a deep breath, half convinced she'll hang up while I do, but I can still hear her breathing on the other end of the line, and I forge forward. "I've made choices since then, some bad, but most really, really good, including the one to come here and start again out of your shadow. And now, not only am I happy, but I see the things that broke me for the minor setbacks they actually were. Whatever else happens between us, I hope you're able to say the same someday."

There's no response, only more quiet breath, and I realize I don't want one. "Good night, Sierra. I'll see you tomorrow."

And then I hang up and head to the stairs to collect my hug.

The next day, it takes both Salem and Sabrina to help me carry my stuff out to where my parents are picking me up, mostly because I'm taking advantage of the round-trip rides to bring home as much laundry as possible. Add to that my laptop, the books I'm bringing home to study from, and my clothes for the long weekend, and it's definitely a group effort.

And okay, yes, maybe I need the extra fortification after yesterday's miserable phone call.

"This is completely ridiculous, you know that," Sabrina

says flatly, readjusting the bag of sheets slung over her shoulder. "Does Rumson not have laundry?"

"Spoken like someone who doesn't have to share her machines with twenty-two filthy, sweaty, horny boys."

"You mean twenty-one filthy, sweaty boys and one who's completely dashing and pristine at all times," Salem amends.

Sabrina and I roll our eyes. "I notice you didn't strike 'horny' for yourself," she points out dryly.

"Well." He gives a slow, languid shrug, and she puts on a dramatic retching show.

"You guys are gross."

"I didn't even say anything!" I protest.

"His hand is literally in the ass pocket of your jeans."

Oh, so it is. "Okay, well, maybe you would find our coupledom less annoying if you would give a certain somebody a chance."

Sabrina rolls her eyes again. I've been trying to get her to at least *talk* to Isabel for weeks, but she's insisted she has no interest in having anything to do with that group of friends, and she's been sticking to it. And since Isabel refuses to do any pursuing . . . "Move on, Skeevy. It's not happening."

"Okay, first of all, can everyone stop calling me that? And second of all, she's *Isabel McEvoy*. And she wants to put her hand in your ass pocket." I pause at that and note everyone's expressions of mild disgust. "I hear how that came out and that is not what I was going for. But you know what I mean. She is literally the hottest girl in this school. How are you not even gonna *talk* to her?"

"Just to be clear," says Sabrina, "in college, when you finally have that 'oh shit, I'm bi' moment, and try the whole 'Whaaat? But there weren't any signs!' thing, I'm going to direct you back to this conversation."

"I'm not *not* feeling threatened," Salem adds.

I roll my eyes. "I don't think I enjoy this Grayson twin onslaught."

"We get that a lot," they say simultaneously, and I groan, but in truth, it warms me to see them getting along so well, even if it's a stark reminder that I'm heading home to a very different sibling interaction.

"That is not a happy face," Sabrina observes, squinting at me. "Are you only just realizing who your boyfriend is? I was afraid this would happen. There's still time to take it back. I'll pretend this never happened if you do."

Salem scratches at his nose with his middle finger, then looks down at me. "Thinking about your sister again?"

"How can I not?" I groan. "What if we just wandered off into the woods? Tell my parents to turn around and go home, would you?"

"You can handle this," Salem assures me, taking my face in his freezing hands, because of course he refuses to wear gloves. "You are a badass. Sierra's got nothin' on you."

I stand on my toes to press my lips to his, circling my arms around his neck, and there's another retching sound before Sabrina says, "That is definitely my cue. Happy Thanksgiving, pervs."

"Bye, Sabs!" I call after her before Salem reclaims me for another kiss, and then another, and then all talk of my sister and going home flees my mind completely as it turns into a full-on makeout.

A loud cough sounds nearby and we pull apart to see Hoffman glaring at us from where he stands with a clipboard, checking off departures as parents come to claim their kids. My cheeks are already rosy from the cold, but I can feel their color deepening and I bury my face in Salem's shoulder.

"You're ridiculous, you know that?" he says, amused, but he holds me close anyway, keeping me warm in the crisp late-fall air.

"Ridiculously cute?"

He yanks my knit hat down over my face. "Sometimes."

"Hey!" I swat his hand away and readjust the hat. "Don't make me send you back inside."

"You wouldn't."

"I might."

"Not in a million years. You kinda sorta like me, remember?"

"Oh, whatever. You kinda sorta like me too."

"Kinda. Sorta." He pulls me into another kiss, but we keep this one brief, for Hoffman's benefit. "This is gross, right? Do we make you as sick as we make me?"

"Sicker," I admit. "But I still like us."

"Me too." He squeezes my shoulders and kisses the top of my head. "Hey, is that your car pulling up to the gate? Black SUV?"

"That's them." I hoist my duffel bag higher up, followed by my laptop bag. "If you wanna bolt in order to avoid a Meet the Parents scenario, you have about one minute."

"Up to you." He rubs a thumb over my jaw, and I melt into his palm. "You met Ted and Naomi. I can be charming for two minutes, if you want me to be."

"Why do I have a feeling they wouldn't come away from this conversation glowing about your social grace?"

"You'd be surprised," he says with a smirk.

"You know, I do believe that." His fingers are cold, but I take them anyway, and his strong arm curling me into his side more than makes up for the chill. "But given everything I already have to talk about with them, I'm gonna give you a pass. For now," I add with narrowed eyes. "No promises come winter break."

"Deal." He rests his chin on my head. "Before you go, I just need to say something nauseatingly romantic, and then I need to retreat like a turtle into my shell for at least the length of Thanksgiving, but *then* maybe like an entire six weeks of winter."

My stomach flutters gently in response. Forthcoming as he is with physical affection, verbally, "It's cool that you don't suck" is about as sweet as he gets. I've been waiting weeks for "nauseatingly romantic," especially considering that's a pretty good descriptor for how I feel about him. "You're mixing up turtles and groundhogs, but okay, go ahead. I'm ready."

He takes a breath and places his hands on my waist. "You're the best friend I've ever had that I also wanna make out with."

I don't know why I let myself get primed for actual romance, but somehow, I got fooled. "*That* was your nauseatingly romantic goodbye sentiment?" I splutter. "God, you really had me for a second there."

"That's not romantic? To feel like being with you is the most comfortable thing in the world but also gives me butterflies? Dude, that's romantic as fuck."

"That . . . actually is pretty romantic," I concede, "but it's not what you said the first time."

"Well, it's what I'm saying," he mumbles, tugging his beanie down until it nearly covers his eyes. "Okay?"

I pull him down for a kiss. "Okay."

His gaze shifts to some point in the distance, as if the drying grass has somehow become the most fascinating thing in the universe. "You get that I'm saying I love you, right?"

Wrapping an arm around his waist, I close my eyes and rest my cheek against his beating heart. "Now I do," I say, listening to the healthy thump as I feel my own race. "You did it, Grayson. That was officially romantic. Romantic enough for me to tell you that I love you, too, even."

He grunts in response, but I feel another kiss ghost the top of my head before my parents pull up and he steps away. "Now get in the car, because that was embarrassing and I can't look directly at you at least until we FaceTime in a few hours."

"I thought it was six weeks, because you don't know the difference between a turtle and a groundhog? Which is much more embarrassing, by the way."

He groans. "I'd like to take everything back now."

"Don't you dare." I rise on my toes one more time and curl my fists into his sweatshirt for a breath-stealing kiss. Hopefully my parents have better things to do than watch us in the rearview. "You're my turtle-groundhog now, and in the animal kingdom, there are no take backs. It's very vicious."

"I have so many regrets," he mutters, but the way he kisses me, cradling my jaw with strong, callused hands, it's like he's never had one in his life.

And maybe I have a few, and always will. But right now, as I get in the car and watch him fade away behind us, knowing he'll be here when I return, I feel extremely good about my life choices.

Acknowledgments

Ordinarily, by your fourteenth set of acknowledgments, you expect to have knocked it down to three or four solid paragraphs mostly just thanking the people who turned the once-nonsensical draft you threw at your wonderful editor with an email that said "Thanks so much for the twelve deadline extensions" into the polished book you now hold in your hands. (Or maybe that's just me? That might be just me.) However, since this book is literally fifteen years in the making (I know, right? But I was doing other stuff in the meantime, I promise), this is gonna get a little long—bear with me. (Or don't! You've already read the book, for which I am very grateful. You're totally allowed to put this down now.)

This book began in a class called Writing for T(w)eens at the University of Pennsylvania taught by the esteemed Melissa Jensen, to whom I am forever grateful for both an excellent education and convincing me this story had legs. I was so convinced of it, even, that over the next couple of years of writing and querying, I asked about a million people to beta this book, and I'm so grateful for all the encouragement and the many sets of notes most of you probably don't even remember giving me at this point, but anyway! Huge thank-you to Marieke Nijkamp, Maggie Hall, Gina Ciocca, Chessie Zappia, Christopher Koehler, Jaz Hillenberg, Dani Leeds, and Aliza Boim for polishing and cheering on the original version of this book, and giving me something to work with before I absolutely shredded it to death for the version you see in front of you.

As far as first real querying experiences go, it was in fact a lovely one, and I'm so grateful to Victoria Marini for ending it with the rejection that was the final editorial note I needed; it honestly changed the course of my writing career in a way I have never forgotten. (So did selling my first anthology, so big ups to Victoria all around, really!)

Fun fact: that version was *still* supposed to make it to publication; it was almost my next Spencer Hill Contemporary book, thanks to the brilliant Patricia Riley, who's been in the business of making my publishing dreams come true for some time now. All's well that ends well, but I will never not be thankful for the vote of faith and knowing I was in the most capable editorial hands.

Anyway, this brings us to now, and the other brilliant and supportive and wonderful Patricia in my publishing life—thank you, always and forever, to Patricia Nelson, who is not only the best person I could've ever dreamed of having in my corner, but who, with one brilliant note, took this book from an inevitable "too quiet" to selling it over a decade after I was certain it was dead. Many more brilliant notes then followed as this book slowwwwly found its footing, and I'm so grateful to both Patricia and my wonderful editor / granter of the many extensions, Vicki Lame, for their insight, patience, kindness, and fight, and for pushing me to turn this book into the best version of itself. Also, thank you to the brilliant Taryn Fagerness, who's worked so hard to bring my books across the world.

Of course, thanks are also due to everyone else at Wednesday who's worked so hard to turn this from multiply revised manuscript to book: to Vanessa Aguirre, ~~assistant~~ editor extraordinaire—three books in together, I could not be more grateful for how professionally and capably you help this process go round; to Devan Norman, who constantly finds new ways to turn my eyes into little heart emojis with gorgeous designs; to Kerri Resnick, whose cover designs have landed me so many accurate comments about being blessed by the gods—thanks to you and to brilliantly talented illustrator Guy Shield for bringing Evie, Salem, Camden, and the infamous rope ladder to life; and to editorial director Sara Goodman, associate publisher Eileen Rothschild, managing editor Merilee Croft, editorial assistant Sarah Pazen, production manager Diane Dilluvio, senior production editor Cassie Gutman, copy editor Terry McGarry, proofreaders Kyle Avery and Susannah Noel, the marketing team of Austin Adams and Brant Janeway, and, of course, publicist Meghan Harrington.

Speaking of the many improvements that went into this version of the book, thank you to its wonderful and insightful early readers—to Keely Parrack and Emery Lord, for polishing those first few chapters and helping me find the right path, and to the generous and talented Michelle Millet, for so helpfully and brilliantly taking it all the way home. Thank you, too, to Clare for the tarot expertise and Colby for the tagline help, and again (always!) to my dearest Maggie, for the early read and enthusiastic texts. And to Courtney Summers, queen of the pep talks—someday we will get those drinks on a Friday.

This is a tough industry on its best day, and I'm extremely grateful for all the Discords, Slacks, group chats, Facebook groups, DMs, and texts that get me through it; I don't know how I'd do this without y'all, especially Katie, Marieke, Maggie, A-M, Lev, Tess, Jen, Jess, and Eric. Love to the entire StoryLoom editorial crew, for generally being awesome, and to all the llamas in the Dahlhouse. It's been a long time, but it was also a damn good time, and I had to memorialize it somewhere. And of course, love to all the bloggers and bookstagrammers who always bring the joy and support.

Finally, to my family, who is bored of these already and I'm pretty sure stopped reading them about five books ago but never stops cheering me on, buying and displaying each title, celebrating each win, and asking how the next one is going (even if sometimes you get nothing but a snarl in response)—I love you.

About the Author

Maggie Hall

DAHLIA ADLER is an editor by day, a freelance writer by night, and an author and anthologist at every spare moment in between. She is the founder of LGBTQ Reads; her novels include the Kids' Indie Next picks *Cool for the Summer*, *Home Field Advantage*, and *Going Bicoastal*, a Sydney Taylor Honor book; and she is the editor of the anthologies *His Hideous Heart*, *That Way Madness Lies*, *At Midnight*, and, with Jennifer Iacopelli, *Out of Our League*. Dahlia lives in New York with her family and a wall of overflowing bookcases.